C000244929

THE ENCODED HEART

She nodded to the side as she said it, gesturing over the handrail. In spite of herself, the Iconoclast followed the gesture. Her eyes moved, just a fraction, but it was enough. Red launched herself forward, ducking under the bolter and striking the woman a massive, back-handed blow.

The Iconoclast didn't even get a chance to fire. The swipe flipped her clear over the handrail.

Red skidded to a halt, cursing herself. She'd acted purely on impulse again. For the crime the Iconoclast had committed up in the dome, she should have made the fight last longer. Made it hurt more.

"Sneck it!" she exclaimed. "And I was getting thirsty, too."

Durham Red from Black Flame

THE UNQUIET GRAVE
Peter J Evans

THE OMEGA SOLUTION
Peter J Evans

More 2000 AD action from Black Flame

Judge Dredd

DREDD VS DEATH
Gordon Rennie

BAD MOON RISING
David Bishop

BLACK ATLANTIC
Simon Jowett & Peter J Evans

ECLIPSE
James Swallow

KINGDOM OF THE BLIND
David Bishop

THE FINAL CUT
Matthew Smith

SWINE FEVER
Andrew Cartmel

WHITEOUT
James Swallow

ABC Warriors

THE MEDUSA WAR
Pat Mills & Alan Mitchell

RAGE AGAINST THE
MACHINES
Mike Wild

Strontium Dog

BAD TIMING
Rebecca Levene

PROPHET MARGIN
Simon Spurrier

RUTHLESS
Jonathan Clements

DAY OF THE DOGS
Andrew Cartmel

A FISTFUL OF STRONTIUM
Jaspre Bark & Steve Lyons

Rogue Trooper

CRUCIBLE
Gordon Rennie

BLOOD RELATIVE
James Swallow

Nikolai Dante

THE STRANGELOVE GAMBIT
David Bishop

IMPERIAL BLACK
David Bishop

Durham Red created by **John Wagner**,
Alan Grant and **Carlos Ezquerra**

Special thanks to **Dan Abnett** and **Mark Harrison**
for character and continuity of the Accord

DURHAM RED

THE ENCODED HEART

PETER J EVANS

BLACK FLAME

To the Middletons
For a peaceful place
In which to get away from all of this

A Black Flame Publication
www.blackflame.com

First published in 2005 by BL Publishing, Games Workshop Ltd.,
Willow Road, Nottingham NG7 2WS, UK.

Distributed in the US by Simon & Schuster, 1230 Avenue of the
Americas, New York, NY 10020, USA.

10 9 8 7 6 5 4 3 2 1

Cover illustration by Mark Harrison.

ISBN 13: 978 1 84416 272 7
ISBN 10: 1 84416 272 9

A CIP record for this book is available from the British Library.

Printed in the UK by Bookmarque, Surrey, UK.

The Legend of Durham Red

It is written that in that year of 2150, the skies rained down nuclear death, and every family and clan lost father and brothers and sons. The Strontium choked our beloved homeworld and brought forth mutants, squealing and twisted things.

Yet such mutants were not weak things to be crushed underfoot, for the same radiation that had created them warped their bodies, making them stronger than any normal human. They became hated and feared by all, and were herded into ghettos and imprisoned in vast camps. There they plotted rebellion and dreamed of freedom amongst their own kind.

Some, it is told, were able to escape from the shadows of ruined Earth, to join the feared Search/Destroy Agency. They tracked wanted criminals on worlds too dangerous for regular enforcement officers. They became known as the Strontium Dogs.

The one they call Durham Red became an S/D Agent to escape the teeming ghettos of her devastated homeland. Shunned even by her own kind because of a foul mutant blood-thirst, she soon found that her unsurpassed combat skills served her well as a Strontium Dog. The years of continuous slaughter took their toll, however, and the tales relate that in the end Red willingly entered the deep sleep of cryogenic suspension, determined to let a few years go by without her.

All know of the unexpected twist that the legend took. Her cryo-tube malfunctioned. Durham Red woke up twelve hundred years late.

While she slept, the enmity between humans and mutants had exploded into centuries of total war, leaving the galaxy a shattered shell, home only to superstition and barbarism. Billions of oppressed mutants now worship Saint Scarlet of Durham – the mythologised image of Red herself! The bounty hunter from Milton Keynes has now become almost a messiah figure for mutantkind – and a terrifying blasphemy in the eyes of humans.

Half the galaxy is looking to her for bloody salvation. The other half is determined to destroy her at any cost. The future is a nightmare, and Durham Red is trapped right in the middle of it...

1. INITIAL CONDITIONS

Sorrelier was dreaming when the alert sounded.

He sat up, breathing hard, glancing about wildly. The bedchamber was pulsing like a live thing, the jewelled walls swelling and contracting as he watched, a dizzying counterpoint to the beat of his racing heart. For a moment the sight baffled him, left him wondering if he had actually awoken, or whether the dream had simply moved into another, even stranger phase. Horror gripped him. His mouth, dry as dust, strained to articulate a single word.

"Lise," he gasped, finally.

A shadow appeared at the end of the bed. Lise, his most trusted sylph, had stepped out of the darkness. Sorrelier saw her eyes flick up to the ceiling of the chamber, where the illuminated panels pulsed softly in time with the alarm.

He let out a long breath. The walls were still solid after all. Only the shadows rose and fell as the lights echoed the alarm's bleating.

He sagged back and shut his eyes. "The bitch is here, isn't she?"

Lise didn't answer. There was much she was capable of, but speech wasn't among her talents.

Sorrelier shivered. He felt empty. The dream had been a strange one, sadistic and surreal, but that was only to be expected. He had taken great pains to design it that way.

Something about a child, he remembered.

The alarm was getting on his nerves, fracturing his memory of the dream. "Off!" he snapped, stilling its noise instantly. Through his closed eyelids, Sorrelier saw the chamber's lights grow steady.

A child, yes. An infant of uncertain gender; smooth-skinned and scrubbed, clad in brilliant silks. A skull-cap of gleaming metal had covered the child's head from the brows upwards, and even now, naked and sweating on his bed, Sorrelier could still see the knowing smile that had played about those dimpled cheeks as the child approached him, dark promise in its eyes.

It had spoken, he remembered, licking his lips. Just once. "Taste," it had said.

And then, with one chubby, soft-knuckled hand, it had reached up and removed the top of its own head.

The skull-cap came off as smoothly as the lid from a tureen. There was nothing beneath; no skin, skull, or even brain. The child's head was an empty bowl, edged in silver filigree and set with a bed of padded satin, upon which lay the most exquisite array of candies and sweetmeats that Sorrelier had ever seen. The sight was mouth-watering.

He had been reaching out for a particularly succulent morsel when that cursed alarm had dragged him back into hated wakefulness.

The shivering was getting worse. He had woken too early – he needed more sleep, more time to dream. But the alarm meant he would have to do without either.

"Lise? I need the emerald. Quickly."

He reached out, and a moment later the jewel was in his hand, cool and smooth. It was as big as the end of his thumb, and easy to hold. Without opening his eyes Sorrelier pressed the end of the emerald to the inside of his left wrist. He felt its coldness there, then the brush of the needle, too fine and brief to be called pain.

Sudden, icy calm filled him, along with a crisp alertness. "Well," he breathed. "That, as they say, certainly hit the spot."

He opened his eyes and handed the jewel back to Lise, making sure the needle had slipped back into its chemical reservoir before he did so. The drug it delivered was one of his own concoction, a delicate balance of myelic enhancers and synthetic neurochemicals that had taken years to perfect. Every dose, tiny as it was, took days of intense labour to harvest. It was far, far too expensive to waste on a sylph, even one so exquisite as Lise.

Sorrelier got up from the bed and smiled at her. "Thank you, my dear. And now, I believe, some haste is required. It would appear the lady is eager to begin."

Tarsus was an unlovely world. Seen from orbit, it was a mottled patchwork of lumpy whites and fibrous greens, as though an apple had been left to shrivel and rot and grow fur. There were few clouds, and those that existed did more to throw the grimness of the planet's surface into sharp relief than to conceal it. In other circumstances, Sorrelier wouldn't have set foot on the place.

Unfortunately for him, he hadn't been given the choice. The assassin wouldn't meet him anywhere else.

The rendezvous point had been agreed days before, during an exchange of highly encrypted data transmissions. Sorrelier's ship, the *Aureus*, had set down exactly where and when the assassin had suggested, every one of her instructions carried out to the letter. Sorrelier didn't like following someone else's path so closely, especially when it led to a rancid sphere like Tarsus. But the situation was far too critical to take further risks.

And so, for the past six hours, the *Aureus* had hunched on its slender landing claws, on a landmass so cold that the cliffs and mountains covering it were more ice than rock. In fact, Tarsus had no exposed ground at all, and its atmosphere would not have supported oxygen if its cold oceans had not been home to continent-sized mats of stinking algae.

It had taken Sorrelier about eight minutes to tire of watching snow whip past the viewports, and the assassin was not due to arrive until dusk. There had been time, or so he had thought, for a dream or two.

It was irksome for him to admit now how wrong he had been.

Fully dressed, with Lise at his heel, he strode on to the circular command deck. "Rimail. Is she down?"

"Almost, sire." Captain Rimail pointed out through the front viewports, to where a splinter of dark metal was dropping through the thin snow. "She made three fast orbits before hitting the planet's atmosphere, and a low pass that only failed to count as a strafing run because she didn't fire on us. She's a cautious creature, it would seem."

"Indeed." The splinter was jetting fire, spitting a column of flame downwards. Smoke and steam billowed, whipped by the dry wind.

Sorrelier touched a control, and a detailed hologram of the assassin's vessel unfolded in the air in front of him, weaving itself from threads of green light. The image was generated in real time. Sorrelier saw its thruster arrays turn slightly to resist the gale, the antimat turrets moving in response.

Every one of the ship's weapons was aimed right at him.

Sorrelier would have expected nothing less, especially since all those on his ship were aimed right back. "Odd looking beast," he muttered. "What do you think, Rimail? Iconoclast design?"

"Maybe it was once." Rimail turned from the pilot's helm to face him. "There's something of a daggership about the pressure cabin and the main drive. But those weapons? And the nacelle clusters... If you ask me, sire, she's stripped that vessel to the keel and rebuilt it by hand."

Sorrelier nodded. Rimail was a fine shipman, on his way to the seventh level of observance. He could be irreverent at times, but Sorrelier hadn't risen to his own level by ignoring the worth of a good second-in-command. He valued the man's opinion. "And if this little standoff turns ugly?"

"Let's just say I'd rather it didn't."

The assassin's ship dropped a single landing spine, and settled in a cloud of superheated steam. Sorrelier heard a faint chiming, and saw that his own ship's data signals warned of an incoming cypher. "Well," he said quietly, "keep a close eye on those turrets, Rimail, just in case."

He took out his comm-linker. Words were scrolling across its tiny screen, decoding a cypher-message. Sorrelier watched it make a couple of cycles, and then sighed.

"Lise, it looks like we'll need our furs."

The wind was cold and horribly dry. The snow in the air was coming down from the ice-cliffs, not from any scrap of cloud cover. Sorrelier crunched his way towards the assassin's ship under a piercingly blue sky.

The woman was already waiting for him, standing halfway between the two vessels. It was symbolically neutral territory, Sorrelier reflected, and far enough away from her ship for the antimat guns to cover without any blind spots. He looked up from under the fur-lined hood of his coat, and saw several of them tracking him as he walked.

There was an honorific these people used, he remembered, a remnant of their troubled past. "Het Nemesine," he smiled, stopping in front of the woman. "Good to finally meet you."

Her head bobbed slightly in a bow. "Likewise."

Sorrelier had known, from prior research, roughly what she would look like. He was still surprised, though.

She seemed so *young*.

Nemesine was small, a full head shorter than either Sorrelier or Lise, and her features were smooth, unlined. Almost childlike. For a moment the dream fluttered behind his eyes, but he forced it away.

She blinked at him, with huge dark eyes beneath a whipping mane of jet-black hair. What he could see of her skin was sand-brown, a heavy breath mask covering her nose and mouth, twin pipes curling down from it to the support systems of her battle armour.

Still very much an Iconoclast, thought Sorrelier. No matter what name she takes.

Nemesine glanced questioningly at Lise. Sorrelier shook his head. "Don't concern yourself. Lise is the epitome of discretion."

"I'm sure she is. Tell her to back off anyway."

Sorrelier hesitated for a second, and then turned to Lise. "Do as she says," he told her gently. "Just a few metres."

Lise tilted her head slightly, and only when Sorrelier repeated the order did she start to move away. Leaving his side in such a situation went against all her instincts. Watching the sylph trudging carefully backwards through the snow, Sorrelier was struck with an odd reciprocal feeling, a sudden glimpse of how empty life would be without Lise.

It was not, he decided there and then, something he ever wanted to experience.

He returned his attention to the assassin. "Het Nemesine, it's cold out here, and there are far more weapons trained upon me than I am used to. May we proceed, or is Lise still too close for your comfort?"

The woman shot him a glance. "Surely you can do without your pet for a few minutes, sire? But you're right. It is cold." She folded her arms. "What's the job?"

"A live capture."

"Tiresome."

"But important."

She shrugged, not easy in battle armour. "You're paying. Who's the target?"

"Durham Red."

There was a period of silence, other than the thin hiss of the wind, and the dry, powdery snow that rattled against Nemesine's armour. Finally, she responded. "If you were just joking, you'd not have come this far. So when did you first develop this psychosis?"

"Trust me, Het, I'm quite serious, and mostly sane. I simply want you to hunt down and capture Saint Scarlet of Durham."

"*Simply*. Of course." She made a clucking sound. "It's all so simple, I wonder why I haven't done it before."

"If anyone in the Accord can do it, it's you."

"I'm flattered, Sorrelier. Though somewhat confused."
She tugged the breath-mask away, dragging in a long breath
of cold Tarsus air. Sorrelier observed with some interest the
long, puckered scar that the mask had concealed, running
along the left side of her jaw. He'd been previously unaware
of it.

"It may have escaped your notice," she was saying, "but
there's already a considerable bounty on Durham Red. At
last count, almost ten times what you're offering me. That's
quite an incentive – I hear she's got at least five hundred
professional bounty hunters on her trail at any one time.
What have I got that they haven't?"

"A personal interest," he replied. "One that outweighs the
professional." He stepped forward, and lowered his voice.
"I'm tired of playing this game, girl. Nemesine the assassin
is a myth. You know it and I know it. A remarkably recent
myth, in fact."

A weapon had appeared in Nemesine's gloved hands, a
slab-sided pistol with a barrel Sorrelier could have fitted
two fingers into. "Meaning?"

"Not so very long ago, I would have been referring to you
as 'major', would I not?"

Her dark eyes narrowed. "You're talking about a dead
woman."

"And what, pray tell, led to her demise?"

Her gaze dropped for a moment, betraying her uncer-
tainty.

"I know about the other hunters," he said. "I've had my
own agents chasing her too. Trust me, no one has even
come close to bringing her in. As far as my research has
shown, the only person that even slowed her down was
you."

"That…" Her voice faltered, and she swallowed. "That
was a long time ago."

"Not so long. Less than a standard year."

"It seems longer."

"A lot has happened to you since." His voice remained low but its tones were gentler, comforting rather than conspiratorial. Despite everything he had heard, it seemed this ex-major would be no harder to manipulate than anyone else.

She looked away, out towards the cliffs. "I'd never find her."

"With my help, you will. I'm not just offering the commission. I can put you on her tail, too."

"Tempting..." Her eyes stayed on the cliffs. "She'd probably kill me, which maybe isn't so bad. And if I succeeded..."

The wind rose in a sudden gust, buffeting Sorrelier. He had to take a step sideways to avoid overbalancing, and heard the weapons turrets on Nemesine's ship whine as they moved to keep him targeted. When he had steadied himself he found both her gaze and her gun in his face.

"Tell me something, Sorrelier," she said. "What would stop me taking your commission, using your data to find the monster, then simply bringing her severed head back to High Command? Clear my name and take a bounty ten times what you would give me?"

Sorrelier smiled. "Because her pain would end when your blade found her neck. Give her to me, and I guarantee she'll suffer the agonies of the damned every second of every day for the rest of her life." He reached out, and gently pushed the barrel of her gun down. "Besides, you don't really think they'd take you back, do you?"

Tarsus was no prettier when Sorrelier saw it from orbit, but he observed with interest as Nemesine's ship engaged its light drive.

The converted daggership seemed to change shape just before it went superlight. The nacelle clusters that Rimail had spotted hinged downwards, and the wings swivelled back to a more rakish angle. It was as if the ship tensed, readying itself for exertion, before the light-drive flared and the little vessel leapt away into the void.

A pleasing fancy, Sorrelier acknowledged. But the ship was simply saving energy by narrowing its profile before opening a jump-point, that was all. Still, it was satisfying to see the assassin set out on her mission.

Sorrelier harboured no illusions about Nemesine's chances against Durham Red. The two had fought each other to a standstill on Lavannos, but the vampire had been weak, still recovering from her time with the Osculem Cruentus, and Major Ketta was at the height of her powers. Now the positions were almost exactly reversed. Ketta was a wanderer, tortured and alone, reduced to freelance murders under a false name, while Durham Red was as strong and as deadly as she had ever been. If the two fought, the results would be very different.

But that, of course, was not the point.

Sorrelier settled back on his bed, and sipped a cool drink while Lise undressed. It was a long way back to Magadan. There was still time for a dream or two.

2. DANGEROUS KNOWLEDGE

One month later, Durham Red sat in *Crimson Hunter*'s engineering cell, frantically waving her left hand about to cool her fingers. "Bastard," she said.

She'd touched the wrong part of the soldering iron again. Red stopped waving and brought her scorched fingertips close to examine them, wincing in pain and wondering, rather guiltily, how much time she had before the ship reached Biblos.

Red had hoped to be mentally prepared for the negotiations to come. She'd allowed herself much longer than normal to get ready, setting her stateroom's alarm chime to wake her at mid-morning rather than her usual noon start. This, she had calculated, would give her enough time for a hot bath, a careful consideration of which outfit to wear, maybe a little research on the library station and the man who commanded it. She might even try to meditate for a few minutes – Godolkin had once taught her some mental calming routines, Iconoclast mantras to still the mind and accelerate the senses. Normally Red's attempts at meditation resulted in her either falling asleep or suffering a fit of the giggles, but the rendezvous at Biblos was, to her, desperately important. As she had told her companions before turning in the previous night, she would do anything to make sure it ran smoothly.

It was a good plan, and a worthy intent. But by the time the star-yacht dropped out of jumpspace and started the final approach to Biblos, Durham Red hadn't done any meditating. She'd not had her bath, or read any of the ship's database entries, or picked out suitable clothes. She hadn't even slept.

As far as mental preparation went, Red wasn't prepared for anything except taking the collection of machine-parts in front of her and hurling them out of the nearest airlock. She was angry, frustrated, and had gun-oil in her hair.

She picked up the trigger assembly to glare at it. "Work," she snarled, not for the first time that morning. "You stupid piece of rusty junk. Bloody work!"

It was entirely her own fault. Just after leaving the command deck the previous night she had decided to drop into the engineering cell for a few minutes before bed, and have another try at repairing her favourite gun. But while the Borstin Auto-Chetter was a wonderful, lethal piece of hardware, it was also irreparably broken.

She was just checking the chrono display on the cell wall when an alert gong began yammering at her. Red recognised its sound: *Hunter* was decelerating from superlight, leaving the compressed dimensions of jumpspace behind and ripping a hole back into the real universe.

She leapt up, sending tools flying. "Sneck!" she yelled.

The engineering cell was near the yacht's stern, an oddly shaped chamber formed by the space between the main drives. Red keyed the door open, sprinted all the way along the spinal corridor, and skated to a halt just inside the command deck's rear hatch.

Behind her, beyond the engineering cell, she heard the light-drive throttle down with a rattling whine.

Harrow and Godolkin were already on the command deck, occupying the two forward thrones. Harrow turned to greet her as she came in. "We're here," he said simply.

Godolkin had manual control of the ship, his hands on the control collectives, tilting the vessel around to home in on Biblos. Red looked past him and through the forward viewports as the stars slid aside and a pallid disc swung into view.

She blinked at it in surprise. "Sneck," she muttered under her breath. "It's Pierrot."

It was a strange first impression. She was looking at a featureless white surface, marred only by a single black tear. It could, in another life, quite easily have been the face of a sorrowful, monochrome clown with closed eyes.

Her perception changed as Godolkin engaged the main drives and the ship moved forward. The face was a planet, a minor gas giant, its atmosphere a pale cloudscape of crystalline methane. And the tear, if the sense-engine returns were anything to go by, was a cone of black metal nearly two kilometres high.

"Is that Biblos?" she asked.

"Good morning, Blasphemy." Godolkin didn't turn as he spoke. "Can I assume that your planned research didn't go as far as you'd hoped?"

"Not as such, no." Red stepped forwards to put a hand on the back of each throne, standing behind the two men. "As you know full well, you sarcastic berk. I got distracted."

"Hmph," Godolkin replied. "The gun again."

"Look, forget about that. How long have I got?"

"Our meeting with Seebo Zimri is due in twenty minutes," said the Iconoclast. He was working the thruster controls; *Hunter* turned over in space, and suddenly Red was no longer looking at a teardrop, but at a titanic ice-cream cone.

She shook her head. "There's no way I can get ready in twenty minutes. Give me an hour, okay?"

"An hour?"

"Yeah." She made circles in the air with one finger. "Drive around the block a couple of times."

"That would be unwise. The Librarian is a difficult man, and insists on punctuality. To arrive late could prejudice him against you."

"Oh, come on, Godolkin! Who turns up on time to a library?"

Godolkin made a sound in the back of his throat, a barely-suppressed growl of frustration. "Blasphemy, I urge caution. Your communications with Zimri have been successful so far, but that is only due to curiosity on his part. Do not imagine him a harmless old man, interested only in his collection of books. He is at best an unstable eccentric. At worst, dangerously obsessive."

The library filled *Hunter*'s viewports. Red could see a narrowing between the upper hemisphere and the cone. That was where the landing bays would be. "I seem to remember you saying exactly the same thing about me."

"I hate to interrupt," said Harrow from the systems throne. "But we have been targeted. Biblos has multiple phalanx turrets locked onto us."

"I rest my case."

"Shut up, Godolkin. He's just being careful. Bad memories from Wodan." She sighed. "Okay, take us in. But can you do it slowly, please? At least give me time for a shower."

"Thy will be done, mistress."

"Good boy." She leaned playfully on the back of Godolkin's control seat and ruffled his hair. He hated that. "Hey, stop worrying. There's a quarter-tonne of Iconoclast platinum back in the hold. That should cheer the old guy up."

Godolkin inclined his head, just a fraction. "I admit the possibility. Nevertheless, I shall accompany you aboard the library, and I will remain armed."

"Good. You can carry the cash." Doors were opening ahead of the ship, saw-edged lakes of metal as big as playing fields. She headed back towards the rear hatch. "And if Zimri calls, tell him I'm trying to find my library card."

Red went straight back to her cabin, undressing as she ran, flinging her clothes all over the gel-bed and jumping into the shower, desperately hoping it would wake her up. Once she was done she grabbed a towel, but she wasn't even halfway dry before the door to her stateroom chimed. It was probably Godolkin, come to complain that she was taking too long. "Piss off!" she yelled.

"Holy one?"

The voice was Harrow's, relayed into the room by the internal sounders. Red sighed and shut the dryer off. "Sorry, Jude. Tell him I'll be out in five minutes, okay?"

"Forgive me, holy one, but Godolkin didn't send me. He's busy scanning the landing bay."

Red opened the shower and padded out over to the wardrobe. The concealed drawers began to slide open as she touched them, one by one. "So what is it you're after?"

There was a pause, then, "I need to speak with you. Can I come in?"

She blinked in surprise. "No you bloody can't. Not yet, anyway." She scanned the open drawers quickly, then reached into the nearest one and pulled out a bodysuit in burgundy leather. It wasn't her first choice, but time was short. "You can talk to me from out there."

"Very well. It's about the data crystals."

"It always is."

She heard him clear his throat. "I've been monitoring the Iconoclast data channels. High Command has just issued new edicts concerning the Lavannos debris. They say that possession of *any* artefact from the Shantima system is now a capital crime."

"Any?" Red gave a low whistle. "Sneck, that's going to piss off the Archaeotechs."

"Archaeotech division has always been something of a law unto itself, holy one."

"I suppose." Red dropped onto the bed, putting her feet into the legs of the bodysuit and pulling it up. It was well known that Iconoclast High Command had already outlawed the transcription of data from the translation drive project, days after the destruction of Lavannos, declaring the knowledge heretical, unholy, too dangerous to learn. But to extend that prohibition to artefacts or wreckage spoke of a greater fear. They must have realised that the data was still out there somewhere, in a form they might not recognise. Crystals of active silicon, for example.

"How much do you think they know?"

"To be honest, I'm not sure." The sound of Harrow's voice changed imperceptibly. Red imagined him turning around out in the spinal corridor, leaning back against the wall. "They must have deduced the history of the project by now. Detailed sense-scans would confirm that Lavannos itself was once Earth's moon, and that it was moved across space by the translation drives. But if that's all they knew, they would have tried to recreate the experiment. Being able to move planets would be a formidable weapon."

Red had the bodysuit half on and was squeezing into the rest. "It would be if it worked," she replied grimly.

In part, of course, the experiment had gone exactly as its originators had planned. The Moon, home to millions of people in Red's day, had been cleared of its cities and projected hundreds of light-years across space, a trial run for the technology that would, one day, send the entire planet Earth off on a similar journey. Four huge hyperspace engines – translation drives – had been buried in the Moon's crust, along with bases containing the scientists who would manage the project. Two hundred years after Red had climbed into her cryo-tube, the drives were activated, and the Moon vanished.

But it didn't come back.

Instead of reappearing instantly in the Shantima system, the Moon had taken a catastrophic detour. As to exactly where it had gone, Red didn't know and preferred not to think about. Wherever it was, it was hot enough to melt its crust into black glass, such an extreme environment that it had driven the scientists trapped inside their bases murderously insane.

Five hundred years later the Moon had returned, glowing hot, to its target system, settling into orbit around the gas giant Mandus. And it was not alone. On its trip to hell it had picked up a parasite, a creature Red could only conceive of as a carnivorous, intelligent cancer, a nightmare thing that had burrowed its way down to the core of the Moon and started to grow. As it grew, it ate out a space for itself.

The Moon had been colonised by a monastic order who called it Lavannos. And while almost none of the monks realised their icy little world was once the satellite of the fabled lost planet called Earth, all of them were aware that the ground beneath their feet was only a thin crust, an eggshell around a gigantic telepathic carcinoma with a taste for human brains. It was their new god, and they served it well.

It was no wonder that High Command had outlawed anything that might come from Lavannos. When Red had encountered the creature it had been comatose for centuries, but its merest sleep-stirrings had cost thousands of lives. Together with an Iconoclast admiral called Huldah Antonia, Red had managed to reactivate one of the ancient drives and fatally wound the sleeping monster. But if it had ever fully awoken, it would have ravaged the galaxy.

Red shivered at the thought, pulling the suit's front seal closed. "So what's your point? Oh, and you can come in now, by the way."

"Thank you." The hatch slid aside and Harrow's face poked nervously around its edge. Seeing Red at least half-decent he relaxed visibly. "My point is that I'm beginning to agree with Godolkin."

Red's eyebrows went up. "That's a first."

"Holy one, please be serious. Your pursuit of the crystals is growing more dangerous with every day."

She got to her feet. "If High Command knew they were here, we'd be surrounded by killships."

"That's not what I meant." Jude walked further into the room, folding his arms across his chest. "Red, I know what these artefacts must mean to you–"

"Do you? Really?" Red rounded on him. "I've got *nothing* in this universe, Jude! Not a snecking thing! Apart from one busted gun the only connection I've got with my own time is the planet where I was born, and somebody stole that while I was frozen!" She stomped back to the drawer and began rooting around inside it. "Nobody in this time knows where Earth is. Christ, most of you don't even know it ever existed. So those crystals are my only clue."

"And what are you prepared to do to get them?"

She found what she was looking for in the drawer – a short leather jacket – and hauled it out, then kicked the drawer closed. "Anything," she said quietly.

"That's what worries me. Holy one, these crystals are a plague. So many people have died because of them: the Harvesters that found them in the Shantima system, the Tenebrae that tried to take them. Death surrounds them like a miasma." He sighed, looking at the carpet. "And I'm afraid for you."

Red glared at him for a moment, but then her gaze softened, and she found herself smiling. "That's sweet," she said. "But you don't have to worry about me."

"In these times, I worry about everything. Especially you."

"You'll end up bald." She crossed the stateroom to open another drawer and began to rummage. "Look, I know that the crystals are trouble. But if there's any chance of finding out where those scientists sent the Earth, I've got to make a play for them. If only to make sure the silly buggers didn't make the same mistake twice." She found what she was looking for and straightened, holding it aloft: a particle magnum, custom-built with an extended power core and double-length barrel. "Besides, you know I'll be careful."

Harrow eyed the weapon dubiously. "That's one way of putting it."

There was no one on the landing bay to meet them. Red knew that Seebo Zimri's dislike of visitors was legendary, but she would have expected a servant, at least – even some kind of robot would have been comforting. As it was, all she could see moving as she left *Hunter*'s landing spine were phalanx turrets, mounted on the bay's ceiling, attached to armoured gimbals. As she stepped out of the lock they snapped smoothly around her to cover her from every angle.

Her stride faltered, and she stopped. "Blimey."

"The turrets are automated," Godolkin murmured, moving to position himself between Red and the nearest guns. He put his carryall down onto the deck, leaving an arm free. The other was buried to the elbow in the gleaming bulk of his holy weapon. "I count six quad-mounts of heavy-calibre particle cannon. Primarily anti-personnel devices, although sustained fire could damage a starship."

"Nice," Red replied. "And you missed a couple." She jerked her head back, at the turrets set on either side of the bay doors, just in case anyone tried to leave in a hurry. "Heard 'em turning."

Godolkin raised his comm-linker. "Harrow?"

"I'm right here," the mutant replied. "Do you want to come back in?"

"Negative. Close the outer lock, but leave the reactor on standby." Godolkin gave Red a questioning look, and she nodded very slightly. "And bring the flayer missiles online. Target the bay doors."

"As you wish."

Red peered about, trying to ignore the way all the turrets moved as she did. The particle magnum was clipped to her belt, but she doubted whether she could take all the phalanxes down if things got nasty, and the bay was almost completely devoid of cover. She'd not want to get into a firefight here.

It was a killing ground, if Zimri wanted one.

"All right," she muttered. "I'll admit it's not quite the welcome I would have liked. But we all knew he was an antisocial bugger."

Godolkin lifted the carryall again. It must have weighed a hundred kilos, with all that cash-metal inside, but if he felt the weight at all he made no sign.

"As you surmised," he said, moving away. "Memories of Wodan must trouble him greatly."

Red made a face, and hurried to catch him up. If the fall of Wodan kept Zimri awake at nights, she could hardly blame him. Every now and then it did the same to her – when sleep evaded her and the cool darkness of her stateroom pressed down like the lid of a tomb, it all came surging back. The reek of burning flesh and burwood, the chatter of Iconoclast bolters, the screams...

Bolters. Red looked over at Godolkin's holy weapon, and groaned. What the hell was Zimri going to say when he saw that?

"Shit," she hissed. "I should have brought Harrow instead."

"And which of you," Godolkin asked, raising the container, "would have carried this?"

"Point taken." Red could have carried the money, but it would have looked bad. Harrow couldn't have lifted it. "You could have brought a different gun, though. That one's not exactly tactful."

"Blasphemy, the Iconoclast operation on Wodan was a direct response to your presence. You are more directly accountable for the destruction of the Great Library than I. We must hope that Zimri has passed beyond that fact."

"Great." The two people Seebo Zimri would most have reason to blame for the destruction of his life's work were walking across his primary landing bay, with every turret in the place aimed right at them.

"Um, Godolkin? Maybe you'd like to pick up the pace a little here?"

"Were I not carrying this container, Blasphemy, rest assured I would do so."

"Right. Do so anyway."

She had only spoken to Seebo Zimri once, over a wobbling and heavily-encoded comms link some weeks before. Just after she had learned there was a very good chance he had the Lavannos data crystals.

The crystals had almost gone to the Iconoclasts, which would have been the second time Red had lost them. It was bad enough that she had taken them to the Aranites of Lyricum to get them translated. Despite their reputation as experts in the field of lost technologies, the spidery little mutants were also, Red had discovered, thieving bastards. They had sold her out so that they could get their hands on the Lavannos data, and given her to a psychopathic mutant terrorist called Xandos Dathan.

While Red had been trying to stop Dathan plunging the Accord into civil war, the Aranites had been downloading everything that lay within the crystals, storing it for their own use or to sell it on. When they had realised Red was still alive, however, they had suddenly decided that they didn't want the artefacts around them any more. Anyone else might have simply thrown the things out of the nearest airlock, but the Aranites were far too avaricious for that. Instead, they had put a call through to the Archaeotech temple-labs on Nicopolis.

The Archaeotechs were a division of the Iconoclast army, but, as Harrow had said, they were very much a law unto themselves. Secretive to the point of paranoia, their techno-priests and warrior-historians travelled the darkest tracts of Accord space, hunting technologies lost during centuries of bloody war. It was well known that they dealt with the Aranites on a regular basis.

So well known, in fact, that Red had been waiting for their procurement clipper when it dropped out of jump-space.

The Archaeotechs didn't have the backing of High Command. As the Lavannos data was proscribed as heretical, they had wanted a secret deal, a quiet exchange of resources that could be easily denied, but all they got was a flayer missile in the drive core. Red had got into the clipper and away with the money so quickly, the crew hadn't even sounded an intruder alert until she was on her way out.

In one risky but exhilarating operation she had not only derailed the Iconoclast bid for the crystals, she had gained enough cash-metal to finance her own. It would have been the perfect solution if Seebo Zimri hadn't stepped in.

But he was already with the Aranites, ready and waiting with his own bag of money. When the Archaeotechs failed to show up, the Aranites had been happy to take on the next highest bidder.

Something occurred to Red as they crossed the landing bay. She hadn't noticed it at first, not with the gun muzzles following her, but she was starting to realise what was bugging her.

"It looks a bit plain," she said.

Godolkin raised an eyebrow. "In comparison to?"

"Almost everything else I've seen in this mad universe of yours." She spread her hands. "Where are the columns, Godolkin? Where are the carvings, or the stained glass, or those creepy metal skulls you people love gluing to everything? Sneck, this place looks almost normal..."

The Iconoclast shrugged, huge muscles sliding under the armoured battle-harness he wore. "Biblos was not always a library," he replied. "It predates the Accord. It was abandoned during the Bloodshed, its original contents lost to Harvesters and other scavengers. Zimri appropriated the gross structure decades ago, and fitted it out for his own purposes."

"Which were?"

"A staging area for his shipments. He roamed the galaxy looking for ancient texts and then stored them here for cataloguing and verification. Shipping them to Wodan was the final stage."

"Ah! So he was here when you cooked the place?"

"Here, or in transit." The Iconoclast inclined his head a fraction. "He might even have watched the Great Library burn."

"Maybe that's why he didn't meet us at the door. He's pissed off at us."

"Undoubtedly."

An armoured hatch, big enough to drive a truck through, led off the bay. As soon as Red and Godolkin drew close it gave a grinding, echoing squeal and started to rise. Red paused, letting the hatch go up, giving the Iconoclast a quick smile as she waited. "This is it, I suppose."

When the gap was wide enough she stepped through, hand outstretched, ready to finally greet the man who would show her the way home.

3. HUSH

Zimri wasn't there. No one was there. The chamber beyond was as lifeless as the bay.

Red had entered a loading hall, a wide rectangular space with steel tables lining one side and a row of cargo sleds parked against the other. A smaller door occupied the far wall, solidly closed, and caged lumes cast a sullen, bluish glare across the plain metal floor.

The sleds were laden with dozens of storage crates, heavy cubes of impact-plastic bound with iron, and more were stacked around the tables. Some of those had been opened, and their contents piled onto the metal surfaces for sorting; great piles of books, scrolls and dataslates spilling across the bright steel.

Zimri had taken possession of a new shipment by the look of things, and not long ago. There was no dust on the books, no damage to the hall itself, nothing to indicate the loaders and sorters hadn't simply been called away minutes before, leaving their work where it lay.

Nothing, save a crawling itch at the back of Red's neck.

She stood still, gnawing her lower lip, listening hard. Apart from the faint humming of air recyclers and her own breathing, the hall was silent. Very carefully, she shifted her weight from one foot to the other, so the barrel of the magnum just touched her thigh and reassured her it was still there.

She glanced over her shoulder as Godolkin stalked in past her. "He's taking this privacy business a bit far, don't you think?"

The only answer he gave was to tilt his great head back and glare up at the ceiling. "Librarian!" he roared, his voice sudden and startlingly loud. "No more games – show yourself!"

Red took an involuntary step away. "Jesus, Godolkin! Say that a little louder, won't you? I still have partial hearing in my left ear."

"What do you suggest, Blasphemy? Wait here until he chooses to answer?"

"I'll let you know."

That itch wouldn't go away, though. She could almost understand Zimri not sending anyone to meet her in the bay: if he was fearful of visitors, as well he might be, it would be the perfect place to rid himself of any he distrusted. But Zimri was an obsessive bibliophile. Ever since the fall of Wodan he had been scouring the Accord for texts, his only aim in life to recreate the glories of the Great Library in this ancient, forgotten hulk of a space station. Why would he call his staff away from these latest acquisitions? If he didn't want Red and Godolkin seeing his newest treasures, he could have sent a guide and led them in by a different route.

Red wandered over to the nearest table and scanned the books lying there. "*Deus Sanguinius*, *The Cling Peach Cookbook*, *Cislunar Hit Singles of 2176*... Quite a range." She turned an ancient tome around to squint at its title. "*Kitab Al-Azif*? Sneck, Dathan had a copy of this! Must be a real page-turner."

"I believe the Abbot of Lavannos may have possessed a similar volume," said Godolkin absently, setting the carryall down next to one of the loading sleds.

The door in the far wall opened automatically as Red got close, but there was no one behind that one either. Together, she and Godolkin moved through another four rooms, each devoted to the storage and cataloguing of books, and each as lifeless as the first. By the time she got to the heart of Biblos, the main section of the Library, Red had pretty much given up on finding anyone at all.

Maybe Zimri had sent them all away. The sense-engine
return Harrow had spotted might have been the entire staff
of Biblos going superlight in the opposite direction,
although Red could never imagine the Librarian himself
leaving this place. Wodan was gone, Seebo Zimri would live
and die in Biblos, she was certain.

The centre of Biblos was behind a larger, more heavily
built hatchway. Red had to open it manually to get through,
rather than wait for it to slide away as she got close. She
wasn't quite sure why, until she saw what the door led to.

Beyond it lay a bridge, a narrow strip of metal meshwork
no more than three metres wide, and maybe two hundred
long, edged with waist-high handrails. At the far end of the
bridge loomed a skyscraper-sized cylinder of greyish metal.
Below was a sheer drop of terrifying proportions.

Eyes wide, Red stepped out onto the mesh, feeling it shake
slightly under her boots, and peered over the rail. "Bloody
hell," she breathed. "That is a snecking long way down."

She was at the heart of Biblos. From what she could see,
most of the conical bulk of the library station was taken up
by one gigantic open shaft.

It was a kilometre deep, at least, and almost half that distance across. The cylinder occupied its centre, topped with
a wide dome of black glass, and Red could see dozens more
walkways, identical to that on which she stood, poking out
from the sides of the cylinder all the way down. They
appeared at odd angles, and not all of them were connected
with anything at all. Those furthest from her, at the bottom
of the library, looked like no more than threads in the hazy
air.

Wind, warm and stale, was blowing up from the base of
the shaft, whistling mournfully through the rails and the
open mesh beneath Red's feet.

"Blasphemy," said Godolkin, nodding at the cylinder.
"Note the sectioning of that structure. I would guess that
each of these bridges has its own segment, and that each
section can rotate independently of its neghbours."

"But why would they rotate? Oh, hang on! I get it." She paced partway out onto the walkway and looked over the edge again. "If the bridges turn, and you can walk around inside the cylinder, then you can get to any part of the wall. Just go from one to another, all the way down." The walkway she stood on would also turn too, hence the difference in the doors. If the door leading out of the cataloguing area had been one that opened on command, someone might go through it when the bridge wasn't connected. Which was not advisable.

Why would Zimri need access to the shaft walls, though? Unless...

Red looked back to the part of the shaft wall nearest to her, and gasped. "Son of a bitch!"

"Mistress?"

"Godolkin, the walls – they're all bookshelves!"

The Iconoclast followed her gaze. "Impressive," he replied quietly.

That was an understatement. Red whistled softly, the sound lost amid the shaft's sorrowful winds. The outer wall of that enormous space was an insane grid of shelves, home to untold thousands of books. The shelves were continuous, angling slightly as they wrapped around the inside of the shaft, spiralling down away from her in an endless helix. Looking more closely she could see hundreds of narrow platforms connecting the shelves, precarious sets of steps, even ladders bolted to the shelf edges. Every now and then, mesh discs stuck out like fungi on a dead tree, each with a small table and a single chair. Reading platforms.

Suddenly, the true scale of the Librarian's obsession became clear. It made her own hunger for the data crystals seem amost innocuous.

There was a hatch at the far end of the bridge, a narrow doorway set into the cylinder wall. Red and Godolkin reached it after a couple of minutes walk – they had slowed towards the centre of the bridge, where the mesh seemed to bounce quite alarmingly in time with their footfalls. Red found herself gripping the handrails tightly when that started to happen, and being very glad indeed that Godolkin had left the carryall behind. There was an arch-shaped keypad mounted next to the door. Red pressed the "open" button and the hatch slid aside, onto the interior of a long hallway, the walls curving away out of sight. In contrast to everything else she had seen on Biblos it was clean and elegant; the floors were of polished wood, the ceiling delicately vaulted.

Godolkin took a few paces around the curve of the hallway, and Red followed, keeping to the outside wall while he hugged the inner, covering him with the magnum. "There's got to be a door around here somewhere."

"Here," the Iconoclast said suddenly. He darted forwards, past a tall panel of dark wood, and put his back against the wall on the far side. As Red watched he reached over his right shoulder and unsheathed his silver blade: the huge sword emerged like a magician's trick as he brought it over and down, extending from an empty hilt into two metres of razored silver in less than a second. "On three," he said. "One…"

Red jumped forwards and kicked the door clean off its hinges. "Three."

She dived through, even before the broken door had finished falling, rolled to one side and came up in a perfect fighting crouch, her magnum up and the trigger halfway back. Behind her, Godolkin barrelled through with his sword held high. "Librarian!" he roared.

Red swallowed hard. "I don't think he can hear you."

Finally, she had found Seebo Zimri. But it was far too late.

She got up from her crouch and walked into the room. It was a big place, open and light, maybe three quarters of the entire upper surface of the cylinder taken up by one vast circular chamber. The impression of luxury out in the hallway continued here – the floor was a sea of carpet, the walls consisting of row after row of exquisitely filled bookshelves.

Soft light filtered down from a ceiling that, unlike the glossy blackness outside, was a dome of elegant silver tracery and frosted glass.

Chamber music filtered gently from concealed sounders. That, even more than the airy comfort of the place, made the horror it contained all the more harrowing.

Zimri was at his desk at the centre of the room, sitting in a high-backed leather chair. His head drooped forwards, and his long white hair hung down and trailed in the pool of blood before him, drawing some of it up like wax up a candlewick. The surface of the desk, pale wood polished mirror-smooth, bore criss-crossing scratches: in his final moments the man had clawed at it, hard enough to drive the bones through the tips of his fingers.

There was much blood on the desk. It teased her nostrils, but it was old, clotted, rank with the stench of death. It made her nose twitch, her stomach tighten. "Whatever went on here, we missed it," she said dully. "Poor bastard's been dead a day, maybe more."

Godolkin had moved past her, to stand by the Librarian's side. He reached down and moved a hank of trailing hair aside. Red saw what lay behind it and stifled a gasp.

The blunt end of an Iconoclast staking pin jutted brutally from his sternum.

There was no mistaking it: Red had seen those awful things far too often to ever forget them. A needle-sharp bolt of silvered steel, the staking pin was blast-fired from the holy weapon of an Iconoclast shocktrooper. Superstitious to the last, the Iconoclasts had designed it as an anti-vampire weapon, part of the holy trinity of bolter, burner and silver blade.

The old man bore neither the marks of cleansing fire nor the beheading sword, but that didn't matter. The staking pin had gone in through his breastbone, shattered his spine and fixed him, like a nailed plank, to the back of his leather seat.

Not wanting to, but unable to stop herself, Red reached over the desk and took Zimri's bloodied head, lifting it.

Immediately she let it fall again, jerking backwards in horror and disgust. "Bastards." she said.

Someone had taken time over the old man. A long, long time. When the end finally came, he must have welcomed the pin's cold kiss like that of a brother.

"There is nothing for us here." Godolkin's voice was low, almost tender. "We should be away."

She shook her head. "No. Not yet."

"Mistress, the Librarian's death is clearly Iconoclast work. The fact that he endured torture makes it unlikely the data crystals are still on Biblos."

"I know." She'd known as soon as she saw the staking pin. The Archaeotechs might have been scientists and historians at heart, but they were still Iconoclasts. They had been stung by both Red and Zimri, stung hard. Their cash was gone, their plan to obtain the crystals completely derailed. They wouldn't even have been able to report the loss.

How naïve had she been to think they would just give up?

"It's over," she said. "By the time we get *Hunter* fixed for another jump they'll be back at Nicopolis–"

"We can speculate on that once we are off this station," Godolkin snapped. He was already heading for the doorway. "We have to leave. Now."

"I said not yet! Christ, show a bit of snecking respect!"

Godolkin had stopped near the door. He looked back over his shoulder, his expression partly anger, but mostly exasperation. "Blasphemy, for once, use the brain God gave you. If the Librarian has been dead that long, who let us into the landing bay?"

4. NEW FRIENDS

Red barrelled along the curving hall, heading for the hatchway back onto the bridge, but Godolkin, restricted by the bulk of his holy weapon, was reduced to a more measured pace. Red was out of the cylinder and onto the walkway while he was still inside. "Get a bloody move on!" she said.

"I see no reason to scramble, Blasphemy. In probability the crystals are already gone."

"Did you see another ship in the bay?"

"There is more than one bay."

"So we check the others first. Ice anyone aboard, then come back for the cash." She licked her lips. If anyone were stupid enough to be waiting around for her, she'd take great pleasure in demonstrating just how bad a decision that was.

What the Archaeotechs had done to Zimri had wiped any thoughts of mercy from her mind. Putting a staking pin through someone's chest was one thing – to most Iconoclasts, that counted as a friendly greeting. But blinding a man whose whole life was reading, carving away his face and his eyes, while he screamed and twisted and clawed his fingers to the bone, was beyond reason.

There was no way she'd let that stand.

Godolkin still hadn't reached the walkway. Red was about to shout at him again when she heard a scraping behind her, a dull slamming of metal on metal. "Great," she snapped. "About bloody time."

There was no answer. Impatiently, Red glanced back, and the insult she had been readying died on her lips.

The sound was not Godolkin's boots on the bridge. It was the hatch slamming shut.

"Shit!" She ran back, slapping at the keypad. That did nothing except emit a defiant "locked" tone, so Red put her hands to the hatch and shoved as hard as she could. She was a lot stronger than she looked, but the hatch didn't budge. Considering its thickness, and the way it was seated deeply in the runners of its frame, she hadn't really expected it to. She couldn't even get a proper grip on its damp, corroded surface.

She gave it one final punch, more to punish herself for being so stupid than in any hope of damaging the door, then took a step back. "Godolkin!" she yelled, up at the dome. "Can you hear me?"

Behind her, something split the air.

She snapped sideways, felt the heat of the staking pin as it seared past her and buried itself in the hatch. Another was already whining towards her: she ducked and whipped out a fist, punching the heavy bolt aside. It struck the cylinder wall behind her and clattered away.

A dark figure was crouching on the bridge, halfway across. An Iconoclast.

Or was it? For a moment, Red wondered if her sense of scale was deceiving her. The figure was small, much more than Godolkin, or even herself. The armour it wore was very much like that of a shocktrooper, a black rubberised carapace with an integral breath mask, but it was also smooth and figure-hugging, free of the usual feed-pipes and support cables. And the bolter it held was compact, more like a stubby rifle than the metre-long metal egg that constituted a holy weapon.

Red bared her fangs. Iconoclast or not, it really didn't matter. The staking pins that had sizzled down the walkway a moment before were twins to that which transfixed the Librarian. Whoever this undersized trooper was, the bastard was as good as dead.

"Not so good against a moving target, are you?" she snarled.

"Actually, I prefer them that way." It was a young woman's voice, filtered through a breath mask. Red saw the warrior straighten slightly, shaking back her dark hair. "Where's the heretic?"

"Out of the picture. I'll go and get him when I've finished with you."

"Pity. He and I have a score to settle." The Iconoclast patted the cut-down bolter with her free hand. "I owe him one of these."

"Yeah?" Red said. "Is that what you said to the old man, just before you pinned him?" She was pacing forward, her stride easy and confident, her hips swinging. It was a tried and tested bluff, a display to throw her opponent off guard. But behind the lazy swagger, she was frantically trying to work out why this woman sounded so familiar.

And why the whole situation felt so totally, sickeningly wrong.

The woman frowned, the brown skin of her forehead creasing over her dark eyes. "The Librarian, you mean?"

"Who do you think?" Red stopped. "And the others, the staff. What did you do with them? Throw them over?"

She nodded to the side as she said it, gesturing over the handrail. In spite of herself, the Iconoclast followed the gesture. Her eyes moved, just a fraction, but it was enough. Red launched herself forward, ducking under the bolter and striking the woman a massive, backhanded blow.

The Iconoclast didn't even get a chance to fire. The swipe flipped her clear over the handrail.

Red skidded to a halt, cursing herself. She'd acted purely on impulse again. For the crime the Iconoclast had committed up in the dome, she should have made the fight last longer. Made it hurt more.

"Sneck it!" she exclaimed. "And I was getting thirsty, too."

There was a dark blur to her left, moving too fast for her to see properly. She turned on reflex.

The blur smashed into the side of her face.

The force of it hurled her across the walkway. The handrail hit her in the side, under the ribs, ripping the breath from her. She bounced off it, pain detonating inside her from head to hip, and slammed into the bridge floor. Rust and oil spattered into her mouth.

The walkway jolted from end to end.

The Iconoclast had come up on the other side and kicked her in the head. Red rolled over to see the woman drop down onto the bridge. Even to have survived Red's blow she must have been immensely strong, and her reactions were incredible.

Suddenly, it all fell into place. She *had* heard the voice before, and only once encountered an Iconoclast who could move that fast. "Ketta?"

"Good guess." The bolter flared. Red whipped aside, and the staking pin scythed past her right hip. It took the particle magnum off her belt, punching a hole clean through the charge-core. The pistol vomited a sheet of sparks and died, the silver pin joining it to rusted steel.

Red leapt up, kicked the bolter aside and put a fist into Ketta's breath mask. Weapon and mask whirled away in opposite directions; Ketta flailed, trying to grab the bolter as it span away. She took Red's next kick right in her belly.

She staggered into the handrail, recovering almost instantly to catch Red's boot in both hands and turn it hard. Red had to spin with it to avoid having her leg twisted out of her hip joint, and took two vicious blows in the back before she managed to wrench herself out of the Iconoclast's grip and flip away.

Ketta darted after her, blurring with speed, giving her a sideways chop to the neck that put her into the handrail again. Red dipped under the next blow and then came up hard, the back of her head connecting with Ketta's chin in a shattering reverse butt. She heard the Iconoclast stifle a cry as she went skidding back along the walkway.

She jumped after her, eager to advance her attack, but Ketta was already up in a fighting crouch. Red paused, knowing from bitter experience how deadly that stance could be.

The woman looked very much as she had done when they had last met, back on Lavannos. Her hair was longer, more ragged, and there was a scar along her jawline that hadn't been there before. She still looked improbably young, though.

Red spat bloody rust over the rail. "Long time, no see."

"Don't try to distract me with your idiocies, monster. I know why you came here, chasing your trinkets all over the Accord. Tell me, how long did the Librarian resist before you had Godolkin kill him?"

Red blinked. Ketta was an Iconoclast special agent, a warrior and an assassin of incredible strength and skill. She was an enemy, of that there was no doubt. But she had never struck Red as one to hide behind lies. If she had taken Zimri apart, she'd be bragging about it.

There was a sharp cracking sound behind her. Fragments of black glass whipped past Red's head, pattering down like rain onto the walkway. She realised what was going on, and grinned.

Godolkin was trying to shoot his way out of the dome.

"Time's almost up, Ketta. Want to give up now, so he doesn't hear you beg for mercy?"

For a moment, an expression almost akin to longing crossed Ketta's face. "Mercy is something I gave up on a long time ago, Durham Red."

Red paused. There had been no humour in those words, not even the desperate jibes she and Ketta had been exchanging a few moments before. It was as if the Iconoclast had let her guard down, just for a moment, and revealed a glimpse of what truly lay behind the armour and the smart comments.

This was not, Red realised, the same Major Ketta she had fought on Lavannos.

Something had happened to the woman since then, something awful. The vicious certainty Red had witnessed at the Church of the Arch was gone, replaced in Ketta's eyes by something quite different. Loss, and hunger. And a dreadful, soul-deep loneliness.

Durham Red had seen all those things in a woman's eyes. Almost every time she looked in the mirror, in fact.

"Walk away," she whispered.

"What?"

"You heard me. You didn't kill the old man, and neither did I."

Ketta straightened up from her crouching position, shaking her head. "When I saw him, I thought..."

"Come on. You really think that's my style?"

The Iconoclast opened her mouth to answer, but Red never got a chance to hear what she would say. For, at that very moment, the entire walkway squealed like a thing in pain and shook hard.

Red grabbed at the handrail to steady herself, and saw Ketta do the same. For a moment she thought that the library station must have been under attack, bombed from space and suffering a massive structural failure. But then she saw the endless walls of books begin to turn slowly around her, and remembered what Godolkin had said about the sections of the cylinder: how they could rotate to move the bridges about.

The top section was doing just that. Someone had disengaged the walkway from the wall at the far end, and activated the motors. In the distance she could see that the bridge had left the hatch she had come in by and was shuddering in empty space.

She was trapped. The door behind her was locked, and the walkway ended in nothing but a thousand-metre drop. The entire structure was bouncing as it crunched around on its tracks; Red could see rust falling from its sides as it vibrated. "Oh, nice one. Now we're really snecked."

"It's them..." A few metres ahead of her, Ketta was throwing frantic looks around the shaft. "They've been waiting for us, to trap us both at the same time. You've walked right into the spider's web, and like a damned fool I've followed you all the way in!"

Suddenly, Ketta stopped where she was. She stiffened slightly, lifting her head as though she heard something over the rattling din of the walkway. "Too late," she whispered. "Monster?"

"Stop calling me that."

"It doesn't matter what I call you. Listen to me. You're no use to me dead, not any more. So if you get a chance to run, don't hesitate. Take it."

"Run?" Red stared at her. "What from?"

"That," said Ketta, pointing up the walkway.

It was another Iconoclast. Even at first glance there could be no mistake. The man was big, two metres tall or more, and powerfully muscled. He was naked to the waist, apart from a battle harness that crossed his chest, and his only other clothing was a pair of black leather trousers and military-issue boots. His skin was corpse-white, his head shaven, and heavy goggles covered his eyes.

He was pacing confidently up the bridge towards them. He had a bolter in his right hand, much like Ketta's, but it wasn't pointed at her.

"The monster and the renegade." He smiled. "Together at last. Truly a gift worth waiting for."

"Hermas," snarled Ketta.

Red moved past her, to square up to the new arrival. She'd taken shocktroopers like this down without even trying. "Do you know this guy?"

"Guard yourself, monster. You've not fought his kind before."

"We'll see." She took a step towards Hermas, feeling the bridge vibrate under each of his heavy footfalls. He was almost close enough to take...

Another warrior landed on the walkway right in front of her.

He came out of nowhere. Red barely had time to react before the man lashed out, his fist catching her in the jaw and spinning her around, his boot crashing into the back of her left knee.

He was insanely strong, far stronger than any shock-trooper Red had fought before. Fast, too. The blow to her face set her head singing and she only just managed to keep upright when he kicked her.

She whirled, blocking the next blow as it came, slapping the fist aside and following through with a punch of her own, square into his nose. It should have killed him instantly, driving bone and gristle right back into his brain-pan, but it barely rocked his head back. He grinned, showing teeth that were filed into needlepoints.

Ketta had been right. These weren't normal Iconoclasts. "Who the hell are they?"

"I'll explain if we survive." Ketta was moving away, back towards the cylinder, giving Red more space to fight. "Another one, monster!"

A third warrior dropped out of the sky, the weight of him bouncing the whole bridge as he slammed into it. Reflexively, Red threw a glance up and saw where the warriors were coming from.

They were on the ceiling, dozens of metres above her head, clinging there like bugs.

"Christ!" She leapt to one side and a blow hissed past. She grabbed the arm, wrenched it around until she felt the tendons shearing under the skin, then put an elbow back into the warrior's ribs as hard as she could. Bones broke, she was sure of it, but it didn't even slow the man down. He lashed out again, striking a glancing blow across her head that made sparks fly into her vision.

This was bad. In a straight fight she could probably have taken any one of these guys, but the walkway was narrow and there were too many people on it already. It was severely cramping her style.

"Here!" she said to Ketta. "You have one." She dived under the next blow that came in her direction, grabbed the battle harness of the warrior whose ribs she had cracked, and yanked him over her head. He was heavy, but off-balance. She threw him off his feet and straight into Ketta.

Then the first one was on her again, aiming a horrifying series of punches at her head. She had to use all her strength and speed to shove the blows aside. If any of them connected it could stun her long enough for the Iconoclast to press his advantage.

From behind her came the sounds of Ketta battling the warrior Red had thrown. The bridge, fixed only at one end and not in the best state of repair, was shuddering like a living beast.

The Iconoclast she was fighting threw one punch too many. Red got past his fists, punched him in the throat, then the centre of his chest. He staggered back, coughing blood, and she whirled her right foot up and around in a soaring roundhouse kick that connected perfectly with the side of his head. He sagged back, into the handrail, and Red simply shoved him through. He tumbled away without a sound, spinning down a couple of hundred metres before he met another bridge. Red saw him strike the handrail and ricochet bonelessly away, trailing pale blood as he fell. "One down."

"You'll pay for that, witch!" Hermas was bringing the bolter up. He had a clear shot at her.

The gun flared, but Red had already jumped out of the way. There was nowhere to go on either side, so the only path was upwards, a massive leap that sent her somersaulting above the stream of staking pins and down onto the bridge a metre behind him. She calculated the jump perfectly, even gauging how far the walkway would move while she was in the air.

There was a hoarse scream from further up the walkway. The stakes had found another target, hammering through Ketta's opponent. Red hadn't anticipated that, but she was never one to pass up an opportunity.

Hermas swung around, trying to bring the gun to bear again, but she was too close. She dived at him, slammed a knee into his groin with shattering force, and sank her teeth into his throat.

Distantly, through the bloodlust, she heard Ketta shout a warning. But it was too late. The Iconoclast's blood was already in her mouth, her throat, spilling down her chin.

Burning her apart.

A scream tore its way out of her, past the bubbling agony that was ripping its way up from her stomach. The Iconoclast's blood was like battery acid. She tore herself away from Hermas, saw him slump with both hands against the spouting wound in his neck, and then she was down on her hands and knees, vomiting pale fluid onto the walkway floor.

Smoke came up. The toxic liquid was starting to burn its way through the metal.

Red coughed weakly. Her stomach felt as though it was trying to turn inside out, her throat as raw as an open wound. She flailed, felt a hand slap against the rail and held on, dragging herself up. She was almost blind. Some of the blood must have got into her eyes.

Another Iconoclast dropped onto the bridge. She felt his boots hit the metal close to her, but there wasn't a damn thing she could do about it. Vaguely, through scalded eyes, she saw Ketta dart into combat with this latest assailant. Something bright flashed down, maybe a blade. The man roared, fell forwards with Ketta on his back, then powered up again. Ketta must have been caught by surprise, because in the next second he shoved her so hard into the handrail that the metal finally gave way.

The agent teetered for a moment, then fell off the edge.

Red snapped a hand out on reflex. She felt her fingers close against Ketta's wrist, and then the Iconoclast's weight slammed her face-down into the bridge floor. She snarled in pain.

Below her, Ketta kicked and span. "Let go of me, monster!"

Red shook her head. She tried to say something, but her mouth was a ruin, her tongue so swollen she could hardly breathe.

It hurt so badly that, for a moment, she barely felt the staking pin punch through her right shoulder.

At first she thought the Iconoclast had stamped on her, his boot crushing her down onto the bridge. Then she saw blood on Ketta's face, fat globules dripping down onto her from above, at the same time that the pain erupted through her back and arm. She moaned, almost letting go.

The staking pin had gone right through her, pinning her to the walkway.

"I have them!" The Iconoclast was standing above her, yelling in triumph. "Commander Hermas, the bitches are ours!"

"I beg to differ," snapped Ketta. Her free hand came up, her trigger-finger tensing. A slab of black metal appeared so fast that Red didn't even see it move, and spat fire.

Above her, the Iconoclast exploded.

Superheated innards cascaded back over the rail. Red reached down with her other hand, feeling her shoulder tear around the staking pin, then grabbed Ketta and hauled her up in one last, massive effort.

It took all that she had. Blackness fluttered around the edges of her vision as she fell against the metal.

Ketta's voice sounded next to her. "Don't think this changes anything, monster."

"Go," Red croaked. "Bloody go."

"I shall. But not alone." She saw the woman's shadow move as the Iconoclast reached down, and felt her body tense.

The pain as Ketta pulled the staking pin free was enough to black her out completely.

"Monster? Are you suffering?"

Red nodded. "Yeah."

"Then the day has not been entirely wasted."

She opened her eyes. Blurry colours leapt at her, light sending spikes of pain through her retinas. Her skull was pounding, joining her right shoulder and arm in a chorus of agony. Her throat was a column of gritty fire, her mouth a nest of thorns. The acidic reek was all over her; she'd vomited again while she was unconscious.

She blinked a few times, trying to clear the fog from her vision. It worked to a degree, but there were patches of stubborn grey in her sight that could only have been scoring on the surface of her eyes. The thought made her stomach flip again, and she forced it away.

If she tried really hard, summoning all her meagre reserves of strength, she found she could move her head a little to either side. The motion set her brain swimming in her skull, but it at least made her surroundings a little clearer. Gleaming outlines of light and shade to either side of her, with a rectangle of darkness above, and a mobile shadow that must have been Ketta herself.

Red might have believed she was anywhere, were it not for the constant, bone-deep thrumming coming up through the base of her spine and making her teeth rattle. They were aboard a starship, but not one that she knew. And the main drives were at full burn.

Her hands were bound, and there was a harness keeping her pressed back into a padded seat. Every now and then a force would shove her this way or that, the ship's changes of course acting on its interior before the dampers could compensate. Ketta must have been hurling the vessel all over the sky.

Red coughed, spitting acid and bits of throat tissue. "Escaped?"

"Barely." Ketta's voice was distant, preoccupied. "Hermas was weak enough for us to get past him."

"Chasing us?"

"No, monster. I'm doing this for amusement."

Red didn't have an answer to that. She squeezed her eyes shut, rolling them behind their lids, and when she opened them things were slightly clearer. At least she'd not been struck permanently blind.

She had a feeling, though, that her troubles weren't over simply because they'd left Biblos.

Ketta had told her, in a moment of desperate candour, that she was no use to her dead. The fact that she was alive, but imprisoned, spoke volumes about the agent's intentions. Knowing the kind of people Ketta worked for, maybe it would be easier for Red if Hermas and his super-troopers did catch up with them.

Then again, the man had called her a renegade. Red almost found the strength to smile. By the sound of it, little Nira Ketta wasn't working for the Patriarch any more.

Maybe she could survive this after all. "Light-drive," she croaked. "Jump away."

Ketta's shape moved slightly in front of her, and the ship swung violently over. "Damn, he's fast."

"Feel sick..."

"I regret that, monster, I truly do." Another lurch. "Considering I'll have to share this cabin with you for several days. But there was a ship waiting outside Biblos when we left... I can only assume Hermas had it stationed there in case we escaped."

"Weapons?"

"I can't bring them to bear! That cursed ship is the most manoeuvrable thing I've ever seen. Vampires included. And he's got some kind of damping field on us, stopping the light-drive from... Oh, dear God!"

Ketta's voice had turned into a cry of raw fear. "What?"

"The field! Some kind of surge..." The ship made one last rollercoaster swoop that almost threw Red out of her seat, harness or no harness, and then all the lights went out. The thrumming of the drives faltered like a dying heart, and ceased.

Red felt wisps of invisible energy crackling over her skin, worming through her hair, over her eyeballs, into the wound in her shoulder and the ragged tissue of her mouth. She screamed in pain.

There was no light at all. She was blind again.

Past the fading crackle of residual energy, she listened. Footsteps went past her at Ketta's cat-light pace, and there was the click and whine of a weapon being readied. From somewhere else came more distant, metallic thumps and crashes.

"They're boarding," said Ketta. "Monster, I can kill you now if you wish. It might save you further pain."

She shook her head; once left, once right. "Take my chances…"

"I'm glad." There was a soft creak of armour as the Iconoclast readied herself. "I was honour-bound to ask, but I'd rather your suffering continued a while longer."

"Charming…" Red gasped, but a fizzing explosion from behind her drowned the word completely.

Her seat rocked, as something vast slammed into the deck. Ketta started firing a second later. One, two shots ripped out into the dark, and then, from behind Red's seat, came a waspish snarl and a faint snap of impact.

Ketta gave a choked cry, and fell heavily onto the deck.

Silence. Then movement. Whispered voices. Red heard soft footsteps padding around her and then, in a sudden burst of light, a face appeared right in front of her.

She jerked back in surprise, a reaction that set her head spinning. The face was bizarre, unreal; a harlequin mask in silver and black, the nose hooked down over a mouth that was half smile, half frown. Jewels glittered around its edge, and as tears beneath the eyes.

"This one," said the mask. Its voice was male, but high-pitched and liquid, its cadences strange. They were not, Red was certain, the tones of Hermas or one of his enhanced cronies.

At that, other forms moved close, and her bonds were carefully cut away. The hands that freed her were gentle, but her injuries were great. There was no way they could have freed her without causing her pain, and nothing she could have done except but collapse into their grasp once the harness was gone.

Despite her agonies, she remained awake through the whole process. Curiosity had her, its impulse almost as strong a motivation as the will to live. It kept her damaged eyes open as the masked troupe carried her out of the darkness and into the light.

5. THE CRIMSON AND THE GREEN

When the hatch between Matteus Godolkin and the Blasphemy had slammed closed, Godolkin had put his holy weapon aside and tried to force the door off its runners. It took him less than ten seconds to realise he couldn't do it.

His strength was prodigious, his bones and muscles augmented by Iconoclast biochemical remodelling, honed by years of combat and hard, ceaseless training. But the hatch remained as solid as the wall. Whoever had caused it to close had activated the locks at the same time – it could have been a series of powerful electromagnets, or even simple metal bolts, that held it firmly in place.

Godolkin drew in a long breath, focussing on it, magnifying the stillness in his soul with an Iconoclast catechism. It was a simple trick, one of the first mental disciplines he had ever learned, but it remained effective. The rush of anger in his chest faded, replaced by a serene certainty. If his tactics were sound and if God was with him he had no doubt that he would prevail.

The solution was quite obvious when he thought about it. If the doors wouldn't open for him, he would make some more. He ran back to the reading room, raised the holy weapon and sent a burst of staking pins hammering up into the ceiling.

The glass panels, delicately frosted and set into an intricate series of curving vaulted silver frames, erupted into a storm of fragments. It took only a few pins to destroy the ceiling completely. The framework had little structural strength, relying instead on symmetry and balance to hold the panels up. Godolkin only had to take out a square metre or two for gravity to do his work for him. In moments, the reading room was a blizzard of tumbling, shattering shards.

He bowed his head as the worst of the storm came down, then looked up to examine what his shots had revealed. There was, as he had surmised, a considerable space between the elegant inner ceiling of the reading room and the thick, black glass of the cylinder roof. The space was filled with a maze of pipework and ducting, power cables and suspended lumes. Little remained in the area he had targeted, but the roof above it was surprisingly intact.

Godolkin moved closer to the wall, switched the holy weapon to single-fire and put one staking pin into the glass.

The pin slammed into the roof with splintering force, creating a crater the size of Godolkin's head. He stepped aside as debris arced down onto the littered carpet, and made a swift mental calculation as to how many pins he would need to get through, along with the best pattern in which to concentrate his fire. Then he began ripping a hole in the roof of Zimri's inner sanctum.

The job took a few minutes. The glass was tough, heavily modified to support its own weight, and layered with a steel mesh for added strength. Part of the mesh must have been linked to the comms shielding too, because as soon as he had made a gap big enough to see through his linker went off.

It was the mutant, Judas Harrow. "Godolkin? Where in the name of God have you been?"

"I've been busy," he replied flatly, then switched channels. "Mistress?"

He waited for three seconds before getting back to Harrow. "Mutant, is the Blasphemy with you?"

"What? Damn you, Iconoclast, don't tell me you've lost her!"

"We were separated," he growled. "I shall look for her. In the meantime, ready the ship, and run a bio-scan. This structure is heavily shielded, but you may still be able to locate her. Godolkin out."

He shut the device down, cutting off Harrow's indignant protests.

A few more pins made the hole big enough to scramble through. He ran to the nearest wall and began to clamber up it, hurling the books behind him as he climbed from shelf to shelf. They had rested on stout planks of burwood, easily strong enough to bear his weight, and in a few seconds he was pulling himself into the opening.

The walkway was turning, but it was close. There were only a few seconds to wait until it was beneath him. He watched it rattling around, vibrating on its ill-maintained runners. And then, against his every instinct, he looked back down into the reading room.

Zimri sat there, eyeless. Decay had already begun to bloat him; the chair was slowly edging back from the desk as his belly swelled. Godolkin's nose twitched at the stench rising from the body. In another day, the atmosphere in the reading room would be unbearable.

Godolkin never intended to return. But still he raised his holy weapon and sent a column of searing flame washing over the corpse of Seebo Zimri.

The burner fire was unimaginably hot, the self-combustion of its fuel approaching the temperature of thruster exhaust. Godolkin had a momentary glimpse of a shape in the midst of the inferno; a blackened skeleton shedding curls of blazing meat, falling off the staking pin and onto the desk. Then even that was gone.

"*Resquiat in pace*, Librarian," he breathed.

It was a waste of burner fuel, but he had plenty. Godolkin turned away from the pyre and jumped down from the roof.

Combat had taken place on the walkway. The signs of it were everywhere.

The handrail was bent and fractured as if from massive impact, and in one place was torn through altogether.

There was blood on the steel flooring, although Godolkin had difficulty identifying its origin. The greater mass of the liquid, surrounding several threads of scorched offal trodden into the walkway, seemed to have a sizeable toxic component. One pool, a vomitous mix of poisoned blood and mutant stomach acid, had even started eating into the metal.

But one small trail of blood concerned Godolkin far more. It was that of Durham Red.

He knelt by its traces, noting the hole in the walkway it had poured through, the discarded staking pin that lay nearby. It seemed certain that the vampire had fallen prey to an Iconoclast weapon. She had been stapled to the bridge by it.

Then someone had pulled the pin out, from metal and flesh alike, and borne her away.

He had no trouble getting onto the landing bay, as the door from the loading hall was back under manual control. It was his biggest clue yet that whoever had been leading him, and the Blasphemy, through this accursed place was already gone. The thought added speed to his steps, but didn't stop him making a short detour to take the carryall of platinum from its hiding place.

Harrow was in *Hunter*'s command cabin. The mutant swung his throne around as Godolkin entered. "What happened?"

He ignored the question, and the accusing stare that went with it. "Have you run the bio-scan?"

"I did, but all I picked up was you. Godolkin–"

"This entire situation was a trap, Harrow. The Librarian was dead when we arrived. Whoever killed him led us through the library and then trapped me in a shielded structure. While I was there, the Blasphemy was locked in combat."

The mutant looked aghast. "Who with?"

"Iconoclasts. There is evidence she fell prey to a staking pin." He set down the holy weapon and the carryall, and dropped into the command throne. "Re-hinge your jaw-bone, mutant. I am certain she lives."

Harrow shook himself, then ran through the last of the yacht's pre-flight checks, tapping the controls quickly. "The Archaeotechs?"

Godolkin shook his head. Even the Custodes Arcanum, the Archaeotechs' dedicated warrior division, wouldn't have been able to bring the monster to heel. She had been attacked by something far more powerful.

The landing bay doors opened at Godolkin's command, and in a few moments *Crimson Hunter* was powering away from Biblos. "Harrow, begin a series of sense-sweeps. Highest resolution: check for plasma trails and ionisation from jump-points."

"Right." Harrow got up and went to the sensor board. Godolkin, his attention on the flight controls, heard two or three keypresses and then a yelp of surprise. "Moon of blood, human! There's another ship out here!"

Godolkin activated a slaving control, directing a holo-display from Harrow's board to his own. It sprang to life instantly; a glowing sphere of green light as big as his head, with a tiny triangle pulsing in the centre to mark *Hunter*'s position.

Off to starboard was something else: a yellow threat marker, surrounded by data icons.

"Range ten thousand kilometres," Harrow reported. "The drives are idle, but she has power." He looked up. "Human, is that an Iconoclast vessel?"

Godolkin was already turning *Hunter* about. "In part. Ready the flayer missiles, and then continue with the sense-sweep. This may be a feint – we have already been led a dance today."

The data icons became more detailed as the range between the two vessels shrank. The other craft was, as he had told Harrow, a machine at least partly based on an Iconoclast daggership, a military interceptor famous for its speed and firepower. But so much of the vessel had been replaced or upgraded that almost nothing of its original outline remained. Godolkin noted multiple weapons emplacements, enlarged sense-domes, hugely overpowered thrusters mounted on variable-geometry winglets; changes that would increase the daggership's range and firepower beyond the dreams of the original designers.

Flying a rather battered luxury yacht, with only two flayer missiles for protection, Godolkin found himself feeling just a little outgunned.

He opened a crypt-link. "This is Johann Fahn of the *Barracuda*. Identify yourself."

For a few seconds the link stayed dead, the screen nothing more than systems icons against a black field. Then the audio cut in. "You're a liar, heretic, and a bad one."

"Major Nira Ketta," said Godolkin, hearing Harrow suppress a gasp behind him. "Why am I not surprised?"

The screen came on. For a second it showed nothing but an empty control throne, and then Ketta slumped into it. Her armour was battered and torn, her dark skin sheened with sweat. She looked breathless, exhausted. "Heretic, if I had time I would love to stay and chat. But I have an appointment elsewhere."

"Your only appointment is with death, agent, unless you hand over the Blasphemy now."

Ketta made an amused sound. "My, aren't we getting protective! A pity I don't actually have her. It would have been fun to watch your reunion." Her dark eyes were fixed on the controls of her ship, below the pickup for the holo-feed. "I'm sure it would have been most passionate."

"Your time as a renegade has affected your sanity, Ketta."

"Godolkin, take care!" It was Harrow, still at the sensor board. "She's charging the light drive!"

The holographic image of Ketta's ship was changing shape, the drive nacelles folding inward. Godolkin half rose from his throne, reaching over to the weapons control board. He tapped at the icons, fast and certain. A heartbeat later there was a third marker on the hologlobe.

A single flayer missile lanced out from *Hunter*'s starboard launch-tube, corrected its course once and accelerated. It hit Ketta's modified daggership in the port nacelle. *Hunter* was close enough for Godolkin to witness it: the engine flew apart, ripped open by the missile's warhead, spilling fire. The image of Ketta on his screen shook with the impact.

She gave a wordless snarl of fury, pulling back hard on a control mechanism just out of sight. Godolkin saw the ruined engine disengage from its winglet, a burst of one-shot thrusters sending it spiralling away in an expanding cloud of metal fragments and fuel. "You'll pay for that, you tow-haired maniac!"

Before Godolkin could reply, the ship was gone, leaping forward into the billowing lightstorm of a jump-point.

He sat back down. "Harrow, do you have her course?"

"There's an ion-wake from the damaged drive." The mutant frowned in puzzlement. "And something else. A return that keeps coming and going on my scopes, but I'm beginning to think it might just be a fault in *Hunter*'s sensorium."

"Given what this vessel has been through, that would not surprise me." Godolkin set the reactors to charge, throttling up the rate of power-feed. Indicators on the board began to crawl upwards. "Give me the coordinates Ketta is heading for. We still have things to talk about."

"There is still much about this situation that puzzles me, Harrow." Godolkin had taken the opportunity for some much needed refreshment – a small cup of cold water and part of an Iconoclast mealstick. "Ketta had us outgunned fifty to one. She is sworn to destroy us both – why didn't she open fire?"

"I think her weapons were offline." Harrow, as befitted a Tenebrae deviant, preferred the foul stuff Durham Red called "coffee". The mutant sipped at his steaming beaker, blinking at the taste. "Hmm. From what I could glean from the sense-engines, her ship was recovering from some kind of directed power-surge. She'll have recovered by now. If we go up against her again the results won't be so pretty."

"We shall prevail," said Godolkin. "The Blasphemy wills it."

Harrow put his beaker aside, and shrugged into a battlemesh jacket. "What I don't understand is why she would be heading for Ashkelon. The world is uncolonised and is close to the Vermin Stars: it makes no sense. Why would anyone go there?"

"A rendezvous, perhaps. Somewhere to hand the Blasphemy over to bounty hunters, far from the gaze of high command."

"Hand her over?" Harrow cocked his head to the side. "You've lost me."

Godolkin finished his water, and stood up. "From what I have gathered, Ketta is no longer an Iconoclast. She disappeared after an operation to gather evidence against Lord Tactician Saulus. Since then, her whereabouts have been rumour, at best."

"I can't think of anyone better at covering her tracks. But one doesn't just leave the Iconoclast special forces for a career change!"

"After Lavannos, she fell into the hands of the Ordo Hereticus," Godolkin replied. "She must have been exonerated, or she would have ended her days as a component of a hunger-gun. But the Ordo's methods are… extreme."

"So I've heard."

"Trust me, mutant. What you have heard is not one tenth of the actual reality. I am not surprised Ketta deserted after they were done with her. I *am* surprised that she is still capable of speech."

Ashkelon was a globe of almost solid green. White caps dusted its poles, and there was a scattering of ocean beneath the cloud layer, but for the most part the planet was a seething ball of rampant vegetation. Without so much plant life the seas would have been three times their size, but the better part of the planet's water supply was permanently bound up in leaf and branch.

It was a wonder, but Godolkin spared it little attention. He was watching the skies. "Any sign?"

"I'm not sure. That anomaly again."

"Ignore it. We are looking for jump-points, or their residue." He returned his attention back to *Hunter*'s controls. "We have only one chance at this, Harrow. Ketta has the means to mask her warp-echoes. If she evades us again, it may take months to track her down."

"I know, but... there!"

Beyond the curve of the planet, flame was erupting from a point in high orbit. Even as Godolkin pushed the throttle control all the way up, Ketta's malformed ship had darted from the jump-point.

Somehow, they had arrived before her. The modified daggership must have been more disabled than he had thought. "Harrow, ready and target the last missile. We can't waste this shot."

The mutant switched seats again, and began bringing up the weapons board. As he did so, the comms screen lit.

"You're persistent, heretic. Not to mention foolish beyond belief!"

"One last time, agent. Give me the Blasphemy."

Ketta made a sound of pure exasperation. "I don't have her! For God's sake, if I did, would you not know by now? The bastards that neutralised my weapons took her from me outside Biblos."

"And you chased them here?"

"I thought I had. But there's no sign."

Godolkin raised his hand slightly off the controls, a gesture to Harrow, who was out of sight of the holo-pickup. If Ketta was telling the truth, and he was beginning to think she was, then it was imperative that he cripple her ship now before she could harm *Hunter* any more.

He didn't have to worry about hitting the Blasphemy any more. "Fire," he said coldly, and watched as Ketta's ship was enveloped in novas of green light.

"Sacred rubies," whispered Harrow next to him. "Godolkin, I've not fired."

Godolkin grabbed the flight controls and hauled them to port as hard as he could. *Hunter* seemed to leap under him, almost sending him out of the nav seat. He caught a glimpse of Ketta's ship diving away, its remaining thrusters sending out a thousand-metre blowtorch of plasma as the agent poured on the power. The green glow from her battered forcewalls was still coruscating over the hull of her ship.

If the defence shields hadn't been up, Ketta would have been atomised in that massive volley.

"Harrow?"

The mutant was hanging onto the nav throne with one hand, using the other to lock his safety harness before Godolkin manoeuvred again. "The anomaly," he gasped. "It's back, and it's gaining…"

Godolkin locked his own harness, then brought up a rear-view holo. Ketta's ship appeared to one side of it, peeling away, but what really caught his attention was the shape in the very centre of his view, a massive silhouette carved from the blackness of space itself.

The shape passed across the orbit of Ashkelon, and the planet showed through, distorted and rippling. "A shadow web."

"What?" Harrow gaped at him. "That's impossible! No one's been able to do that since the Stealth Wars!"

"It would appear that the technology has been rediscovered." He dragged on the controls again, feeling the dampers struggle to compensate, but this time he wasn't fast enough. Ragged bolts of yellow light were ripping towards the ship.

"Hang on," he said. "This could be unpleasant."

As the words left his mouth, *Hunter* was struck so hard that it physically turned upside down.

Godolkin roared in fury, hanging onto the controls like grim death and watching the planet's horizon whirl around in the viewports. The whole ship was shuddering, the throne hammering up into the base of his spine, the controls fighting to slide free of his grip. There was an awful noise from the aft sections, a metallic tearing. "Harrow, what have we lost?"

"Most of the port wing," the mutant replied. "And the port drive is venting fuel." His fingers danced over the icons, shutting the drive down. Godolkin felt the shuddering die away, but the controls were suddenly heavy in his hands.

"And the starboard drive?"

"That's not looking so good either."

Wisps of orange light began to speed past the viewscreens. The ship was skimming the planet's atmosphere.

Godolkin engaged the lateral thrusters, bringing *Hunter* level again, but the prow wouldn't come up. Fragments and trails of vapour were still spitting away from his rear-view holo, a trail of catastrophe through Ashkelon's cloudy sky. The yacht's main drives were tearing themselves to pieces.

Hunter could make a good landing with only the manoeuvring thrusters, as long as the wings were fully extended for atmospheric flight. But with only one wing, Godolkin was running out of options.

And sky.

Sea skimmed below him, grey-blue, a billion infinitesimal ripples catching the edges of dawn light. *Hunter* was heading for destruction, shedding speed and altitude at roughly comparable rates.

"We're going to crash, aren't we?" said Harrow dully.

"We are going to *land*, mutant. However, we may do so rather quickly." Godolkin touched an icon, readying the last flayer missile. "Brace yourself, Harrow."

There was no answer, save a whispered prayer to Saint Scarlet. Godolkin snorted derisively, and fired the missile, watching as it streaked away, a vanishing spot of searing light that cut a slender track of smoke through the air.

The upper layers of the forest were light, the branches delicate, the leaves sparse. The flayer missile carved its way through kilometres of such foliage before it struck something substantial enough to detonate its warhead.

Godolkin saw the explosion through the viewports, far ahead of them; a circular shockwave slammed out from the point of impact, expanding through the forest at a rate too fast to track. At its heart, raw light became flame, a growing billow of greasy fire, the outer skin of it peppered with tree trunks.

The inferno raced towards him. Godolkin dragged hard on the controls, hard enough to bend the collectives, and triggered every thruster he had.

Hunter's deck came up like a sledgehammer and hit him.

The deceleration was dramatic, far too much for the dampers to handle. Godolkin's head pounded as much of the blood in his body was shoved upwards into his brain, and his spine felt as though it was being squeezed to half its length.

There was a crater in the forest, a gaping, blazing wound the size of a sports stadium. It was the last thing Godolkin saw before *Hunter* crashed, with shattering force, into its heart.

6. THE LADDER

Durham Red almost died on the way back to Magadan.

It was a bad time for Sire Saleph Losen. As the man tasked with rescuing her, it was up to him get her back to the citadel of Trawden safe and alive. Had she died, he would have lost, at best, several levels of dominance. At worst, his head.

If there was one single factor that contributed to Red's survival on that long phase-jump home, it was Losen's almost complete ignorance of what he had walked into. His orders, in as much as a dominus of the citadel of Trawden was ordered by anyone, were simply to find the mutant and bring her back to Magadan before anyone else got to her. He had been warned that there were other players in this particular game, all of which were converging on the vampire's last known position, but what their intentions towards her might be was left very much to his imagination. Losen wasn't even sure if Red would accompany him willingly, or whether she would have to be subdued. Or indeed, given what he had been told about her, if she *could* be subdued.

And so, not knowing whether he would be entering a library or a war zone, or if he was undertaking a rescue or a kidnapping, Saleph Losen had done his best to prepare for any situation he might encounter. He had double the usual compliment of guard-sylphs aboard his ship when he left Magadan, along with a troupe of assassins, a fully fitted mobile infirmary, more weapons than he had space for and a small prison.

As it transpired, the guard-sylphs were a waste of space, and the extra weapons were not needed at all. The prison had its uses – Losen had so overloaded the ship with personnel and equipment that he ended up using it as a stateroom. But not everything he had brought along was superfluous. The assassins proved their worth in boarding the renegade human's starship and removing Durham Red from her clutches, and it was the infirmary, run by a senior physician called Compasso and staffed by mind-linked servilants, that saved her life.

When the troupe brought Durham Red aboard she was in an awful state, covered in bruises and contusions from the brutal fight she had been involved in, bleeding heavily from a gaping wound in her left shoulder. Something viciously sharp and as thick as two fingers had punched clear through her, tearing through skin and muscle before putting a ragged, splintered hole through her shoulder blade.

Worse still was the damage done by the blood she had ingested. Even though she had brought most of the stuff back up immediately, it was so violently acidic that it had burned her from lips to stomach, causing the scorched tissues to swell dangerously. Before Losen's troupe had managed to get her into the ship's infirmary she was having trouble breathing, her ruined throat closing in on itself. She blacked out as the servilants were sliding a breathing tube down into her lungs.

Losen, whose exposure to violent death had been restricted to poisons of exquisite subtlety, found the whole business very distressing.

He had gone into the infirmary with her, and watched as Compasso directed his servilants to remove the mutant woman's torn clothing and dress her wounds. The servilants were mindless, their brains even more altered than those of sylphs, but the command chips grafted to their frontal lobes made them extensions of Compasso's will. They worked with such precision, such unity, that at times

Losen thought he was watching one single creature at work, a many-armed being, quick and sure.

After several minutes work, Compasso turned away from the contour-bed on which the mutant lay. Behind him, the servilants were busy connecting diagnostic engines to her skin. "I believe our guest is stable, sire."

"Thank the Prime." Losen went to wipe beads of sweat from his forehead, and realised that he still had his mask on. He pulled it away and dabbed at his face with a silk kerchief. "I had no idea she'd be in such a state."

"The injuries seem severe, sire, but I don't think it's anything her body can't handle." Compasso pulled his own mask away, although his was far less ornate and more functional than Losen's. Behind it, though, he was elaborately moustached. "Her powers of recuperation are startling. Some of the smaller bruises are already starting to heal."

Losen saw the look in Compasso's eyes, and grinned. "Don't get any ideas, my friend. She has to stay in one piece, by order of the Magister. No trying to dissect her while no one's looking!"

"Sire, I'd not even–" He paused, looking back over his shoulder. One of the diagnostic engines had begun to emit a mournful gonging sound.

The servilants froze, and then stepped back from the couch as Compasso darted towards it. "By the Father!" he snarled. "Poison!"

"What?" Losen ran to join him. "How?"

"The blood she drank. It wasn't just corrosive." Compasso was tapping at the engine's controls with one hand. On the other side of the couch his servilants were already responding to his mental commands, readying syringes and ampoules. "It's reacting with her body chemistry."

Without warning, the engine began to howl. Losen stepped back from it, startled by its volume, but as he did so the mutant suddenly arched up from the couch, teeth bared in a rictus of unconscious agony, hands clawing at the air. A second later, she collapsed, limp.

Another engine began its own cacophony, and another.

"Cardiac arrest," snapped Compasso, before Losen could even ask. "The poison's reached her heart. Sire, I must ask you to leave."

Losen gasped, hardly hearing him. "I was supposed to keep her safe."

"I know, but that is my task now. Sire, please! I need the space!"

The hours that followed were difficult for Losen. Unable to help either Compasso or Durham Red, he was reduced to pacing the decks, trying not to trip over any guard-sylphs or weapons. And the facilities in the prison were so uncomfortable that he didn't even feel like taking one or two of his own sylphs in there to help pass the time.

Luckily for him, Compasso's skills proved a match for whatever toxins the mutant had ingested. Red's vital signs had stabilised before the ship was even through the Logic Gate.

Since then, Losen had kept the most careful eye on his new guest. He had prepared a minor villa for her use on the eighth stratum of Trawden, in the heart of his domain. In accordance with the Magister's instructions the very structure of the rooms had been reinforced, the doors and windows sealed and guarded, and extra surveillance devices had been installed. This, he guessed, was to ensure that Red didn't escape and cause havoc on the stratum, having been brought to Magadan against her will. However, the villa certainly wasn't equipped to house a critically ill young woman, no matter what her powers of self-healing. Losen and Compasso had to work very fast upon their arrival, to transform the villa into a makeshift medical centre without drawing too much attention.

And so, for the first few days of Red's stay, the villa seemed more like a hospital than a home. She healed fast, though, and within two days was able to breathe again unaided. In three she had come out of her coma, and was trying to wake up. On the fourth day she rolled out of the contour couch, and Compasso decided that it was time to put her into a proper bed and start removing the diagnostic engines. They were expensive, he informed Losen, and there was every chance that the mutant would wreck them in some kind of barbarous rage.

After that, Durham Red's recovery seemed to accelerate. Knowing that she needed blood to survive, Losen fed her sylphs, sending them in at carefully regulated intervals. They were the only people she met, during those first few days, although many others saw her through the various visula feeds dotted around the villa. Losen, in particular, spent a long time keeping watch on her.

The mutant never turned into the savage monster Compasso had feared, once she had regained her senses. She often became angry – the silence of the sylphs Losen sent in tended to infuriate her. Every time one came into the villa Red would follow the same pattern; she would try to engage it in conversation, fail, grow angry, and bite the unfortunate servant on the neck. She hadn't actually drained one yet, and seemed able to survive on quite a small amount of blood each day, leaving the sylphs dazed but alive. She was also happy to indulge in the other dishes Losen had laid out for her while she slept.

She seemed particularly fond of anything flavoured with quantities of garlic. Losen, despite himself, found that quite endearing: it so effectively belied all the old vampire stories he had been told.

Naturally, imprisonment did not suit Red well. Her escape attempts broke a little furniture, but nothing that couldn't be replaced. Her ranting at those watching her – for she seemed to have an instinctive awareness that she was under surveillance – was a revelation in terms of her vast and florid vocabulary of cursewords, and her willingness to use them in the most amazing combinations. However, she was still weak and such outbursts tended to be few.

Through most of the nine days Losen held her alone in the villa, she did little but sleep.

Finally, on the tenth day, Losen decided that it was time he and the vampire spoke face to face.

She was asleep when he entered, but he was careful to wear a suit of bio-carapace armour under his robes. Losen was no coward, but neither was he suicidal.

He took the mask with him too, just for insurance.

Once inside the villa he sat down on a chair in her bed-chamber, content to watch her sleep for a time. She was stretched out on the bed with her back to him, lying on her side, half-covered by a silken sheet. Her hair, a vivid scarlet striped with jet black, lay tousled on the pillow, and the sheet did nothing to conceal the curves of her slender body. She was, Losen admitted to herself, quite attractive in an alien, feral way.

For a time he just sat, watching, until she spoke. "You the snecker who's been spying on me?"

She hadn't moved, hadn't changed position in the slight-est. Losen wondered if she had been asleep at all.

"One of them," he admitted.

She rolled over. Her eyes, which he had seen on numer-ous visula screens, were a clear, calm blue. When she became angry they seemed to reflect the light oddly, shin-ing vivid scarlet.

They were red.

"You spoke," she said quietly.

"It's a habit of mine."

"The others didn't share it."

"The others were sylphs. A servant class. They don't speak."

"Which puts you in charge." Without warning she sprang up from the bed, flipping the sheet away, grabbing Losen by the throat as she barrelled into him. He crashed backwards out of the chair and she rode him all the way down, slam-ming him into the carpet.

It wasn't the first time Saleph Losen had been on his back with a naked woman atop him, but seldom had the experience been less pleasant.

The armour was protecting him from being strangled, but only just. "So," she said, her face very close to his. "This is where you start answering some questions. Like what the sneck is going on!"

If Losen had wanted to, he could have brushed Durham Red with the needle projecting from his signet ring. She would have been unconscious before she hit the floor. But he realised he was in no real danger. The woman wanted answers more than she wanted blood.

"I'll tell you anything you wish to know, my lady. That's why I came in. If you like, I can tell you from down here on the carpet, or we can do this in a more upright stance." He let his gaze flick down, purely for effect. "After all, if anyone were watching us now, they might get the wrong idea."

Losen seriousely doubted that his comment would embarrass Red. She had few inhibitions about her nude form, and the clothes she had been wearing in the library were not exactly modest or demure. It was the scars she still bore from that place that seemed to bother her more.

Red got up, and allowed Losen to do the same. While he was retrieving the chair from the floor, she fetched the sheet and draped it over her shoulders.

"There are clothes," he said. "In the wardrobes."

"I know, I saw." She took a slightly shivery breath. "I don't like them."

"I'll have some made for you, something more to your taste. In the meantime..." He smiled, took the mask from his robes and tossed it across to her.

She snapped it out of the air, insect-quick despite her weakness. "Christ," she breathed.

It was the mask he had been wearing when he had taken her from the renegade agent's daggership.

"It was you," she muttered, turning the mask over in her hands. "I thought I recognised your voice, but I wasn't sure..."

"You were rather distracted at the time." He favoured her with a slight bow. "Saleph Losen, at your service."

"You got me away from Ketta, brought me…" She made a vague gesture. "Here. Wherever here is."

"We call our world Magadan."

"Never heard of it."

"That's rather the point. We've been extremely careful to make sure no one has."

Without warning, Red flipped the mask back to him. "So, what's the catch?"

"Catch?" He snatched the mask out of the air. "There is no catch, not this time. The Magister has a personal interest in meeting you, but his motives are quite benign. When it became known to us that you were walking into a trap, a rescue mission was dispatched."

"I don't buy it. Benign reasons? Trust me, pal, no one does a bloody thing for benign reasons, not in this universe. As far as I know I've never been to anywhere called Magadan and I've not met any Magisters. So why is someone I don't even snecking know going to go to all that trouble and expense to pull my fat out of the fire?"

Losen couldn't help but smile. "My lady," he began gently. "The chair I am sitting on is hand-carved from ebony-crossed burwood, and inlaid with about two kilos of solid gold. The sheet you are wearing is prime-grade silk woven with gold thread, as are the pillows, the bedspread, the curtains and the hangings. The carpet is hand-tufted, the walls inlaid with platinum and lapis lazuli, the surfaces marble. In short, this room alone is worth more in monetary terms than most Accord citizens earn in a lifetime.

"There are nine room in this villa and a hundred villas on this stratum. There are fifty strata in this citadel and five citadels in the Grand Keep, and the Magister owns all of it. *All* of it."

He stood. "Now tell me, my lady, how could he possibly consider your rescue and treatment expensive?"

After Losen left the villa, making sure that the door was firmly locked behind him, a sylph approached. She was a neutral, dressed in the soft linens of the Concourse and she carried a message tube.

Losen accepted the tube with courtesy and good grace, but behind his outward calm he would far rather have been handed a live snake.

He took the tube to a café in the nearby piazza, and sat at one of the tables to open it. As was customary, he slipped on a pair of gloves before doing so. It would have been extremely bad protocol to poison the scroll within, or modify the seal; as far as Losen knew, no one had done such a thing in his lifetime. Trust, though, was not something he was familiar with, or even particularly approved of. Besides, the tube was marked with the seal of Cados and the Cadosi could be a strange crew.

The message was written by hand on fine parchment. Its content was deceptively simple.

Losen had climbed a long way up the ladder of the Magadani hierarchy, all the way through servitude, observance, and onward to the giddy heights of domination. But the higher one climbed, the wider the gaps between rungs, and the more painful the fall should one misstep. Saleph Losen liked the altitude, and he had no intention of risking a tumble just yet.

He took the tube back to his own villa, on the outskirts of the eighth stratum, and sent a request for audience through the visula. In a few minutes the little screen brightened, and the patterns on it resolved into the features of Sire Brakkeri, a third dominus and Losen's direct patron-superior.

Losen bowed low before the visula's circular screen. "Sire."

"Hello, Saleph." Brakkeri smiled thinly. "A visula call in the middle of the afternoon? You must be keeping busy."

"Forgive me, sire. Ordinarily I would not have intruded, and certainly not in such an impolite manner. But this is a matter of importance, and I urgently need your advice."

"Hmm." The old dominus leaned closer to the screen. "Does it concern our guest?"

"It does."

"I thought as much. Proceed."

Losen took a deep breath. "I just received a message scroll from a rival dominus."

"Did you now?" Brakkeri's bushy eyebrows rose a fraction. "It would hardly have been from a friendly one, would it?"

The use of message tubes was an old custom, a rare relic from a bygone era. Few but the highest-ranking domini would ever have seen one. Most people used a visula to communicate over distance and would never think of doing anything else. When it became necessary to send more secret messages, the services of a trained word-bearer might be employed – in these troubled times they were seldom out of work. There were even ways to modify a sylph to carry data internally, although the methods of retrieving it were often fatal.

The most polite method of communication, the one that denoted greatest respect, was simply to travel in order to impart the message. "If something is worth discussing," the maxim went, "it is worth doing so face to face, and preferably over a glass of wine."

But to write out a message, enclose it in a message tube and then hire a neutral sylph to transport it sent out a signal all of its own. Only an enemy would send off a missive in this manner.

An enemy with resources. "It's from Vaide Sorrelier," Losen replied.

"Ah." Brakkeri stroked his chin thoughtfully. "That dog. I knew he'd find out we had her, but not so quickly. Perhaps your security needs to be looked into, Saleph."

"It will be. Nevertheless, dogs do sniff. And Sorrelier scents a bitch."

"What does he say?"

"That he wants to meet me. The guest list for the Masque concerns him, and he wants to make sure there are no omissions."

Brakkeri chuckled. "Now that's obvious, even for Sorrelier. The loss of his prize must have hit him hard."

"Twice she's slipped from his fingers," Losen agreed. "He won't rest until she's strung up in his factory with a tap in her spine."

The older dominus sat back, steepling his fingers. It was a gesture Losen knew well, from years under Brakkeri's patronage, and he braced himself.

"Sorrelier is slipping," the man said quietly. "He's carrying too much weight, and it's time he fell. Saleph, make sure Cinderella goes to the ball. If she's unwilling, persuade her. I want to see what happens when Sorrelier finds her out in the open."

Suddenly, it all became clear. "He'll try to take her."

"He may." Brakkeri made a dismissive gesture. "And be prepared for the wrath of the Magister to fall on you, Saleph, if that should happen. You might even shed a level or two." He must have seen the look on Losen's face just then. He raised his hands slightly. "Be calm, my friend. I'll see to it you're not at the sixth for long. And Sorrelier will summon far more spite down upon his head, believe me. We've known for a long while that he's been planning something impolite. This could be the best way of directing the Magister's attentions to where they are best needed, wouldn't you say?"

"I…" Out of sight of the visula, Losen had slipped a small ampoule of Dream from a concealed pocket, and pushed the tiny integral needle into the base of his left thumb. In a heartbeat a wave of stillness had risen from his core, flowering behind his eyes like black satin. He smiled. "Of course, sire. It's too valuable an opportunity to miss. How should I reply to Sorrelier?"

"However you wish." Brakkeri waved the question away. "If at all. He'll be at the Masque in any case."

"I'll be sure to greet him appropriately. Thank you for your counsel, my sire, and enjoy the afternoon."

Once the visula screen had returned to its patterns, Losen relaxed back into his chair. His hand went to the message tube, fingertips tapping its cool metal surface, brushing the broken seal. "Sardonic old bastard," he muttered, without much malice.

He had been used, but it was the lot of the Magadani to be the instruments of those higher up the ladder. Now that he could see the whole of the plan, he was too impressed by it to be angry. In the grand scheme of things, what did it matter if he had been selected for sacrifice, his neck on the block from the moment he had set off to find and rescue Durham Red?

Perhaps, when the Dream wore off, he would think differently. For now, there was etiquette to consider.

So he took a piece of the very finest parchment, considerably better than his enemy had used, and composed a reply. He wrote that, while he was far too busy to meet with Sire Sorrelier at this time, he could assure him that the guest list for the Masque was complete. No one who should be there would remain uninvited.

He rolled the message carefully, placed it back in the tube and sealed it with his signet ring, the tiny heating element it contained re-melting the wax perfectly. Then, the job done, he summoned one of his sylphs to take it down to Concourse.

"Here's your bone back, dog," he said, as the woman walked away. "Let's see you choke on it."

7. BELLE OF THE BALL

As soon as Losen had left the room, Red got up from the bed, padded quickly over to the door and rattled the handle. It was locked.

"Crap," she snarled.

She wandered back to the bed and sat down on the edge, nibbling her lower lip. She'd missed an opportunity, her curiosity getting the better of her again. Instead of talking to Losen, trying to get answers out of him, she should have just knocked him aside and gone out to find her own.

She was still tired, still weak. But now that she was getting stronger, she'd do it right next time.

Perhaps she'd been overly startled by the sound of his voice. Apart from him, everyone who had visited her had remained completely silent – even when she had bitten them. They had offered their throats to her, these wordless, beautiful men and women, and not emitted even a whimper as she had taken their blood. But when Losen had spoken to her, the possibility of getting some information from him had put all other thoughts aside.

That was most unlike her. The poisoned blood she'd drunk on Biblos must have done more harm than she'd thought.

But she was also finding it hard to focus in such surroundings. The rooms were so different to anything she'd ever known, before or after the cryo-tube; so opulent and comfortable, so richly adorned. What had Losen said about the sheets?

Gingerly, she lifted the corner of one and brought it close enough to see the weave. It glittered in the room's pearly light, impossibly fine. Silk thread and gold.

She'd never seen anything like it.

Sneck, she'd bled all over them when they'd first brought her in there! She'd been delirious then, injured and poisoned, but the memories still pricked at her. More than once she'd clawed the dressing away from her perforated shoulder, and the blood had come freely. She remembered the warmth of it on her skin, slick at first and then sticky, coating her, its smell a torment.

How many times had she done that? Twice? More, perhaps? And each time, people had come running into the room within moments, calming her with soft words and sharp needles, never more than a minute passing between the bandages coming off and the drugs hitting her bloodstream. She had watched them take away the gore-soaked bedding and clean her body while new sheets and pillows were provided, and even in the depths of her delirium had known that she was being spied upon as she slept.

Red groaned and rolled over. She never trusted people who were too nice to her, or people who were too wealthy. Rich people being nice imbued her with a crawling horror. But, for all the warning signals going off in her head, she couldn't deny that without Losen and his mysterious Magister, she would either still be on Ketta's ship or at the mercy of someone worse.

The thought gave her a chill. Red grabbed a sheet, and drew it over herself.

Losen was a strange one. At first glance, Red might have taken him for nothing more than an ineffectual dandy, elegant to the point of effeminacy. His voice was soft, his manner cultured and almost impossibly polite, his face powdered and his cheeks rouged. Under the surface, though, was something very different. Just as his silken robes had concealed a suit of protective armour, so his foppish demeanour was a façade; behind it was a cunning intelligence, bright and sharp. Red could feel it poking through his mannerisms like the tip of a hidden blade.

She didn't have to wait long.

Towards the end of her conversation with Losen, she had felt the tiredness creeping back again, the sluggish weakness in her limbs. Her body was using every scrap of spare energy to repair itself. Naturally, Red had tried to hide this fact from her benefactor, and had believed she'd done a pretty good job, but maybe she'd underestimated him. Within a few minutes of his leaving, she realised that someone was entering the villa.

Red curled up on the bed, feigning sleep, the sheet still drawn over her nakedness.

She kept her eyes closed, but sight was the least of her senses. Outside the bedchamber, soft-shoed feet padded almost silently across the polished floors – almost, but not quite. There were four intruders, Red could hear, two with the measured pace of the sylph.

She drew in a breath, through her nose; she could smell oil, antiseptic, pomade. A doctor or nurse, she thought to herself, and a soldier. Very close, just outside the door.

The handle turned. Silently, so as not to wake the sleeping captive. Red felt it move.

She launched herself from the bed, sheet flying, and ripped the door open. The two sylphs were behind it, one male and one female; she struck the man first, the hard edge of her hand catching him where his shoulder met his neck. The blow would have killed if she'd invested it with a quarter of her normal strength, but something about the sylphs made her hold back. Their silence, she had decided, was not through choice.

The man fell over sideways. Red stepped alongside the woman and hit her in the temple with her elbow, then followed through with more vicious kicks to the moustached physician and the guard behind him. No lives were taken – her

restraint was intentional, as no one in this place had yet done
her harm, but it was hard not to break a bone or two.

The female sylph was unconscious from the elbow blow,
but hadn't quite fallen over yet. Red caught her as her knees
finally buckled, and swung her over to the bed.

She was tall, this one, a little taller than Red herself, and
catwalk-slim. Like all the sylphs Red had met she wore a
simple uniform of pale green, with black leather boots and
a long coat of heavy satin.

None of it was very difficult to remove, and when Red put
the uniform on she found it fitted surprisingly well.

Moments later, Durham Red opened the door to the villa
and stepped out under an artificial sky.

She hadn't been exactly sure of what she expected to find
outside; the villa's few windows were translucent, letting in
light but no detail, made of a substance that had more in
common with steel than glass. She had given up trying to
break them, or even catch a glimpse of what lay beyond. But
her conversation with Losen and his boastful talk of strata
and towers had made her think of something enclosed, like
the interior of Biblos. Chambers connected by networks of
tunnels and corridors, dotted with the occasional assembly
hall. Elevator shafts and ladders and stairwells.

Nothing like this. She wandered away from the villa, letting her eyes drink the place in.

She was standing in a vast, open space. The ceiling
soared above her, a hundred metres or more, hazed by artificial clouds and sending down a warm noon light. Behind
her, close to what must have been one of the stratum's
boundaries, rows of villas ranged around in a long, shallow
curve, ranks of them sloping upward as if set inside a crater.
The spaces between them were a mass of greenery, and
here and there small trees grew, overhanging the balconies
and balustrades.

Ahead of her, past lawns and tiled squares and white
marble fountains, rose a huge column of iron and gold, a

central support so vast that the lower half of it was home to a great cone of buildings. Layer after layer of brightly painted structures hugged the column and spread out into a series of paved walkways beneath.

Between the ceiling and the ground, slender bridges spanned the space between the distant walls and the column.

Red suppressed the urge to whistle, remembering that she was supposed to be mute, and moved on. There were hundreds of people in sight, some dressed as Losen had been, others even more outlandishly. Many were sylphs, clad in green, hurrying about on their wordless errands. On the lawns, between the feet of gilded statues, children played.

No one spared her a second glance.

She could lose herself here, she realised, with no effort at all. Sylphs would probably be restricted as to where they could go, being a servant class, so she would need to ditch the uniform soon and move up in the world. After that, she would find her way to the nearest spaceport.

She headed away from the villas, towards the column. It was obvious that the stratum was circular, even though she couldn't see more than a part of the outer wall at any one time. Long streets led inwards between wedge-shaped lawns, and the suspended walkways arched overhead from their apex like the legs of a particularly huge and spindle-limbed spider.

It didn't take long to reach the outskirts of the column. The stratum was large, but not remarkably so, perhaps a kilometre from edge to edge. Smaller than Seebo Zimri's library, although it certainly didn't seem that way.

Walking between the shops and eating places, Red was so entranced that she almost didn't notice she was being followed, until she spotted, in the reflection from a café window, someone ducking out of sight.

She cursed, startling several passers-by, and bolted. Back in the villa surprise had been on her side. Since she was being actively hunted things might turn out very differently. She didn't know if she was followed by only one sylph, or by many. They might have been the local equivalent of a police force. If things went very badly, some idiot might even start shooting.

Had the idiot in question been her, she could have dealt with that. But she'd not held a gun since Biblos.

There was a crowd up ahead. She headed towards it, hoping to lose her pursuers there. It wasn't a chase she could keep up for long: while her strength had largely returned, her stamina had not. She was puffing already.

The crowd she had joined were moving toward the entrances in the tower's flank, filtering through large, glass-fronted doors and into the chambers beyond. The interiors of the boxlike rooms were so exquisitely decorated that, for a moment, Red didn't even realise they were elevators: silk wall hangings and polished brass seemed oddly out of place, in a device designed simply to get people from one level to another. Red found a place and stood still, watching with some satisfaction as the doors closed in the face of a pursuing sylph.

She tried not to pant, but her breath seemed reluctant to stay in her lungs.

The elevator chimed softly, then rose. Red closed her eyes for a moment, trusting that no sentient creature on an elevator ride would look at another until they got out again. Her respite, however, was short. In less than ten seconds the elevator slowed and stopped. The chime sounded again and the doors swung open.

Red cursed inwardly, and let herself be carried forward by the crowd. No one stayed in the chamber. It emptied in moments, and was then filled by several dozen Magadani waiting patiently to take the reverse journey. All she had done was move herself up to bridge-level.

She set off along the bridge, keeping to the centre like the other sylphs she could see. The outsides of the bridge seemed to be reserved for those capable of speech. Exotically dressed Magadani crowded the spaces between the centre and the safety wall, enjoying the height and the view.

Only the sylphs, with their complete lack of curiosity, walked with any degree of purpose along the bridge. Everyone else meandered, chattering idly or enjoying the sights, as if hurrying was a coarse, uncultured thing.

She increased her pace, heading for the stratum wall. It rose up in front of her like a waterfall, an endless curve of startling white stone, meeting the ground in a foam of villas and markets. At its top it curved over her head to become the domed sky-roof of the stratum, and the space between was home to row upon row of windows and balconies. Red could see, that the wall was only an inner surface. Dozens of floors lay behind it, connected by long stairways and ramps.

Light, cooler than that from the artificial sky, poured in through the windows ahead. It flowed over Red as she passed through the door at the end of the bridge, and into the cavernous space beyond.

The air was suddenly cool. It was the crisp, echoing coolness of cathedrals and museums, mansions and palaces. The floors here were dark marble, gleaming in the harsh light, and the ceilings high. Red stumbled forwards, across the expanse of polished floor, her pretence at sylph-hood forgotten. There was just too much to see.

To her left, mighty staircases curled up to meet three separate balconies, crossing tens of metres above her head. To her right was a series of enormous arches, carved columns soaring up to frame huge statues of robed men and women in gleaming stone, chased with gold. And before her, across the marble floor, was a solid wall of glass.

The base of the wall was a mass of people, ten deep at least. Most had their backs to Red, staring entranced at what lay beyond.

That crowd was Red's final chance of concealment. She used the last of her strength to reach it, then began edging her way in. She drew disapproving looks, and the occasional hostile word – sylphs were obviously an unwelcome sight here – but she ignored them. If she could get to the

glass, behind these hundreds of gawping tourists, she might
be able to stay hidden long enough to catch her breath. If
she could just stay a while and rest, she was certain that
she could recover fully enough to continue her journey
away from the stratum.

Finally, after an age of insistent, silent shoving, she made
it to the base of the transparent wall. The last layer of people parted for her, and the scene outside was revealed in all
its glory.

Past the glass, the Grand Keep reared in every direction.

Red gave up all pretence, and gasped. Losen had men-
tioned the five towers to her already, their profusion of
strata and the magnificence of their contents, but nothing
he said could have prepared Red for what she saw.

From there, she could see all four of the other towers. The
glass wall faced inwards, to the centre of the Keep, and the
great citadels of Magadan were clustered about her. They
were close together, only a few hundred metres between
them, but each one was gigantic. Cylinders of glossy blue
stone, each one several kilometres across, rising up so far
that they extended past the boundaries of the window, and
almost as far downwards. Thousands of metres below her
the towers became one, widening into a sea of detail: scaf-
folding, at a distance, turned into a tangle of silvery threads.
Cranes rose above them, and past that, hugging the rim of
the vast main cylinder, were the clouds.

She was in the sky.

The sight, the perspective, was dizzying. Red stumbled
away from it, shutting her eyes tight as vertigo swept over
her, cold and terrifying.

It was then that her pursuers found her. They swarmed
about her in a cluster, taking her arms and leading her gently away, but she saw nothing.

All she could feel, until the touch of a needle, was the
yawning distance between her feet and the cloud-shadowed
surface of Magadan.

8. MASQUED

"That," Losen told her later, "was foolish."

"What did you expect?" Red tipped the chair back on its rear legs with her boots on the bed. "You locked me up and spied on me. I don't take kindly to that."

Losen sighed. He was languishing on the bed, legs outstretched and crossed at the ankles. A sylph, Annia, lay blankly next to him, and two more waited by the door. "You were locked away for good reason, my lady. My people got to you only just before those from a rival citadel. Believe me, had the Cadosi reached you first, your present surroundings would be considerably less pleasant than these."

"What, they'd lock me up too?" Red snorted. "Big deal. Prison's prison."

"You are not in prison."

"Well, that's what it snecking feels like! Ow!" She winced, rubbing her shoulder. "Sneck, that's sore."

"I'll have Compasso look at that for you." Losen's expression darkened for a moment. "As soon as he comes out of the infirmary."

"He was in my way."

"You broke three of his ribs!" For a moment, Losen looked almost as though he was going to get angry. Then he took a breath and calmed himself. Anger, Red thought to herself, must have seemed as far beneath the upper-class Magadani as haste.

She felt his eyes on her. "What are you staring at, Losen?"

"The uniform. I do wish you'd take it off."

She snapped, glaring around at him, "What did you snecking say?"

He gave a sort of facial shrug, as if using his shoulders would be too much trouble. "It's a sylph's uniform. To see someone wearing it, and speaking – it's, well, unnatural."

"You're kidding me," she said flatly. "Christ, I've heard some excuses to try and get me naked, but that's got to be the lamest ever."

Losen carried on as if he'd not heard her. "Besides, as my guest at the Masque, I'd hoped you would wear something more striking. I know that nothing we supplied took your fancy, but I'm sure we can do better next time."

"Next time? Masque?" Red jumped up, sending the chair over backwards again. "What, did I fall asleep during that part of the conversation?"

The Magadani sat up straighter, looking ever so slightly stricken. "Did we not discuss this?"

"We've discussed exactly two things about my attending anything, Twinkletoes. Jack and shit."

"My lady, this is devastating. I cannot believe I've been so remiss." He swung himself off the bed and got to his feet, bent over in a bow. "Please forgive me."

"Oh, stow it." Losen's insipid politeness was grating on her nerves. "Just tell me what the sneck you're on about."

"Of course." He nodded sideways to a sylph, who stooped to right the chair. "There is a masked ball tonight on one of the common strata. It is a regular event, a time for domini from all the great citadels to gather." He smiled, rather wolfishly. "It's terribly exclusive."

Red put her hands on her hips. "Let me get this straight. You and Cados, normally you bastards are one stage shy of outright warfare. But every two weeks someone puts on a running buffet and suddenly it's all handbags and glad-rags?" She shook her head, chuckling. "Christ, talk about blood on the dance floor. Does anyone survive these things?"

Losen seemed pained. "My lady, you do us an injustice. There hasn't been open conflict in the Grand Keep in living memory. There are systems of behaviour laid down by the Magister himself, just to prevent any such thing from taking place. And as for the Masque, it is far more than a buffet. It is the beating heart of Magadani society, an antidote to the stagnations of petty rivalry and mistrust."

"Right," said Red slowly. "And you want me to be your date for the prom, eh?"

"You could put it like that."

"Um, actually I can put it like this." She folded her arms. "No. Snecking. Way."

"But my lady, the Masque is unmissable!" He put his arm to her shoulder. She felt the heat of his fingers there and a sudden itch. If he moves that hand a millimetre in the wrong direction, she though sourly, he's going to take it home in a carrier bag.

"A spectacle beyond compare!" he went on. "Certainly something with which to regale your friends when they arrive. And weren't you saying earlier about how much you disliked your imprisonment here? Wouldn't it be the perfect opportunity to leave these walls, and see the best of Magadan?"

Red frowned. If she was honest with herself, the idea of spending another night cooped up in the villa was pretty intolerable. And even if things at this Masque got ugly, she was in good enough shape to handle herself.

And when had she last been to a party anyway? "I don't know… Maybe. If…"

"If?"

She rounded on him. "I choose my own costume. None of this bustles and bows shit, but something I'll look good in, okay? And I get to wear a mask? Like in the vids?"

"They are required."

"Cool." She puffed out a breath, feeling quite cheerful. "Okay, you got a date. How long have I got?"

"About four hours. If we hurry, we can be dressed and ready by then."

Red waited a second for the punchline, but then realised he meant it. "Christ. Okay, you go powder your wig, I'll do mine."

"I'm delighted." He smiled, and bowed again. "At eight, then?"

"Eight. And no dancing."

"It is far from compulsory."

Losen arrived late, but Red was expecting that. She had used the time to put the finishing touches to her costume.

By the look of things, the dominus had used every second of his four hours plus getting into his attire. Red had never seen such a combination of layers and textures; from the white silk of his ruffed undershirt to the topshirt, waistcoat, jacket, coat and sash, he looked more like an exotic bird than a man. His hair was swept back in a jewelled clasp, a narrow sword swung from his belt, and the lace of his cuffs almost entirely concealed his hands.

"Bloody hell," muttered Red, as the sylphs showed him in. "It's the dandy highwayman."

His reaction to what she was wearing was no less derogatory. He bowed as soon as he came in, carefully sweeping the sword back behind him, but as he rose his eyes widened. A second later, he threw his head back and roared with laughter.

Red's eyes narrowed. "What?"

With some effort, he recovered his composure. "My lady," he began, dabbing at the corner of his mouth with a silk handkerchief. "By the Prime, that really is the most wonderful costume. Pray, what are you supposed to be?"

She looked down at herself. "It's not that bad, is it?"

"Bad? Of course it's not bad! It's merely unique " He began walking around her in a slow circle. "After all, who else would combine the armoured boots of a guard-sylph with the silk leggings of a pageboy? A courtesan's bustier with a soldier's breastplate? And who, but you, would round off the ensemble with the coat and gloves normally worn by the artisans concerned with the cleaning of paint-work?"

Red threw a glance at the nearest mirror. Unique it might be, but the outfit was practical in the extreme. The boots were high, covering the knee-length cuffs of the leggings, and nicely capped with a good, solid steel toecap and heel. The bustier wasn't that different from what she normally wore, but the breastplate was chased silver over a woven polycarbonate mesh, and would stop bullets, lasers, and even the slender needle-guns of Trawden's guard-sylphs. As for the coat and gloves, they were well cut and flexible, no hindrance if she needed to punch her way out of trouble.

Okay, she could have doubled as a shiny space-pirate. But she actually looked considerably more masculine than Losen did.

"Lucky for you, Twinkletoes, men and women wear different masks. That way no one will mistake me for a guy and get any funny ideas about you."

He smiled languidly. "Variety is the spice of life."

The elevator that took them down to the common strata was one of dozens that ringed the citadel's outer walls. To get to it, they had to walk almost exactly the same route that Red had taken on her ill-fated escape bid. In fact, she noted sourly, she had nearly made it. In her exhaustion, she never realised how close she had come.

They went masked as soon as they left the villa. Losen's was a full-face creation of gold leaf and diamonds, while Red's was more discreetly feminine. It was a black domino mask, satin and chased with silver. As soon as she put it to her face it clung there, conforming instantly to her features with a grip that was firm but gentle.

For all their pseudo-historical finery, the Magadani were possessed of some fiercely advanced technology. Not for the first time, Red wondered how this place had escaped the gaze of the Iconoclasts.

They began to join other masked couples on the stratum bridge. Losen greeted some politely, some warmly, while others were pointedly blanked. The same kinds of reactions were directed, in turn, back at Losen himself with equal mix. Red noticed that he didn't appear particularly upset, no matter what was thrown back in his face, and neither was anyone else. They would take note of what was said, and change their own behaviour in turn – a reflexive verbal dance, following rules Red couldn't begin to follow but which Losen and his peers seemed born to.

It was a kind of ritual, she realised. An elaborate game based on social standing, on manners and decorum. And though he appeared to be merely walking and swapping choice comments with his fellow Magadani, Saleph Losen was playing it for all he was worth.

The doors were already open, held aside by uniformed flunkies. As their little procession passed through – Losen, Red at his side, a small cadre of sylphs behind them – one of the flunkies raised himself to full height and bellowed that the Lord and Lady Nightshade had entered the Masque.

There was a smattering of polite applause, to which Losen bowed as though receiving an award. Red gave him a sideways look. "Nightshade?"

"I felt it suited the mood. Besides, I could think of nothing more deadly."

There was something about those words that gave Red a fleeting moment of puzzlement, but it passed very quickly. For the crowd in front of her had parted, and she now could see the Masque.

"Bloody snecking hell," she said.

The Masque's venue was easily as big as any sports stadium Red had ever seen, and rose about her in much the same way. Instead of benches full of howling spectators, though, these rising tiers were wide enough for tables, hundreds of them, both open and enclosed in private booths. Above the highest step was a ring of pillared arches that must have stretched a kilometre before coming full circle, and behind it the walls shimmered with a holographic trompe l'oeil, a simulated panorama of sea and sky glittering beneath a golden sunset. It was as if the entire stadium had been set on its own island, surrounded by a tropical ocean.

None of which was half as stunning, to Red's eyes, as the people who crowded it.

Hundreds of Magadani were on the paved field of this blinding place, a solid wall of colour. More crowded the tiers, seated in couples or groups, or stood watching the crowds with tiny pairs of opera glasses, conducting the continuous business of social manoeuvre.

Each of them, from those closest to her to the farthest groups, was dressed in finery so outlandish as to beggar the imagination. She had thought Saleph Losen to be ornate, but compared to some of these people he was almost minimalist.

And there were sylphs, too. Armies of them. She first spotted those in the pale green uniform of Trawden, but those from the other citadels were there too; in midnight blue, in purple, in pale orange and silver grey. Almost all of the sylphs were in motion; a very few stood in attendance by their masters, but the vast majority were walking between the chattering cliques, carrying drinks, drugs, messages.

Orchestras sat up on the highest tier, playing in fractured counterpoint.

"The blue sylphs," Losen murmured to her, "are Cadosi. Be careful around them. And if they offer you something to drink, don't accept it."

"You and Cados don't get on, eh?"

"Stay a while. In all likelihood you'll find out."

She would have asked what he meant, but he was already moving into the first of his social sparring matches. At first Red did her best to follow the conversation between Losen and the pair of domini he had cornered, but she quickly lost

interest in his with, and instead wandered further onto the
paved field, her metal heels clicking on the polished floor.
The crowds around her moved with an odd, liquid precision, a constant motion that enabled everyone to keep a
slight but significant space between their fellows, no matter
how expansive their costume. Red was able to walk freely
through the mass, because everyone reflexively passed
around her as she did so.

This isn't something learned, she thought. This is what
rich people do, as natural as breathing. It was in their
bones.

Somewhere behind her she heard Losen's laugh rise
above the general hubbub, but he sounded distant. She
turned back, and as she did so someone leaned close and
whispered in her ear: "Perhaps, lady, you shouldn't stray
too far from your companion. It would be easy to get lost in
these crowds."

"I've been lost for a long time, pal." She looked around,
into the face of a golden wolf.

The man who had spoken was quite tall, perhaps Red's
height, although the carved mane of the wolf's head made
it difficult to tell. His costume was mainly black and gold,
with a few telling touches in midnight blue. Cadosi, thought
Red. A rival of Losen's.

This, she decided, could be interesting.

He bowed slightly, although his eyes, glittering behind the
mask, never left hers. "The Lord Vulpus," he said. "At your
service."

Red grinned widely. "Lady Nightshade, I guess. So tell
me, wolf-boy, where does a lady have to go to get a drink
around here?"

9. BAD WOLF

The edges of the Masque's floor area were more sparsely populated than the centre, but only just. Vulpus led her through the crowds to the base of the first tier, where long tables stood covered in elaborately woven cloths. Each was piled high with delicacies: candies and sweetmeats, glasses of wine and tiny ampoules of coloured fluid. Sylphs stood behind the tables, handing out refreshment to anyone who drew close. It really wasn't a place Red wanted to be anymore, but she was starting to think that Losen could be useful. With the correct persuasion, of course. "It's noisy here," she told him, leaning a little closer. "Don't you think it's noisy?"

"Maybe a little lively for my taste, lady."

"You know," she breathed, getting very close, "Losen told me to watch out for you people. He thinks you're dangerous."

Vulpus raised his mask slightly to take a sip of his own drink. "The Cadosi, you mean? Well, yes, he would say something like that."

"Why? Are you dangerous?" She ran her tongue, quite slowly, along the rim of her glass. "Should I be careful?"

"You have nothing to fear from me, my lady."

"Pity." She stepped away, back towards the refreshment tables.

Behind them, set into the wall of the first tier, was a tall, arched opening. Red had spotted it earlier, when Vulpus had been leading her here. "Where does that go?"

"The arch?" Vulpus seemed momentarily confused. "It, ah, leads to quieter places."

"Really?" Red grinned. "Sounds interesting."

"Hardly. When I say quieter, my lady, I mean more dull. Courts of silence, meeting halls, galleries. Rooms for those tired of the Masque to rest, nothing more. Nowhere private."

"Chill out rooms? Great." Red moved quickly away from him, between the tables and into the archway. "Come on."

She walked away, steel boots clicking on the hard floor. Through the arch was a short corridor, ending in a tall, polished wooden door. Red headed directly for it. She didn't need to look around and make sure Vulpus was following her; the hallway was already quieter than the Masque hall itself, and she could hear his footfalls.

As she drew close the door opened, and a trio of Magadani stepped through it. They were smiling, talking in relaxed tones about some rival or another, and more followed, brushing past Red with polite nods. Vulpus had been right about the spaces beyond the arch not being private, but that was fine with her. If her new companion thought she was planning anything untoward here, he was going to be sorely disappointed.

Just to keep his hopes up she threw a seductive glance over her shoulder as she opened the door and went through.

It closed behind Vulpus, and the noise of the Masque fell away completely. Red found herself in a long, wide hallway, its walls and vaulted roof carved from creamy stone, the floor dark granite burnished to a mirror shine. There were no windows, but big paintings, each wider than Red was tall and set into gilded frames, ranged along both long walls.

At first it was the sheer scale of the pictures that stopped Red in her tracks, but as she gazed up at them something about the subject matter seemed to hold her fast. She hadn't gone far into the hall before her pace faltered, just enough to bring her level with the first painting.

The scene it showed was deceptively simple: a man stood there, clad in thick, velvety green robes. In his right hands he cradled a human skull, while his left gripped the pommel of an ebony walking cane. His face was cruel and imperious, his hair long, his chin defined by a small, neat beard. Red could feel the intensity of his gaze, captured expertly by the artist, resting on her like a physical weight.

The callousness in his expression, the lazy, indolent spite, was depicted so skilfully that it lit something within her, honed an edge of familiarity that she could feel, yet not name.

From what Red could see, all the other pictures lining the walls of this gallery were the same in both subject and tone. "Who are they?"

"Prior Magisters," he said, his voice low. "No one that would interest you."

"Oh, I don't know. You'd be surprised what I find interesting..." This wasn't getting her anywhere. Red tore her attention away from the pictures and turned it back on Vulpus, giving him a predatory smile, a tiny flash of fang. "I like doing all sorts of things."

"I'm sure you do."

He moved towards her, but she slid out of his range, reaching up to strip away the domino mask. "There," she smiled. "Isn't that better?"

"Oh, much." He reached up and unclasped his own disguise, shaking his long hair out from behind it.

He was pale – Red had been expecting that – but not excessively so. There was little powder on his face, and only a hint of rouge at his lips. His eyes were as dark, his nose narrow and straight. The way his black hair was brushed back made his forehead look strikingly high.

Even without the mask, Red decided, Lord Vulpus had something of the wolf to him.

"Nice to finally put a face to the voice," she smiled. "I don't think you're as bad as Losen made out."

"Losen's opinion of me is not high." He sounded almost sad. "The old rivalries, you see. He takes them all so personally."

"Rivalries?" Red felt an itch at her left shoulder, and she rubbed it absently. "Sorry, Wolfie, but I don't follow you. What did you do? Criticise his curtains in a former life?"

A strange expression passed across the Cadosi's face, as though he had suddenly remembered something. "Of course," he whispered. "The off-worlder!"

"What, I've got a reputation already? News travels fast in this place!"

"Sometimes, my lady, it's the only thing that does." He chuckled, and Red saw to her surprise that his canine teeth were quite long and pointed. Not up to the standard of her own fangs, of course, but certainly noticeable.

Suddenly she wanted to be out of the gallery, and its lines of dead Magisters. Their stares were making her skull throb. Her shoulder felt as though someone had a hot needle in it, and beads of sweat were beginning to prick her brow. The good mood she had attained back in Losen's villa was starting to fade, leaving her feeling humid and ill.

She turned her back on Vulpus and began to walk, quickly, towards the doorway at the far end of the hall. The Cadosi called out after her, once, but she ignored him, just ran to the door and tugged it open.

Coolness, damp and delicious, washed over her from beyond.

Beyond the gallery was a fountain court, a broad disc of blindingly white marble surrounded by a low wall. At its centre was a pool of bright, clear water, set rushing and leaping by the fountains within, and in the very heart of the place reared an immense golden statue.

The place was exquisite, but its setting was ever more so. Beyond the pillared wall lay kilometres of open parkland.

Red padded inside, eyes wide with wonder. She was not alone here – Magadani, plainly refugees from the Masque, sprawled about her on stone benches – but she ignored them, walking past the pool to the far edge of the circle, and leaning out over the wall. Below her, trees swayed in an artificial wind.

"The flooring has been cut away in this area," said Vulpus quietly. He had stepped up behind her, his footfalls masked by the crystalline sound of the fountains. "All around this court, around the Masque hall, everywhere. The forests you see are maintained on the next stratum down, with no supporting pillar to mar the view. That has been built into the Masque hall itself."

Red just stared down at it, feeling the breeze ruffling her hair, cooling the sweat on her brow. "Why? I don't understand, Vulpus. This is incredible, the amount of work to make this. Why not just go outside?"

"The outside is toxic, my lady. Lethal. We all live here because it's the only we place we *can* live."

She snapped around on him, aghast. "You mean the air's poisonous?"

Vulpus smiled grimly. "If only it were something that easily overcome. But no, my lady, the surface of Magadan is tainted, in the foulest way."

"I don't—"

"Disease, my dear. Plague. The ground is seething with it, the air a drifting sea of spores. Only the Prime himself knows how the first of us survived here, but the only way we can live now is by sealing ourselves away in the Keep. Anyone who walks outside must do so in protective clothing, and then undergo weeks of decontamination upon their return."

Red shuddered, feeling unholy itches crawl up and down her spine. All the time she had spent trying to get away from this place, not knowing that the world outside those vast windows was boiling with hungry bacteria. "Bloody hell, Wolfie! That's awful! Has it always been like that?"

"As far as anyone knows." Vulpus pointed up at the statue, waiting until Red had turned back to it to continue. "You see him? That is the man we call the Father, the Prime Magister. He brought us here, over a thousand years ago; found the richest planet in the galaxy and gave it to us as a gift." He snorted derisively. "His great bequest to us was a poisoned chalice – he trapped us on a plague world. The greater part of our heritage is wondering what it was our ancestors did to upset him so much."

Red remembered the row of paintings back in the gallery, the parade of long-dead Magisters. Each of them had been holding a human skull. The gift of death.

The golden form rearing above her was in the same stance, one hand gripping a walking cane, the other a jaw-less skull. It wore a flowing frock coat and ruffed shirt, and instead of a beard a drooping moustache outlined a full, slightly sneering mouth. The hair was long and straight, framing a gaunt, angular face.

Red squinted up at the carved man. Once again, some weird recognition was tickling the back of her mind, just as it had done when she gazed up at those painted despots.

Or in fact at Vulpus. What was it that these people reminded her of?

It was a distracting, worrying feeling, drawing her atten-tion away from the reason she had led Vulpus on this dance. She shook herself. "You could leave. You've got starships, Wolfie. That's how I got here, remember?"

"Perhaps we could, but the Magister controls all space travel, and he fears the universe. Even the domini are not free in the Keep. The terror of disease holds us here, in our citadels, unless the Magister or the Board of Arch-Domini sanction it."

Red could well understand that. Sealed away for hun-dreds of years, the Magadani would be a prime target for disease. An alien infection could run riot in a place like this. "So there's no other settlements at all?"

"There are none. Why would there be? Everything we need is here."

Red gazed out over verdant grass and swaying treetops, and could only agree. The Magadani had built themselves a world inside these towers.

· · ·

She turned away from the wall, and gazed back up at the statue. As she did the tickling behind her eyes came back, that sudden, dislocating sense of recognition. It was the same as she had felt back in the gallery, from the prior Magisters. But now she could see that she had recognised them only because they had fashioned themselves after the Prime, the Father.

She tried to imagine this man as he would have been in his lifetime, a thousand years ago. His hair dark, his gaze bright and cruel. A knot of tension began to form behind her sternum.

"Vulpus?" she asked quietly. "This Prime bloke – what was his name?"

"His name was Simeon," said Saleph Losen, striding towards her across the marble floor. He had a trio of sylphs with him, one wearing a breastplate very much like Red's. A guard. "Sire Simeon of Isis, Prime Magister of Magadan, and a damned fool."

There were gasps at that, from the Magadani ranged around the fountain court, but Red barely heard them. She was staring at Losen, her heart bouncing inside her chest like a maddened animal. "Isis," she whispered.

"You whelp," Vulpus was sneering. "Still running errands for that old pederast Brakkeri?"

"And speaking of damned fools, here's Vaide Sorrelier. What are you up to this time, Vaide? Testing your pathetic powers of seduction one more time, or just tasting the fruit before you start juicing it?"

Vulpus spat back some threat or insult, but Red didn't even notice what the man was saying. She was still staring up at the statue, at the chiselled, golden face of Sire Simeon of Isis.

Or, as he had called himself when Durham Red knew him, Simon D'Isis, the Gothking.

Suddenly, everything about the Keep made a sickening kind of sense. The paintings in the gallery, centuries of Magisters modelling themselves on their long-dead progenitor.

The pseudo-historical fashions, languid cruelty and callous disregard for life hiding behind paint and powder. The drugs, pervading all levels of Magadani society so completely that they were given out like candy. All of it stemmed from one man, one name.

Red closed her eyes, wincing at her own stupidity. Of course, the drugs!

Losen had drugged her.

That touch upon her shoulder, the itch. He must have stuck her with a needle, one so fine she hadn't even felt it go in, and introduced a narcotic compound into her bloodstream. And the next thing she knew she was swanning round this ridiculous party, dressed up like a fool, thinking herself free for a night when in fact she was just as much a prisoner as before.

She turned smoothly on her heels, and before Losen could react or cry out she had him by the lapels, swinging him over into the air and down onto the wall, halfway over the balcony. She felt a movement of air behind her and kicked out, sending the guard-sylph spinning across the marble.

Losen was struggling, eyes wide with terror, looking down over a drop of a hundred metres or more.

Red shook him. "You snecking son of a bitch. You even think about putting another needle in me, and I'll rip your guts out with my bare teeth."

"I never–"

She didn't let him finish the denial, just heaved him slightly further over the drop. "Don't try. If I ever see you again, I'll kill you. You know I'll do it, and you know I'll be smiling when I do."

With that, she dragged him upright, planted a kiss on his clammy forehead, and threw him into the fountains.

Vulpus was standing as if frozen. She winked at him. "Thanks for the drink, Wolfie."

And she ran.

. . .

Perhaps if the Grand Keep hadn't been filled to the brim with narcotics of every description, Red would have found it harder to believe that her old enemy, the Gothking, had led the people that would one day evolve into the Magadani. But now that she knew some of the history behind this place, they conformed to her memories of him perfectly.

The Magadani's reverence for him made her smile, though. Simon D'Isis had built an empire on the sale of illicit drugs, and one toxic little planet in the middle of nowhere would be nothing to him. There must have been something he wanted from the place, back in the dim and distant past, but in all likelihood D'Isis had visited the world once when the first drugs factories were being set up, and then promptly forgotten it. If his memory was revered by the people that lived here, then more fool them; there must have been a hundred worlds that bore his mark.

A movement ahead of her brought her back to the present with a jolt. A dozen sylphs stood in silent formation between her and the elevator doors, and every one of them was dressed in midnight blue.

Red slowed. "Get out of the way," she growled.

None of them moved. Red stopped where she was, unwilling to go straight through the servants without at least giving them a chance. Something about these wordless, impossibly beautiful creatures was both pathetic and deeply worrying.

She put herself in front of the nearest, a blonde with fashion-model cheekbones beneath her empty eyes. "Look, I don't know why you serve these people, or even if you've got a choice. But I'm going into that lift. If I have to go through you to get there, I'll do it."

The sylphs stayed where they were. Then one of them reached for her.

She ducked the grab, slapped the hand away and heard a bone break as she connected. One sylph staggered back, and then the others were all over her.

They were quick, much more so that she had been expecting. Her next few blows didn't even strike; the silent guards simply moved fluidly around her fists, leaping away if she got too close, reaching in and then darting out of range. Red changed tactics, kicking the legs from under one woman, knocking another cold with a blow to the back of her neck.

Now she had the hang of it. She rolled her head around, hearing the clicks as she loosened her stance.

She'd spent too long fighting shocktroopers, brutish men who traded speed for raw power and the protection of heavy armour. These sylphs were a different proposition entirely. One blow in the right place and they were out for the count, but actually getting a punch to land was the hard part.

Red traded a lightning series of strikes and parries with one, then got a straight-arm into the man's sternum and sent him skidding away on his backside. Another leapt in from her left, making her duck to avoid a blow, before she swept his legs away and punched him hard on the way down. A woman came up from behind, another to her right – Red blocked their flurry of kicks with her shins and forearms, and put her steel-tipped boots to good use, breaking a kneecap, a thighbone, a hip.

She found herself hoping that wounded sylphs weren't just taken out and shot, like racing beasts.

Perhaps the thought distracted her, or maybe Losen's drugs had slowed her up. But it was then that one of the sylphs got close enough to scratch at her.

Red whipped aside, her hand coming up to the place on her cheek where the sylph's nail had broken her skin. There was fire in that small wound. Suddenly, all the fight was gone from her. She slumped back against the nearest wall, gasping.

More drugs. The Grand Keep was a catalogue of toxins.

She waited for the sylphs to press their attack, but instead they just moved aside. Only the one who had scratched her – the woman with the cheekbones – moved forward, in order to take her arm in a gentle grip. Red didn't even have the strength to pull away.

She heard footsteps, and raised her heavy head to see who was coming. She was less than surprised to see Lord Vulpus striding purposefully down the corridor towards her.

As he drew close, he nodded to the woman who had Red's arm. "Well done, Lise. Do make sure you clean that nail, though, won't you?"

"Vulpus," Red slurred. "Losen was right about you bastards…"

"He was indeed." He leaned close, and smiled. Small fangs gleamed. "In answer to your previous questions; yes, I am dangerous, and yes, you should have been careful. Oh, and Vulpus is no more a real name than Lady Nightshade."

What was it Losen had called him? "Sorrelier…"

"Sire Vaide Sorrelier, third dominus of the citadel of Cados. Thanks to you."

She let her head fall forward again. It was hard to keep upright. "Me?"

"Oh yes, Durham Red, I owe you a very great deal. You raised me two full levels, before you slipped my grasp. Oh, and just because I lost you at Biblos doesn't mean you'll escape me again." He grinned, fangs shining. "Third time lucky, eh?"

10. TIME TO FLY

There had been times, in the past few weeks, when Vaide Sorrelier had almost given in to despair. It was a common enough affliction among those of his kind, especially the domini, and once it took hold it was difficult to shake off. More than one Dominus had left Cados the hard and fast way – out through one of the flight harbours or observation decks, plummeting straight down to the ground far below.

Sorrelier had never seriously considered taking his own life. He had far too many scores to settle before his time was up. But there had been nights spent lying awake in the cold darkness, with Lise at his side, when the problems of life without Durham Red had seemed almost insurmountable.

By the Prime, anyone would think he was in love with the creature.

He ran his tongue over the tips of his fangs and smiled to himself, sparing the mutant a sideways glance. She was a pathetic, ridiculous sight, gasping and shaking as the drug coursed along her neural pathways, only keeping upright with the help of the sylphs on either side. Without the chemical in her she could have shrugged their grasp away with ease, but the scratch on her cheek had restrained her more effectively than chains or shackles could ever do. Not for the first time, Sorrelier congratulated himself on the drug's design.

Even her eyes were moving sluggishly in their sockets.

Still, there would be time to admire his handiwork later, and in safer surroundings. The surveillance visulas in this area had suffered a fortuitous failure just a few minutes before his sylphs had assembled, but he couldn't be certain they would stay offline for much longer. It was time to be gone.

He walked briskly to where the fight had taken place. He could see three of his servants shaking themselves awake as he approached; the mutant had knocked them senseless, but refrained from damaging them further. Three others were not so lucky. One had a broken arm, which could be dealt with later, but there were two who would require surgery if they were ever to walk again. Had they possessed voices, Sorrelier knew that the halls would be echoing with their screams, but instead they writhed in mute, shivering distress.

He gazed down at them for a moment, deciding whether or not they were worth saving, quickly coming to the conclusion they were not. He gestured at a couple of his upright sylphs, and within moments the broken ones were being dragged away.

At his signal, the remainder hauled Durham Red into the elevator.

Sorrelier went in last, checking one final time to make sure they hadn't been observed. The mutant, he observed as the doors closed, had her eyes shut, and she was shaking her head violently, as if trying to clear the sluggishness from her brain.

"I wouldn't bother," he told her. "It's a neural inhibitor. The production of acetylcholine along your neural pathways is being modified. Not blocked, obviously. I wouldn't want your heart to stop now, would I?"

"Obviously," she snarled, the word slurring from her lips. She opened her eyes and glared at him. "How long?"

"Oh, until I give you the antidote." He turned briefly to the elevator's control panel, setting the controls to take them down several strata, towards the eastern flight harbour. "If I decide to. I must admit, you're far less trouble now."

There was a pause. The mutant must have been searching for something clever to say, but she'd lost the knack of it. A muffled "Bollocks," was all she could muster.

Sorrelier couldn't help but chuckle. "You know, I'm sure that's just what you said to me the first time we met. Not that you'd remember that, of course."

During the time Durham Red had been held by the Osculem Cruentus she had been a source of exquisite product. The drugs fashioned from her distilled spinal fluids had been of a quality almost unheard of in the Grand Keep; not since the days of the Prime himself had such chemicals been available. Stimulants, calmers, sexual enhancers, even poisons of sublime subtlety, Sorrelier had fashioned them all from what the Osculem sent him, and the money and prestige they brought him had raised him two entire rungs up the ladder of dominance.

That was when Sorrelier's taste for power had truly become a hunger. When Red had escaped the Osculem Cruentus – a mistake that their high-priest had paid for dearly – that hunger had almost overcome him. Now she was back in his power, it might finally be sated.

Suitably restrained, and regularly milked, she would provide him with the means to rise higher and faster than any Dominus in Magadani history. His great plan, placed on hold ever since the cultists had let her slip away, would be back on track within a month.

And as for any remaining debt, he'd not even had to pay that incompetent Ketta. She had vanished while following Losen's ship, and had never made it through the gate. It was bad news for her, very good for Sorrelier. And Saleph Losen, the cocksure little snake, had done all Sorrelier's work for him.

The elevator shivered to a halt. The doors slid apart, letting in cool air, and the smell of fuel.

Sorrelier stepped out, looking left and right, then motioned for the sylphs to follow quickly. Like most of the areas beneath the five towers, the flight harbours were open to Magadani of any citadel, but the sight of a Cadosi Dominus and his entourage carting a drugged mutant around would draw attention anywhere. Sorrelier was anxious to avoid that kind of curiosity.

He took a linker from his robes, and spoke quietly into its pickup. "Rimail?"

"Here, sire." He had left Rimail to ready *Pinnacle*, his personal schooner. "Do we have a cargo to transport?"

"We do. And slightly less in the way of passengers, more's the pity."

"Think of the saving on fuel, sire."

Sorrelier grinned, and shut the linker off. *Pinnacle* was docked close by, on one of the lower deck levels.

It wasn't a long walk to the schooner. He set off briskly, knowing that Lise would keep the mutant and the other sylphs close by him.

The flight harbour was a stark, functional place, little more than a maze of decks and launch-cradles, ramps and stairways. It was home, however, to some of the most advanced pieces of technology Magadan could muster; all manner of vessels rested here, from short-ranged fliers to massive harvester gunships, and each was a thing of elegance and perfection.

Dozens of technicians worked on the decks, along with hundreds of sylphs. Despite his growing impatience, Sorrelier took a circuitous route from the elevator to *Pinnacle* that avoided most of the Trawden artisans. Losen would have his own sylphs out looking for the mutant, and Sorrelier had no intention of advertising his new acquisition just yet. The time would come for that, once the milking had begun.

He reached a balcony, overlooking several schooner-class berths. The closest one was occupied, the glass-nosed torpedo of *Pinnacle* filling it from end to end. The schooner's wings were folded back into its sleek hull, and the refuelling ducts were already retracted. Rimail had played his part; as soon as the passengers and cargo were aboard, *Pinnacle* could be out of the launch tube in moments.

They were alone on the balcony. Sorrelier stopped at the rail, and drew Lise aside. "Make sure she's secured as soon as we get her aboard," he told her. "This is going to be a short flight, but a swift one. I don't want her blundering about in the cabin and hurting herself–"

There was a noise behind him, a sudden, meaty impact. It cut him off mid-sentence, and made him turn, just in time to see the sylph to Durham Red's left sliding bonelessly to the ground.

Sorrelier tried to shout a warning, but before the words were out of his throat the mutant had torn herself free of the other sylph holding her, swinging the unfortunate slave about before felling him with the least cultured, yet most effective headbutt Sorrelier had ever seen. Blood spattered high into their air as their skulls met.

There had been nothing sluggish about those actions, nothing remotely like the moves of a woman whose nervous system was doused with neural inhibitors. Impossibly, the mutant was free of the drug, and she was free of the sylphs, too. The one she had butted had gone down like an empty sack. Sorrelier didn't even have time to avoid the gush of blood from the man's shattered face before she was on him.

He saw Lise flung aside, and raised an arm to protect himself, but it was only halfway up when the mutant struck him a sweeping blow that thrust him, with agonising force, into the handrail. He rebounded, too shocked by the pain even to cry out, and slammed down onto the mesh. The mutant drew back a foot and kicked him under the rail.

He rolled with the kick, off the balcony and into space.

A deck came up and hit him, hard, in the side. The impact tore a cry from him, and he turned over, expecting the mutant to be leaping down on top of him. Instead he saw her slender shape darting away, barrelling down a ramp to one of the centre decks and out of sight.

He groaned, and spat blood. There was a fire in his chest, along his ribs. He wondered if any had been broken by the impact of the handrail, or the kick that followed it.

Sorrelier was aware that Durham Red was quite capable, in normal circumstances, of kicking his head clean off his shoulders. The very fact that he was alive meant that either the mutant was still weakened by the drug, or she had restrained her blows.

Had Vaide Sorreilier been a betting man, he would definitely have laid money on the former.

He cursed, and struggled into a sitting position. As he did so, Lise landed on the mesh next to him, dropping into a crouch. She reached for him, but he waved her away, and pulled the linker from his robes. "Rimail, she's running. Do you see her?"

"Sire, are you–"

"By the Prime, tell me you see her!"

"I have her on visula, sire."

Sorrelier raised a hand, and Lise took it, helping him to his feet. "Good. Keep her there. I'm coming aboard."

The deck where he had fallen was much closer to *Pinnacle*'s entrance hatch than the balcony; Durham Red had done him that small favour, it seemed. Sorrelier and Lise were inside the schooner in moments, locking the hatch behind them.

Sorrelier left Lise and stumbled forward, along the main corridor and into the cockpit. "Our cargo is more resilient than I'd anticipated, Rimail. Where is she?"

Rimail spared him a concerned glance as he entered, but quickly returned his attention to the visula screens. He knew better than to fuss at such a time. "She's heading for the skiffs, sire. Some artisans tried to stop her, but she went through them without slowing."

"I share their pain." Sorrelier glared at a technician until the man got out of his seat, then dropped into it. "Show me."

Rimail angled a screen towards him. There, clear on the visula disc, was Durham Red, stalking between rows of gravity skiffs. "What's the bitch doing?"

"Choosing one she likes, I think."

Sure enough, she was reaching down to the cockpit cover of a golden airboat, sliding it back. Sorrelier watched her jump inside it, and groaned. No one had told her how they worked. "That lethal idiot is actually going to try and fly out of here, isn't she?"

"It looks that way, sire."

"Inform the harbour master. Tell him to get the tubes locked down, or I'll be eating my evening meal out of his brainpan."

Rimail's eyebrows went up under the peak of his cap. "Sire?"

"Yes, I know it's stupid! Tell him anyway – if she gets out of the tube we'll be lucky to get her back in pieces."

With that, Sorrelier sat back in the technician's seat and put a hand to his face, probing the bruises that flowered there, despair welling up in him once more. He'd been so close. The bitch had actually been in his grasp – as had the future, however briefly.

The future of Sorrelier's plans looked about as likely to survive as Durham Red. He could see her on the visula, hopping into a skiff and pulling the canopy down, ready to fly from the Keep to freedom.

She couldn't know about the security locks, installed in every Magadani craft to prevent unauthorised access to the poisoned lands outside. No one would have told her that flying such a vessel away from the Keep, without express permission from the Magister himself, would cause the power plant to go critical within a few kilometres.

If he couldn't turn her back, Durham Red would die, and all his plans would go with her. Down in flames to meet the hard ground of Magadan.

11. ASHKELON

The forests of Ashkelon were thick and uniformly impenetrable. During almost two weeks of travel Harrow and Godolkin had gone no more than a hundred and fifty kilometres from the landing site.

"Landing" wasn't a word Judas Harrow would have used out of choice, but the phrases he might have preferred – "crash", perhaps, or even "impact", seemed to unsettle Godolkin. Without Durham Red around to mediate between the two men, Harrow thought it safest not to antagonise the Iconoclast any more than necessary.

Still, the fact was that *Hunter* had "landed" at something close to five hundred kilometres per hour, hard enough to bounce his skull off the navigation board and black him out for an hour. To his credit, he was not the only man aboard to have been knocked senseless as the yacht came down; Godolkin had lost consciousness too, although only for a few minutes. When Harrow had regained his wits, the Iconoclast was already unlocked from his harness and attempting to bring the ship back to life.

The landing had gone almost to plan, but not quite. *Crimson Hunter* had come down in the centre of the flayer's blast crater, which had saved it from being battered to pieces by tree trunks, but the manoeuvring thrusters hadn't been enough to slow it down. Later, after they had left the ship, Harrow had been able to see what had happened to it; how the yacht had belly-flopped onto the ground, bounced, then dropped again prow first, and embedded itself in the forest two hundred metres past the forward edge of the crater.

Crimson Hunter was hanging among burned trees, prow down, its shattered drives pointing at the sky. When Harrow had awoken he had found the deck sloping under him by an angle of about forty-five degrees, and the ship's nose a metre off the ground.

It could have been far worse. The yacht was still largely intact, most of its systems functional and the reactor undamaged. Harrow considered it unlikely that *Hunter* would ever leave Ashkelon under its own power, but the ship was far from dead.

The comms system was damaged, but repairable. Miraculously, the sensorium had survived largely intact, and it was this that Godolkin had been working on when Harrow had come round. He had been trying to locate the other two ships, and to find any trace of Durham Red.

He had failed, on both counts.

From what the sense-engines had been able to tell them, neither Ketta's bastardised daggership nor the craft with the shadow web were in orbit. If they had landed, they must have done so some distance away, far enough for the forest to block their energy signatures. And there were no other vessels in detection range.

While Godolkin worked on the sensors, Harrow had unstrapped himself and climbed down to the communications. He had tried sending a signal to Durham Red on every cipher he could think of, but there was no reply. Either she was not on Ashkelon, or she was not capable of answering him.

Neither thought gave him much comfort.

It was much later that first night when the sense-engines finally gave a sign of hope. Harrow had been sorting through the equipment lockers, setting aside any undamaged tools or apparatus they might need in the days to come, when there was a chiming from the sense-feeds. The event that caused the alarm was short-lived, and Harrow wasn't able to get back to the nav board in time to see it. Luckily, *Hunter* had recorded the incident.

Out in the darkness, almost two hundred kilometres due north, the forest had come alive with power. The energy spike was so vast and so sudden that Harrow initially mistook it for an explosion. But a few minutes more at the board convinced him nothing had been blown up among the trees. Instead, a device of immense electrical potential had activated, increased its output to a peak and then shut down, all in the space of a few seconds.

There had been nothing more. Come morning, neither man had been able to pick up any other sign of technological activity on Ashkelon. The decision to head north was not a difficult one.

On the eleventh day, Judas Harrow rose with the sun, as he always did. He looked up to see Godolkin standing by the portable fusion heater, holy weapon at the ready. That was where he had been when Harrow had finally drifted off. The Iconoclast didn't look as though he had moved all night.

Harrow gave him a sour look as he sat up. "One day, human, I'll see you sleep. I swear it."

"If you're so eager, perhaps you'd like to keep watch tonight." Godolkin lowered his weapon, and surveyed Harrow's crumpled form with undisguised contempt. "Although something tells me you need the rest more than I."

Harrow declined to answer. He never found it easy to sleep at the best of times, and curling up among the wet leaves of Ashkelon's endless forest was no way to get a restful night. He spent most of the hours of darkness lying awake, listening to creatures fighting and tearing each other among the trees. Ashkelon seemed as rich a source of fauna as it was flora, but whatever was screaming out there in the forest remained well hidden during the day. Harrow hadn't seen any creature larger than his own thumb since he had arrived.

He began stowing the heater away, collapsing the vanes and the baffles until he was able to fold the device up in its own casing, and stash it in his backpack. "Since you stood watch, human, I'll lead the way for a while."

"Very well." Godolkin handed him the dataslate. "*Hunter* recorded no more spikes during the night, nor any orbital activity."

Harrow nodded, studying the slate's display. The slate was a flat pod of systemry the size of his hand, heavily strengthened for battlefield use. It belonged to Godolkin, Iconoclast standard issue, and had proved an essential item on the journey so far. For one thing, it contained an inertial compass, without which they could have trekked no more than a hundred metres without becoming completely lost. It also had a direct cipher-link back to *Hunter*'s onboard computers.

He called up the overnight recording, which was as blank as Godolkin had reported, then checked the day's route. *Hunter* had generated their path for them, taking into account the terrain features it had scanned on its initial orbits of Ashkelon. Harrow didn't doubt that it had saved them days.

"We're close," he said finally. "Ten hours, maybe twelve."

"I estimated the same," nodded the Iconoclast. "With luck and effort we could reach our destination by nightfall."

Harrow let out a long breath. "That's good news," he replied.

Another day hacking their way through the forest would be less than pleasant, but nothing he couldn't handle. He had survived eleven days of Iconoclast mealsticks and filtered water, roasting in the sodden heat of the daylight hours and freezing at night, all the while under Godolkin's baleful gaze. Had their destination been further away, however, Harrow wasn't entirely sure he could have made it.

Although what the alternative might have been, he wasn't prepared to think about.

He clipped the dataslate to his belt, took a long, curved vibrablade from his backpack and swung the pack over his shoulder. Godolkin had already done the same, his rucksack bulging with a hundred kilos of equipment and ammunition. Most of its weight was comprised of spare fuel and replacement staking pins for his holy weapon. If they ran into Ketta again, or anyone from the shadow-ship, the Iconoclast would be fully equipped for the encounter.

He wasn't the only one. Harrow hefted the vibrablade, triggering the power for long enough to send the weapon sweeping effortlessly through an arm-thick pole of vegetation. "Bring them on," he whispered.

Godolkin had taken up position a few metres behind him. "Did you speak, mutant?"

"Hmm? Oh, I said we should get on."

"Of course you did."

There had been three more power spikes since the first. *Hunter* had recorded them all, and Harrow had reviewed the data whenever he had been able. However, neither he, nor the yacht's data-engines had been able to explain what might be vomiting gouts of raw energy into the skies of Ashkelon.

The only constant that the spikes shared was their location. Each had happened at exactly the same spot, but they varied wildly in both duration and intensity. The discharges didn't happen at regular intervals, either. Two had been within minutes of each other, the next days later. It made no sense.

There was much about this world that made no sense. Harrow had almost given up pondering its mysteries.

He had been cutting his way through the undergrowth for almost two hours now, and the ground ahead was beginning to slope downwards. He skirted a tangle of tree boles, used the blade to sever some of the vines blocking his path, and then paused for a moment to check the dataslate. He stuck the vibrablade into the ground while he did so, to keep his hands free. Without his finger on the trigger it was no sharper than a rough machete, and stood perfectly vertical.

A bug landed on the back of his neck and he flattened it reflexively. None of the myriad insects he had encountered had actually tried to bite him yet – presumably his physiology was as alien and unappetising to them as theirs to him – but he didn't like to take chances. One of them might pluck up the courage.

He frowned at the slate. A new icon was blinking there. "Godolkin? What do you make of this?"

The Iconoclast trotted up to join him, and leaned over to study the screen. "How long ago did this appear?"

"A minute, maybe two." The slate had its own detection equipment, adding to the more powerful sense-engines aboard *Crimson Hunter*. "We got close to something."

"Hmph." Godolkin looked up, glaring out between the trees. "These readings denote a source of energy. It is of low yield, but the signature denotes a fusion core."

"A ship?"

The human nodded slowly. "If it was powered down, yes."

Harrow took a deep breath. *Hunter* had been watching the skies ever since they had reached this world, and nothing had landed here since their arrival. Which meant they had either stumbled across Major Ketta's daggership, or the mysterious stealth-craft that had attacked them on the way in. In both cases, no one aboard would be pleased to see them.

Unless it was Durham Red.

"She might be there," Harrow said.

"I'm aware of that. In addition, this vessel could provide us with a replacement for *Crimson Hunter*. Whether we find the Blasphemy alive or not, we will require a functioning starship."

"Well then," Harrow replied. "I think a short detour might be in order, don't you?"

They left their backpacks at the base of a nearby tree, along with a tracer set to remote activation – if they needed to find the packs again in a hurry, a touch of the right dataslate icon would cause the tracer to send out a signal.

Along with the mealsticks and other survival equipment, the packs contained a sizeable selection of weapons. Harrow put the vibrablade aside and took out a short-barrelled plasma carbine, checking it was fully charged and set to burst-fire, while Godolkin unsheathed his silver blade. Harrow watched it extend from the handgrip, unfolding itself with a sibilant, metallic hiss into a sword-blade two metres long and scalpel-sharp. The third symbolic weapon of the elite vampire killer.

He looked away. The weapon had been designed for one specific purpose: to separate Durham Red's head from her neck. "Take care how you swing that blade, human. We may have to fight in an enclosed space."

"In which case, heed your own advice." Godolkin whirled the sword around, testing its weight with one hand, his right forearm still enclosed by the holy weapon. "Perhaps our journey ends here, Judas Harrow."

Harrow didn't answer. He wasn't exactly sure what sort of conclusion the Iconoclast had in mind.

The vegetation was growing thin by the time they saw the source of the power reading, the first time Harrow had seen it do so. He could feel the temperature rising as the canopy grew more sparse above him, the morning sunlight striking down in shafts. Sweat began to run under his mesh armoured jacket.

He ignored it, watching Godolkin move on through the trees. The two men were a few metres apart, so as not to hinder each other's movements or provide too tempting a target. And while Harrow's slender frame leant itself to stealth, the hulking Iconoclast padded forward with an effortless silence. There was a deadly, predatory grace to him, the calm poise of the elite warrior.

Harrow hoped it would be enough. There was no telling what kind of odds they might be up against. He stepped between two tree boles, over an expanse of wiry creepers, and put his foot down on something cold and hard.

His heart jumped in his chest, and he froze. For a moment he was convinced that he had trodden on a land-mine, that in the next instant he would be blasted limb from limb, but there was no explosion.

Matteus Godolkin appeared next to him like a ghost. "What?"

"I'm not sure," Harrow breathed. "Something underfoot."

There had been rocks beneath his boots – the ground here was treacherous, littered with stones, rotted wood and all manner of debris under the covering of leaves – but this was different. It was smooth and flat, a wide block that felt inflexible and hard.

Nothing natural felt like that. This was manufactured.

Silently, Harrow shifted some of the leaf cover away with the side of his boot, and confirmed what he had suspected. He was standing on a paving slab.

The stone was old, the edges worn smooth by time, but there was no mistaking the artificial nature of it. Godolkin nodded his acknowledgement, and moved on, modifying his footfalls for the new terrain. Taking extra care not to make a sound, Harrow resumed his own path, his feet finding more slabs, less leaves. Before he had gone a dozen metres, he was under the open sky.

He couldn't help glancing up. It was the first time he had seen clouds since leaving *Hunter*.

Ahead of him, the thinning trees seemed to reach a line and then cease altogether. Beyond that boundary, grey stone glinted in the sunlight. Harrow could see structures there; some intact, others torn down to piles of vine-clogged rubble. Further away, tiers of rough steps rose skywards to cast a long shadow over what must once have been some kind of courtyard, and decayed stone faces gazed impassively back into the treeline.

In the midst of this ancient ruin, dark metal gleamed.

Harrow dropped into a crouch, easing back behind the nearest tree. Ketta's modified daggership was resting in the centre of the courtyard, some of the slabs below it scorched black by the heat of its thrusters. Others lay shattered beneath the vessel's landing spine. Ketta had come down hard too, it seemed, although she had been able to choose a more suitable landing site than Godolkin's blast crater. If her drives had been failing, the stone town must have been as welcome as a spaceport.

There was the faintest rustle next to him. It was Godolkin. "I see we weren't the only ones to have drawn fire from that stealth-vessel."

Harrow looked more closely, wiping the sweat from his forehead, and saw that the human was right. Molten holes were stitched along one of the daggership's winglets, and ragged tongues of metal were ripped back from a gaping wound in its flank. There was a drive nacelle missing too, but Harrow had seen that go. "What do you think?" he whispered. "Is it spaceworthy?"

"It appears to be," Godolkin replied. "However, Ketta will have encrypted the vessel's control codes. We cannot operate it without them."

"It's an Iconoclast ship, isn't it? Can't you override the encryption?"

"Possibly. But it would take time."

"If we can get Ketta out of the way, we'd have time." Harrow chewed his lip nervously. "Easier said than done, though. She's a tough one."

"Aye." Godolkin stood up. "Still, one way or another we need to be aboard that ship. You have the data-pick with you, yes?"

"We'll have a long walk back if I haven't." Harrow reached down to a pouch on his belt, and pulled the pick free. He handed it to Godolkin. "Lucky us."

"Mutant humour," growled the Iconoclast. "One day you must attempt to explain it to me." He stood up, and grabbed one of the tree's lower branches. Harrow saw the muscles in his arms bunch under the battle harness, and heard the squeaking of overstressed wood. A moment later the branch splintered away from the trunk; Godolkin stepped around the tree and threw it high into the air.

If the daggership had been on sentry mode the branch would have hit the ground as ash, but it seemed Ketta's ship had been powered down. The antimat turrets remained still, even as the branch tumbled end over end and clattered down onto the stone slabs.

"Hmm," Godolkin murmured, and stepped out of the treeline. A second later he launched himself into the open, darting away towards the ship.

Harrow followed him, out from the forest and into the ruins. The stone walls on either side of him felt momentarily cold, before he stepped back out in the full glare of the sun, his boots crunching on old stone as he hammered across the courtyard to the ship's landing foot. It was hard not to crouch as he ran, even though the ship's weapons stayed resolutely inert. There were a lot of guns on that thing.

By the time he reached the foot, Godolkin was already working at it with the data-pick. Harrow stopped behind him, nosing the carbine left and right, casting nervous glances around the courtyard. These ruins were the first signs of habitation he had seen on Ashkelon, and even though they were covered in creepers and turned halfway to rubble by time, they were still impressive. People of considerable skill and imagination had once made their homes on this steaming, hellish world.

The data-pick chirruped, and the outer lock doors slid aside. Holy weapon at the ready, blade held aloft, Godolkin ducked into the landing foot. Harrow took one last look over his shoulder, and then followed.

It didn't take long to discover that the ship was not only powered down, but completely unoccupied as well. "Bugger," muttered Harrow, echoing Red's casual profanity as he dropped into the pilot's throne. "I should have known that would be too easy."

"All the more reason to press on, mutant." Godolkin handed him the data-pick. "Ketta would not have left this vessel quiescent unless she had good reason to do so. She may be heading for the source of the power spikes, or may even be responsible for them. But I am certain of this: when we find Ketta, we will find the Blasphemy."

Harrow frowned. "She said that Red had been taken from her. But she must have been lying."

"It is a talent at which she excels." Godolkin began striding across the darkened bridge, towards the spinal corridor. "We should waste no more time here."

"Can't we even see if she has any decent food first?"

The human spared him a backwards glance. "Ketta is, or was, an Iconoclast special agent. To her, mealsticks are a delicacy to be prized."

Harrow stood up. "What about a grav-chute?"

"I have already checked. Move yourself, mutant!"

Godolkin deactivated his silver blade on the way down the landing spine, stowing it back over his left shoulder. Harrow, following close behind him, was glad to see the awful thing deactivated. Doubly so when Godolkin stopped without warning as the outer lock opened and Harrow almost slammed into his back. Had the blade still been in evidence, he might very well have impaled himself upon it. "By the saint, human! I thought you were in a hurry!"

The Iconoclast held up a hand for silence. He was sniffing the air, turning his head this way and that. Harrow instantly fell silent. Godolkin's senses were as greatly enhanced as his physique – he could tell a human from a mutant at twenty paces by smell alone, or sniff out an enemy from ten times that distance. If his sense of smell had called him to a halt, that was reason enough for Harrow to fear.

"Is it Ketta?"

The Iconoclast shook his head. "No. At first I thought I smelled shocktroopers, but there is a taint to them. Familiar, but in a way I cannot determine."

He stepped forwards and a staking pin hissed out of the sunlight to score a track of blood across his shoulder blades.

Harrow saw the wound appear, the bright steel of the staking pin clattering off the far wall of the courtyard and yelled a warning. Godolkin was already down on one knee, in the cover of a landing claw, bringing the holy weapon up to send a pair of bolts slamming back into the treeline. Something was moving out there, impossibly fast and another bolt whickered towards the Iconoclast, missing by centimetres as Godolkin shrugged out of the way.

From the corner of his eye, Harrow saw another figure dart between two structures ahead of him. He raised the carbine and sprayed fire into the ruins.

Stone shattered into superheated fragments, each plasma bolt sending up a fountain of white-hot dust and carbonised plant matter. The burst was far too slow, not even coming near the figure Harrow had seen, but the effect of the plasma fire was stunning. He saw the running man stumble as the blast-wave took him, only just finding his feet.

Staking pins whined back in return. Harrow ducked back, and the razored projectiles shaved peelings of metal from the landing foot. "Sneck! How many of them are there?"

"We are taking fire from two directions," snapped Godolkin. "Do the maths."

Harrow looked wildly about. He couldn't see either of the assailants – one was hidden in the treeline and the other was somewhere past the courtyard walls – but the angle of their attacks was widening. The Iconoclast out there in the ruins was working his way around the courtyard, hoping to cut into them from the other side. "Godolkin, we're being flanked!"

The Iconoclast muttered a curse. His back was a slick of blood, horribly bright against the pallor of his skin and the stark black of the battle harness. The staking pin had cut him deep. "I concur. Harrow, we need to be among those buildings."

"We'll never get across the courtyard! Let's get back into the ship while we still can!"

"Mutant, listen to me – if we enter the daggership we will be trapped, and if we stay here we die." He jerked sideways as a pin parted the air next to him, shattering a carved face fifty metres away. "With stone at our backs we might stand a chance."

"Damn you, Iconoclast! Doesn't being right all the time ever tire you?"

"I'll let you know." Godolkin swung his weapon around. "Now run!"

Harrow ran.

There was a series of gaps around the courtyard walls, some left intentionally by its builders, but far more caused by time and the inexorable advance of the forest. Harrow bolted for the nearest, off to the right of Ketta's ship, hearing staking pins carom off the slabs behind him. The attacker in the trees was trying to take him down with long-range fire, but there was no sign of the adversary Harrow had shot at earlier.

For a few seconds, he almost thought he would make it. The space gaped in front of him, half blocked by the tree that had grown through it, and he could see more stone beyond, layer upon layer where buildings crowded the base of the stepped structure. If he could just make it past the wall he would be among them.

Then, when he was halfway there, he saw the warrior step out from behind the tree, already firing.

The first staking pin was shrieking towards Harrow before he could even shout. With the Iconoclast directly ahead of him he could see the flare of the bolter like a minor sun among the shadows, the light spitting a stream of brilliant metal straight at his face. He dived aside and the bolts whipped past him, but there was no way he could avoid the next volley.

He dragged the barrel of the carbine up, hoping to get at least one burst off before the pins found his heart, and as he did so the air between him and the Iconoclast turned to fire.

The courtyard was illuminated by flame, a great stream of searing, billowing heat that scorched the skin of his face from metres away. He had seen that fire before, more times than he cared to count, but never had he been so pleased to feel the wash of it. Godolkin was directing a jet of cleansing flame across his path, blocking the other warrior's aim.

Harrow hurled himself to the ground, rolling aside as staking pins stitched a line through the firestorm. He answered with a salvo from the carbine, just as the flame sputtered and died – Godolkin could only keep the burner activated for a few seconds, or risk the holy weapon blowing up in his face.

Those seconds were all he needed. Harrow leapt at the next gap in the wall and dived through.

He landed on rounded cobbles, cool in the wall's shadow. There was a narrow street that looked as if it ringed the whole courtyard, although it was so choked with rubble and plant life that it was hard to see for more than a few metres in either direction. One thing Harrow knew for certain was that the warrior must have been close by. Perhaps only a few broken rocks and a smouldering tree-trunk or two separated them.

With that firmly in mind, he scampered off the cobbled road and into the ruins beyond.

The buildings here were low, few rising higher than a single storey, and their walls were angled steeply. Many were totally destroyed by time, some with roofs collapsed inwards, others little more than heaps of stone blocks. But a few were still standing. Harrow made his way towards the closest intact structure and ran inside.

His feet came down on something that creaked and snapped like old wood. Creatures, hand-sized things with too many legs, rustled away in panic, and dust sifted down from the ceiling. Harrow froze where he was, still terribly aware of the open door at his back, but even more conscious of the way the stone roof had shifted perceptibly above him.

He took a tentative step inside, shifting more of the wood away with his boots. Something rolled away and hit the wall, startling him afresh, and he tracked it reflexively with the carbine.

A hollow gourd, he told himself, or a wooden bowl. The floor was a litter of artefacts, worn thin by time. Whoever had lived here must have left in a hurry, without clearing their mess away.

There was a square hole in the wall, a few metres along, admitting a shaft of sunlight. Harrow edged towards it, trying not to tread on too much of the dusty, broken debris on the floor, and stood with his back to the wall. Fragments of ancient glass turned to powder under his boots, and he winced. Even that tiny sound was too much.

He peered outside and saw no one. The street was empty of all but trees and shattered masonry. He let out a breath that he hadn't even been aware he was holding, and lowered the carbine. For the moment at least, he was alone.

He was reaching down to take the comm-linker from his belt when he heard the gourd roll again. He tried to turn around, to get the carbine back up and pull the trigger, but before he could even move the Iconoclast warrior slammed into him like a wall of iron.

The man was sickeningly strong. Harrow went flying backwards, the shadows whirling around him, and crashed into the floor in a cloud of dust. He tried to level the carbine but it was snatched from his grasp, yanked clean out of his hands and flung against the wall. Thin chains, launched at him by the warrior, had wrapped themselves around the barrel and wrenched it from his fingers.

He saw the carbine strike the wall and spin away in two sections.

The chains whipped back into the warrior's grip, then sang out again. Harrow felt them hit him in the face, the neck, and he cried out. There were hooks at the end of the chains, barbed things as sharp as needles, and they sank effortlessly into his flesh. He reached for them, trying to drag them from his skin, but the warrior barked out a laugh and pulled the hooks back. Harrow tried to keep his teeth tightly clenched, but he screamed anyway.

The Iconoclast held him up for several seconds, then let him fall back down. Harrow hit the floor and twisted in pain, his face in the dust. The debris around him clattered, hard edges of it cutting into his skin, and in the dusty sunlight from the window-hole he finally saw how wrong he'd been about the fate of the building's previous occupants. They hadn't left in a hurry, as he had first thought. In fact, they hadn't left at all.

Blood streamed from where the hooks had him, and it fell on bones so old they were halfway to powder.

The warrior dropped to a crouch next to Harrow, the chains in one fist, a cut-down staking bolter in the other. The muzzle, still hot, brushed Harrow's cheek. "A mutant?"

The man's teeth were filed into points, and tipped with steel. Harrow sagged back, forcing himself to relax, to ignore the pain and the hammering in his chest. His hands fell away from the hooks, to the bone-littered floor. Shards of thighbone moved beneath his fingertips.

"Why are you here, mutant? Do you seek the Blasphemy, or the Renegade?"

"I seek no one."

The warrior shrugged, muscles sliding and knotting beneath corpse-white skin. "Pity. You found someone."

"I'm willing to forget it if you are."

The warrior grinned, a barracuda smile. "I'm almost tempted to keep you alive for a time, scum. I'm sure you'd be entertaining company for an hour or two." He put down the bolter and took a long combat knife from a sheath at his belt. Harrow felt the tip of the blade at his neck, scoring upwards to his jawline.

"Past experience tells me your idea of entertainment and mine would differ somewhat," he replied, trying to keep his voice steady. Down at his sides his fingers had found what he was looking for, and gripped it tightly. He'd only have one chance at this. "But maybe we could work something out."

"Maybe. But I've tarried too long as it is." The knife came up, bloodied. "Just time to have your eyes out, and then I'll be gone."

"Don't forget to write," Harrow said, and slammed his right fist up and into the side of the warrior's head.

The Iconoclast howled and leapt up, scrabbling at the side of his skull. A long shard of bone was protruding from his ear, already soaked with blood. Harrow had explored the length of that bone with his fingers, and knew that a good amount of it must now reside inside the warrior's head.

The man was staggering back, his chains forgotten. Harrow snatched up the bolter, flipped it around and hauled on the trigger. It jumped and flared in his hand, stinging his fingers, and the warrior's howls stopped at once. The blunt end of a staking pin had appeared between his eyes.

He sank to his knees, opened his mouth as if to speak, and pitched forwards into the dust. His arms and legs moved fitfully for a moment, but it was only as a reflex. In a few beats of Harrow's leaping heart, the Iconoclast became still.

"I was here to offer assistance," said Godolkin from the doorway. "But it appears you need none."

Harrow sagged. "I'll settle for a trauma kit. What happened?"

"I followed the other one into the trees, and staked her, but she survived and escaped." Godolkin nudged the fallen trooper with his boot. "Harrow, these are not shocktroopers. They have been enhanced, considerably."

"As long as he stays dead, I could care less." Harrow got up, the hooks still dragging at him. He raised his hands to one and began to work it from his skin. "Help me get these things out, and then we'll be away. This building is ready to collapse, I think."

"It and you both." Godolking started towards him, then froze. "Mutant, look at this."

"What?"

In reply, the Iconoclast held up a bone from the floor. It was half covered in the dead warrior's blood. As Harrow watched, the bone sagged, bubbling, and fell in two.

"I have seen this ichor once before, Harrow." Godolkin dropped the hissing, dissolving relic onto the warrior's back. "On Biblos. The Blasphemy tried to drink from one of these creatures."

"Sacred rubies." Harrow was aghast. If Red had taken a mouthful of that stuff.:. "What are they?"

"Iconoclasts with a vastly modified physiology. Toxic blood chemistry, acidic body fluids, heightened reflexes…" The man looked down, and gave the dead warrior a vicious kick.

"Harrow, these are the Omega warriors of Lord-Tactician Saulus!"

12. STORM WARNING

It was raining on Magadan. Fat raindrops the size of finger-nails slapped down from the sullen sky, splashing back up in tiny crowns when they struck the ground. They fell on the rough roads that tangled away from the Grand Keep, and lifted the cobbles on beds of sludge. They beat the leaves from the trees and flattened the grass. They turned soil to mud, mud to slurry, the debris fields surrounding the Keep into endless, sodden mires. And worst of all, they fell on Durham Red.

"Snecking rain," she muttered.

It had been a day, she had decided, for learning new things. She would have been quite content with what she had discovered about the Magadani, and the debt they owed to her old enemy the Gothking, but it seemed that the universe hadn't finished with her schooling quite yet. There was more, some unforgiving power must have decreed, that she still needed to know.

For example, she had learned that the aerial vehicles berthed in the Keep's hangars were beautifully constructed, luxurious to pilot, and fatally booby-trapped. The aircar she had stolen had taken her no more than ten kilometres before it had started berating her in a variety of automated voices, and only another five before the controls had ceased to respond. From what she had been able to discern from the voice-warnings, the ship hadn't been given clearance from the Magister to leave the Keep, and, to prevent conta-mination by the outside world's many airborne diseases had been programmed to nosedive at full speed into the surface. Luckily, the patch of ground it had chosen to impact was totally waterlogged, more swamp than solid. Red had waded out of the wreck shaken but largely unharmed. The flier, on the other hand, had promptly sunk.

Red had also learned that the coat she had worn to the Masque, while it looked substantial, was not remotely weatherproof, and was in fact starting to fall apart at the seams. The gloves were still in the flier, where she had discarded them to get a better feel for the controls, and the rest of her costume was turning out to be much more suited to the temperature-regulated interior of the Keep than to adventuring in the outside world.

The breastplate had grown heavy on her. She'd dumped it a kilometre back.

It had been a very long time since Durham Red had been as cold, wet, muddy and thoroughly miserable. In the day's favour, she had learned one more thing: that the surface of Magadan, far from being a poisoned wasteland, was instead fertile and quite benign. If Sorrelier had been right about the plague-ridden nature of the place, then either such diseases were a lot slower to act than many Red that had known, or she was fighting them off quite effectively.

She had still taken a terrible risk. Getting into the aircar had simply been the quickest way of escaping from Sorrelier, but once she was out of the Keep she had found that she didn't really want to go back. She'd decided to fly on and then set down somewhere quiet for an hour or two, just to think and work out what to do next. But the booby-trapped ship hadn't given her the chance.

Red had been trudging along for more than an hour, through a landscape that had turned slowly from swampland to sparse woods, and then to a kind of hillocky scrubland. The grassy slopes around her were broken by shards and boulders of dark yellow stone, some as big as skyscrapers, as though the planet's crust had shattered beneath the soil and thrown fragments of itself up into the

light. Some were close enough to overhang the road, and
Red had sheltered beneath more than one during her trek.

Another was ahead, looming through the mist and the
spattering rain. Red increased her pace until she got under
the great roof of stone and was finally able to lift her head.
Normally the weather didn't bother her – she quite liked to
feel the elements against her skin, especially if she was
dressed for it. But the rain on Magadan was less like
weather and more like a beating. Red's hair lay plastered
over her head, a sodden conduit for cold rain to slide down
the back of her neck and into her clothes.

She stretched and wiped her face with her hands. It felt
good to raise her head and ease the kinks from her back,
but if she didn't stoop over when she was walking the rain
hit her in the eyes and gummed them closed. She shivered
and wished that she'd worn a hat to the Masque.

Her stomach growled. "Shut up," she told it.

It had been a while since she'd eaten, and too long since
she'd been properly nourished. She could fill her belly with
food, and enjoy it, but it was blood that she really needed.
Nothing else would sustain her, no matter how full she felt.
Without a supply of fresh blood, Durham Red could starve
to death in a restaurant.

She licked her fangs, feeling the sharp points of them
against her tongue, and thought about biting Vaide Sorrelier.

That, Red was certain, would be a meal worth taking, and
when she finally sat down to it she'd not stop until she was
full and Sorrelier was an empty husk.

She could almost see him, moving among the sylphs she
had fought, casting an appraising eye over the wounded as
though sorting through broken crockery. She had seen him
gesture at one he must have considered worth saving, waving another's agonies away with the merest brush of his
hand. Only the nerve-blocking drug she was sedated with
prevented her from leaping forward and ripping the head
from his neck.

If only she'd recovered from the stuff sooner. Red scowled and booted a nearby pebble out into the rain, trying to forget what the drug's effects felt like. Whatever concoction had been on his sylph's fingernails it had been viciously potent. One scratch had turned her to water where she stood. Thankfully she had been able to fight the stuff off, just as she had Losen's happy juice back at the Masque. Sorrelier clearly hadn't expected her to recover from it at all.

Her physiology and metabolism must have been very different from that of the average Magadani.

Red shook her head, violently, whipping some of the rain from her hair. Thinking about Sorrelier was making her feel angry and hungry at the same time, not a great combination for a girl with little but a long walk in the rain to look forward to. But there was something about the man that forced her mind to keep curving back to him, a nagging edge of familiarity that she couldn't set aside.

His similarity to the Gothking, probably. Now that she knew the connection between the Magadani and Simon of Isis, she could see how alike Sorrelier and her old nemesis were.

Betrayers, poisoners, drug fiends... The two could have been twins.

Red rubbed her shoulder through the sodden coat, trying to remember how long it had been since she and the Gothking had last crossed swords. Four years, she guessed, since he had gatecrashed that party on Lethe to tell her that the price was finally off her head. Maybe five.

Suddenly the right answer came to her, and she barked out a laugh. Almost thirteen hundred years had gone by since she had last met Simon D'Isis – while she had slept the centuries away, he had died and gone to dust. It felt like nothing to her; the memory of his face was still fresh in her mind, but he must have grown old wondering where she had hidden herself, his dark hair going grey, his angular features sagging, his gallows wit leaving him one brain cell at a time. Maybe, deep in the court he had built for himself on the planet Isis, the Gothking had faded into memory with her name on his lips.

It was an oddly pleasing thought, but it was far more likely that D'Isis had died at the hands of a rival, or even that the law had finally caught up with him. One doesn't become the head of a drugs syndicate spanning hundreds of planets without making a few enemies.

In either case, Simon D'Isis was dead a thousand years, remembered only by one rather soggy mutant and a castle full of social climbers who couldn't even get his name right.

"Nice legacy," Red muttered, thinking aloud. "How the mighty have fallen, eh Simon?"

Sneck, she was talking to dead men. She'd been standing there too long, the sound of the rain hypnotising her. It was time to be away.

Red cursed under her breath, pulled the collar of her drenched, sagging coat up over her head, bent forwards and stepped out into the rain.

There had been a time, back in her days as a Search/Destroy agent, when D'Isis and his people had been the most dangerous part of Red's life, although it was a matter between her and a man called Jayem that had started the trouble. Jayem was a drug dealer, the head of a minor criminal operation who distributed psychoactive compounds of esoteric manufacture and brutal intensity. Someone Red had known well, and liked a lot, had died from Jayem's wares. So Red had gone after him – and, after a calamity or two, had got close enough to him to express her displeasure.

He hadn't survived it.

Which would have been the end of things, had Jayem not been the nephew of the Gothking, a different kind of man entirely. While Jayem had been a brute, his uncle was refined. Jayem was a fool, but Simon of Isis possessed a frightening intelligence. And Jayem was in his grave, and out of the picture, while the Gothking rapidly became the focus of all the woes in Durham Red's world.

The Gothking's empire was vast: it spanned cities, nations, worlds, webbing whole sectors together in a network of illicit profit, and that had made Red's life very difficult indeed. There had been few enough places she could go to get away from trouble, even before she had come to the Gothking's attentions. Once his eye was on her, she was hunted wherever she went.

Eventually, the price he had placed on her head – more for threatening his authority than for the killing of his nephew, as the two men had never been close – had become insanely huge. Red had been forced to take extreme measures in order to get the Gothking off her back.

They had worked, after a fashion, although her plans had cost the life of a good friend. D'Isis had visited her on Lethe, during that friend's post-funeral party, to let Red know that her debt was cancelled, as long as she stayed out of his way.

Well, she had stayed out of his way for a very long time indeed.

As she walked Red found herself mentally cursing Sorrelier and his kin for bringing such foul memories back to mind. She'd largely forgotten about the Gothlord – this new universe she had awoken to boasted horrors that made his influence pale in comparison. He was in her head again, which was yet another reason to make life unpleasant for Vaide Sorrelier the next time they met.

That, of course, would depend on whether Red ever found her way out of Magadan's increasingly unpleasant wilderness.

It had finally stopped raining, the deluge turning first to drizzle and then to a watery mist. As it did so the landscape around her changed again, quite rapidly. The mud and grass were replaced by broken stone, the vegetation became scraggy and beaten until it finally faded out altogether. Before long Red was standing in a place where nothing grew at all.

The ground beneath her boots was pale grey, a kind of compacted, dusty gravel topped with layers of flat, shale-like

stones. The air was cold, misty, a deepening, colourless twi-
light. There was no sign of a sun above her, or a moon on
the horizon. Other than a few boulders scattered around,
nothing broke the monochrome drabness surrounding her.

Red shivered. Somehow, this was worse than the rain and
the mud. That had just been uncomfortable, but at least it
had been *alive*. Where she was standing was a dead place,
the corpse of a world.

She began to trudge away.

The ground started to slope upwards, rising into what
looked like a series of low hills. Red climbed up a little way
then paused, listening for any signs of danger, sniffing the
air.

Nothing. Just dead rocks and dust and mist.

Far away, past the bottom of the slope and the scrubby
hillocks beyond, past the gradual darkening into muddy
fields and boulder-strewn woodland and drenched mountains of debris, the Grand Keep rose like a knife hilt,
buried blade-deep in the surface of Magadan. From this
distance there was no solidity to it. It was flat, like a paper
cut-out, a tall rectangle of blue-grey against the darkening
sky.

Red turned to the hills again, glad to put the awful place
at her back, and started to climb.

The going wasn't easy, but she'd known worse. The
slope seemed quite constant, with little in the way of irreg-
ularities to trip her, although the flat rocks sometimes slid
beneath her boots. The mist, however, was not so constant,
and thickened continually. Red had expected it to thin out
as she climbed higher, but the stuff stubbornly refused to
conform to any physical law she knew, and just kept getting worse.

Eventually there came a point when the mist became so
solid that Red was utterly blinded by it. A jolt of panic
jumped in her chest, but as soon as it flared in her she felt
the incline reverse direction. She had reached the peak of
the hill, and was now heading downslope.

The mist, finally, began to thin.

Red felt herself grinning. The old excitement, the need to see what lay beyond the next corner, was back in control, that curiosity that had led her on so many adventures, into so much peril. She began to speed up, skittering down the rocky slope, hearing the pebbles slide along with her in dry, rattling avalanches behind her bootheels.

It was with some disappointment, then, that she saw the vista opening up in front of her was very much like the one she had left behind. The boulders were of similar dimensions, the mist was just as chilly, the sky as featureless as before. Even the landscape at the limits of her vision was–

She stopped dead where she was, gaping. The Keep loomed ahead of her.

Red blinked, rubbed her eyes with her fists, but to no avail. There was no mistaking it. It wasn't a structure of similar dimensions. The scene in front of her was the same as the one she had left. There was no difference at all. Even the marks her boots had left among the gravel were there, a few metres to her right.

She was right back where she had started.

"Oh no," she growled menacingly, at no one in particular. "Don't give me that. No way did I turn around."

But there was no denying the evidence, whether she did so out loud or not. Somewhere, up in that thickening mist, she had slipped or changed her direction so subtly she'd not even noticed, then happily trotted back down the same slope like an idiot.

"Shit," she cursed. There was nothing for it but to go up again, and do it properly this time.

On the next ascent, she remained resolutely focussed on her direction. Every few paces up the slope she would pause, and turn to look at the trail of footprints she had made, then carry on, eyes fixed ahead. Her night-vision did her no good at all, and the mist became more and more blinding as she got higher. Once again, there came a time when she could see nothing through it at all.

That was where she had made her mistake last time. Very carefully, ignoring the panic fluttering behind her ribs, she took one long, straight stride over the brow of the hill and onto the downwards slope.

This time she knew, as surely as she knew anything, that she was heading the right way.

Which made her curse all the louder when she got far enough down the hill to see the Keep again.

It was unbelievable, impossible. She could make a mistake like that once. After all, she'd not been concentrating, had been thinking too much about Gothking and his strange legacies. Lost in those thoughts, she could very easily have accidentally retraced her steps. But the second time, she had been careful.

There was only one thing for it. She ran sideways along the slope, well away from her previous route, and made the journey again.

The results were exactly, distressingly, the same.

Red gave up, dropping to her haunches on the dry rocks. The Keep reared up in front of her, just as it had before.

"Just what," she asked desperately, "is going on?"

Her only answer came from the sky. The low growl of engines, changing course.

Red stood up and waved. She couldn't see the flier, but she could feel the vibration of it through her boots, in her hair and her teeth. She should run – she knew that to stand still and attract the vessel's attention was an insane thing to do. She would be captured, returned to the clutches of the people she most desired to be away from.

But there was nothing here for her but madness. The only way she would get off Magadan – if indeed there *was* a way off – lay through answers, not shoe leather. And those answers lay in just one place.

The drone of the flier's engines changed tone. Red watched it emerge from the mist, landing with its legs extended, and prepared to go back to the Grand Keep.

13. NOCTURNAL PREDATORS

Night began to fall before Harrow and Godolkin reached the source of the power spikes. Their plan, back when the sun had just risen, had been to slog uninterrupted through the forest along the path *Hunter* had mapped for them, and to reach their destination before it grew dark. That strategy, however, was now irrevocably changed.

They moved slowly, and silently when they could. Both walked with weapons drawn and primed, staying separated by a few metres, each watching the forest at his side. When the undergrowth grew too thick to move in that manner they took it in turns to forge ahead – one man would lower his gun to cut a path through the greenery, while the other would hold position and keep watch. Then when the scout had gone far enough they would swap roles.

Ten hours had passed like this, pacing forward together or in leap-frog fashion, and their progress had dropped to a crawl. But to go faster would have been to invite death. Ever since the encounter at Ketta's daggership, Harrow and Godolkin had been hunted.

There were more Omegas out among the trees, how many could only be guessed at. One of the two warriors that had attacked them in the ruins had survived, and escaped into the forest. There was no telling how long she had survived – according to Godolkin, her wounds had been extensive – but it must have been long enough for her to alert the others.

This had already been proved several times during the day. If it hadn't been for Godolkin's martial skill, he and

Harrow might have been discovered and killed on three or four occasions. One time, an Omega had passed so close to Harrow's hiding place that he had been able to smell the warrior's sweat, to hear his breathing.

Harrow was certain that the Omegas had never been more than a kilometre away from them since the ruins.

It was a nerve-shredding, terrifying situation. But in spite of the fear, Harrow was almost glad of the lessening in pace. His encounter with the Omega warrior had left him battered and shaken: the gouges on his face and neck stung and itched beneath their covering of hardened antiseptic foam, and his chest ached from the blows he had taken. In other circumstances he would have liked nothing better than to lie down and sleep for a week, but that could never be an option here. Besides, after he had defeated one of the Omegas single-handed, his pride wouldn't let him.

Soon, he hoped, Durham Red would discover how he had prevailed against the enhanced Iconoclast, without asking for a moment's respite afterwards.

All he had to do was find her.

The terrain had taken another one of its downward slopes, although it was often hard to tell; the greenery here was so thick that it obscured the ground completely. Harrow crouched near the base of a tree and watched Godolkin use his silver blade to scythe a way through, cutting through the tall, pulpy stalks that grew around the tree boles, severing loops of vine and glossy, hanging leaves the size of bed-sheets.

It was hot. Harrow sweated under his mesh jacket and resisted the impulse to scratch his wounds. The Omega's hooks had gone deep into him, and although Godolkin had sprayed his cuts with bio-foam they still itched horribly. The temptation to rip at them with his fingernails was horribly strong, but he forced himself to resist: there was no telling what kinds of infections lurked in this steaming hell, and which might have the tenacity to find a home in an alien bloodstream. There was a chance, since he had not evolved on Ashkelon, that the forest's local diseases might have no foothold in his system, leaving him free to walk with open wounds and drink whatever water he found. But it wasn't a risk he was prepared to take.

Instead he concentrated on keeping Godolkin in his gun-sights.

The Iconoclast was nearly out of view. He could normally go much farther before needing to stop and let Harrow over-take him, but the light was failing fast. Harrow was just about to signal him when he saw the man stop, raise his head slightly, then turn around and pad back along the path he had cut.

"What do you smell?" Harrow asked him, as he reached the tree. He was starting to trust the Iconoclast's sense of smell better than his own eyesight, especially in this dwindling light.

Godolkin crouched next to him. "Ozone."

The smell of electricity. They must have been closer to their objective than he had thought. "Close by?"

"Reasonably. At this pace, perhaps half an hour."

Harrow frowned. At the rate the light was failing, half an hour would put them in pitch darkness. Hacking their way through the forest was dangerous enough in daylight, but Harrow didn't even want to attempt it in the dark. It would be just his luck to trip over and break a limb so close to the journey's end.

Until now, the problem had never arisen. By the time darkness fell Harrow was usually at the end of his strength anyway, and more than ready to make camp for the night. He was tired enough to do the same. But if there was a way of getting to the source of that ozone smell without waiting until morning he would happily forgo sleep, and make up the difference later. "Godolkin, do you have your sense-enhancers?"

The Iconoclast had a set of enhancer-goggles as part of his basic equipment. Harrow lacked the surgery required to make use of most of their functions, but knew the image-intensifiers were probably powerful enough for his eyes too.

"I have. In fact, I was about to suggest you try them anyway."

"Really?" It wasn't like Godolkin to offer his wargear to Harrow. The man tended to guard it jealously, probably thinking it would be tainted if used by a mutant. "That's generous of you."

"No, it's not. But there are Omega warriors between us and the source of the ozone. I am more likely to survive an encounter with them if I am not encumbered by a blind man."

Minutes later Judas Harrow was up a tree, waiting for the Omegas to arrive.

He could see quite well in the darkness, thanks to the sense-enhancers. Everything he saw was green, but in this environment that wasn't much different from daylight hours. And although a tree was a less than perfect place for an ambush – there simply hadn't been time to prepare anything better – it made a good enough sniper position. It also gave Harrow the chance to see the creatures whose death-cries had robbed him of so much sleep.

Before this, their shapes and actions had been confined to his imagination, but perched at a junction of branch and trunk high above all the foliage, he could see that his mental images of the conflict had been sadly lacking.

The forest was a battleground. Everywhere Harrow turned the lenses of the sense-enhancers, he saw life. And death, too.

Scuttling things that looked like animated tangles of bone and thorny vine darted amongst the undergrowth, leaping with eerie shrieks to tear at the necks of fat, many-eyed leaf eaters. Winged creatures whined through the air between the towering boles, some longer than Harrow was tall, all bearing lethal scythes along the leading edges of their wings. Harrow watched them swoop, emitting piping whistles, to slice flesh from the loping, stilt-mounted spheroids that formed their ground-based prey. Occasionally a limb or head would be struck from its owner so violently that it would spin, gushing, into the air. Each time it happened, another flier retrieved the morsel before it touched the leaf-strewn ground.

Teeth sank into flesh, claws ripped through bone, a ceaseless dance of bloody predation. By day, Harrow thought to himself, the forests of Ashkelon were simply an inconvenience. By night, they were a killing ground.

He found himself pressing his back firmly against the tree trunk, and keeping a very tight grip on the carbine. The Omegas, it seemed, were not the only hunters he and Godolkin should have been wary of.

The discovery of surviving Omega warriors on this planet had horrified Judas Harrow. He had hoped that the enhanced Iconoclasts would have been destroyed along with their creator, and the entire Omega Solution shelved as a ghastly mistake. But somehow, before he had been taken by the Ordo Hereticus, Lord Tactician Saulus had freed the first batch of his unholy children.

The Omegas were mad, there was no doubt of that. The one Harrow had fought had been clearly deranged, and little wonder – the manner of their creation had been unimaginably traumatic.

Driven by his hatred of all mutants, Durham Red in particular, Saulus had ordered tens of thousands of Iconoclast shocktroopers to be set at each other's throats, forcing them to fight each other to the death. Only the handful of survivors on each of his battlefield planets were deemed worthy of the Omega upgrades, and then subjected to the most agonising surgeries in order to increase their effectiveness.

Designed with the massively increased speed and strength of a special agent like Ketta, yet to be as numerous as shocktroopers, the Omega warriors had bones that were more metal than living tissue, plus toxic blood chemistry and acidic bile. Their senses were enhanced even beyond

the superhuman levels displayed by Godolkin. They were
tireless, fearless, unstoppable.

They had also, somewhere along the line, developed serious psychoses. Had the warrior Harrow battled been sane,
there was no way he could have survived. Godolkin would
have arrived to find the Omega butchering his corpse.

How much that would have displeased him, Harrow
couldn't say.

The human was waiting ten metres away, in another tree.
The plants were vast, their lower limbs as thick as a man's
torso, the places where they joined the trunk wide enough
to rest on quite comfortably. Harrow sat with his legs dangling and his rucksack hooked over one shoulder,
surveying the illuminated world below him along the barrel of his carbine.

And he was still in that same position a few minutes later,
when the killing stopped.

Harrow saw it happen, tinted green through the
enhancers; saw every creature down there pause in their
butchery, raise themselves in their myriad ways as if to sniff
the air, then leap away. There were a few seconds noise as
their exit rustled the undergrowth, then silence. Even the
flying things tilted and merged among the trees.

A moment later, one of the Omegas walked right underneath him.

Harrow's breath caught in his throat and he froze. The
enhanced Iconoclast was pacing silently past the base of the
tree, weapon held at high port, looking left and right as he
moved. He wore no enhancers, but Harrow had no doubt
that the Omega could see as well, if not better, than he
could. The warrior moved easily, as though in daylight.

He was bare-chested, his pallid torso crossed only by a
light battle harness. Harrow pulled the carbine tight
against his shoulder, sighting along the barrel, knowing
that a single plasma bolt at this range would be enough to
blast that corpse-white torso clean open. His finger tight-
ened on the trigger.

Just then, at the edge of his vision, another pale figure strode into view.

Harrow released the trigger, just a fraction. With two Omegas in the picture he would have to co-ordinate with Godolkin, taking the warriors down simultaneously. If there were a gap between one shot and the next, the surviving Omega would have shot him full of staking pins before he could even take his second aim. Instead, he glanced over at Godolkin, tilting his head questioningly.

The human glared at him, indicating which of the Omegas he was aiming for and then holding up four fingers. Harrow started to count down from four in his head, bracing himself for the recoil, and then a third warrior appeared from the undergrowth, signalling to the others in quick, practised battlesign.

Harrow cursed mentally. Godolkin was holding his arm up, his hand making the battlesign gesture for "hold fire."

Then another sign. Harrow squinted, trying to make it out. Godolkin had only just started teaching him the silent language – another Iconoclast secret he was loathe to pass on to a former enemy – but it looked an awful lot like the signal for "jump".

Harrow made a sign of his own: *signal lost, repeat communication*.

In response, Godolkin simply held up something he had taken from his belt. A remote detonator.

Harrow jumped.

He tumbled, a reflexive yell escaping his lips, through the air and into the undergrowth below. The Omegas were brutally quick – a stream of staking pins followed him down – but as Harrow struck the ground there was a deafening whiplash of sound behind him, and the air filled with flying wood.

The tree had exploded, blasting itself to splinters.

Harrow had come down hard, but the greenery of the forest floor had broken his fall enough to let him roll and avoid injury. He stayed down, though, as the tree blew itself to ruin, hearing the whip and snarl of plank-sized fragments shredding the leaves and vines just above his head.

He kept his face to the dirt for several seconds, until the undergrowth stopped shaking, then he burst upwards with the carbine ready.

There was an Omega in front of him, still standing, but the tree had caught him. The man was impaled by dozens of splinters. Most were small, finger-sized or less. But the ones that took him through the heart and the throat were more like spears.

Whatever had opened his belly must have been even bigger than that.

As Harrow watched, the man toppled messily, landing in a heap amidst his own guts. Another lay nearby, head ripped off by a blade of wood. Harrow couldn't see the third warrior at first, but after a few moments the man stumbled into view, his skin so torn by splinters he was practically flayed. He stumbled a few paces, then fell, moaning.

Godolkin stalked out of the greenery to where the fallen warrior lay, and silenced him with a single bolt from his holy weapon. "*Resquiat in pace*," he muttered.

"Human!" Harrow's ears were still ringing from the blast. "What the hell did you just do?"

"There was ten grams of detonex at the base of your tree. I set it off."

"While I was there?"

The man gave a shrug. "What better way to draw the Omegas close?"

"So you used me as bait."

"Not for the first time, mutant, nor the last. It's a role to which you are uniquely suited." He paused and sniffed the air. "More," he snapped.

"How many?" Harrow said.

"Enough. Start running."

"Any idea where to?"

"No," Godolkin replied. "But follow me anyway." And he leapt away.

Before Harrow knew what he was doing he was crashing through the greenery. There was no time to cut his way through the sea of plant life in his way, not if he wanted to keep Godolkin in view. All he could do was follow the man's path as accurately as he could, running over what had already been trampled and jumping the rest.

In daylight, it would have been a nightmarish journey. In pitch blackness, his vision an artificial jigsaw of blurring green forms, it was a hellish flight. Harrow doubted he would have gotten ten metres if the plant life hadn't been starting to thin out.

He was heading downhill. Maybe there was water ahead, a river or suchlike, the soil beneath his hammering boots giving way to rock. But that wasn't what his nose told him. "Godolkin," he panted. "Something's burning."

As he spoke, the Iconoclast stopped dead in his tracks, and swung around. The holy weapon came up and Harrow only just managed to leap aside as a stream of cleansing fire erupted past him.

The forest became bright, lit like day by a vast wall of flame. Harrow heard the enhancers whine in protest, and his vision darkened to compensate. A hundred metres behind him, infernos raged between the trees, layered firestorms that sent twisting columns of flame whirling up into the canopy.

"It is now," Godolkin said flatly.

Harrow watched him turn, and then lope away. Back in the forest trees were cracking and splitting in the heat, vines were shrinking away, creatures were running and howling in terror. Some of the trees had been home to nests of flying, scythe-winged predators. Harrow saw then swooping away, panicked, several catching fire even as they flew.

Below them, three figures burst through the flames, running too fast to burn.

Harrow cursed roundly, brought the carbine up and unleashed a hail of plasma at the pursuing Omegas. Two ducked easily away, swaying around and under the bolts, but one seemed confused by the fires. Plasma struck him in the shoulder and blew his arm clean off, spinning him into the undergrowth. The other two paused, looking back at their stricken companion. It was all the encouragement Harrow needed. He turned tail and raced away into the trees.

Staking pins sliced past him, but not closely. Harrow leaped over a nest of thorny vines, battering through some hanging leaves, and then pounded down the slope. The ground was clearing rapidly, and even though he could no longer see Godolkin he was able to increase his pace until he was running flat out. There was no way he could outrun the Omegas, but a respite of even a few metres might have been enough to find another firing position. It was no certainty, he knew all too well, but right then all he could trust was luck.

Which, a few paces later, ran out entirely.

Before he knew it, he was in the open. The trees had simply stopped, vanished, even more suddenly than they had around the ruins. Harrow skated to a halt, but it was too late. He was already exposed, and there was another warrior heading right for him. He had just the vaguest glimpse of a slender female form wrought from green light before it struck him.

The blow was powerful. Harrow flipped into the air and fell with enough force to knock the breath right out of him. His carbine went one way, the enhancers another. Only his backpack stayed put, and that just served to unbalance him even further. He rolled messily to a halt, ash and burned leaves in his mouth.

There was some light in the clearing. An edge of watery moon peeked over the forest canopy, just enough for Harrow to see his carbine spinning out of reach. The female warrior ran over to it, snatched it up off the ground and pointed it at his face.

He saw her grin, a flash of white teeth in the scant moonlight, and then she was turning away.

"Stay on the ground where you belong, mutant," she said. "You'll live longer."

Harrow knew that voice. "Ketta?"

"Oh do be quiet." She had the carbine in her left hand, a cut-down bolter in her right. Harrow's eyes were adjusting quickly, now that he was free of the enhancers. In the forest he would have been sightless, but although there wasn't much light here there was at least enough to let him focus properly.

He could see the treeline, stretching away into the night, a ragged curve of burned and broken trunks. The ground beneath him was scorched too, as though he were lying in a blast crater. For a second the awful thought hit him that he might be right back where he started, in the circle of destruction left by *Hunter*'s flayer missile, but then the truth hit him: he had found the source of the power spikes.

Whatever had been releasing all that energy into the forest had not done so carefully. It had scorched out a disc of ashes he could have landed *Hunter* in.

It was a revelation, but one he had no time to dwell on. The Omegas were leaping from the trees, firing as they did so. One of them, a female, jumped right into a stream of plasma bolts unleashed by Ketta and exploded, the energy superheating her innards and blasting her open from the inside. The other was faster, and ducked the staking pins that came his way. He was on Ketta in an instant, backhanding her aside.

He was big and powerfully muscled. Round-lensed goggles covered his eyes, held in place with a strap around his shaven head, and he wore a heavy battle harness over his pallid, naked chest.

For all his size, though, he was terrifyingly fast. Ketta had gone over hard after the blow, but she had leaped to her feet more quickly than Harrow might have believed. The Omega matched her, though, sweeping her legs from under her in one kick and catching her viciously in the head with another.

"Give it up, renegade," he snarled. "I'll make this swift."

Ketta scampered upright. She'd lost the guns. "I was about to offer you the same deal, Hermas."

"Don't be so quick to dismiss it, woman. Believe me, I've spent many a dream stripping the veins out of you."

"You've dreamed of me? How sweet! No wonder your biceps are so well-developed."

"Sacred rubies," Harrow groaned, sitting up. "Will you two hurry up and kill each other? Or are you completely in love with the sound of your own voices?"

He heard Ketta chuckle. "Actually, Hermas, he's right. You do talk too much."

Hermas straightened slightly, indignant. "Since when was mutant scum like that right about anything?"

"It happens," said Ketta quietly.

As she spoke, there was a flat, meaty impact. Harrow saw the Omega shoved forward by half a metre, his boots sending up clouds of ash as he skidded. He coughed, wetly.

The point of a staking pin, glowing with heat, was sticking out of his breastbone.

The warrior's head dropped forward, as if to study this wonder more closely, but then it just carried on dropping. Hermas toppled forwards and hit the ground like a felled tree. Ash came up in a cloud, settling down on him as he twitched once, then stilled.

Ketta puffed out a breath, visibly relaxing. "You took your time, Godolkin. I can only keep an adversary talking for so long, you know. Even a wordy braggart like this one."

"I was transfixed by your wit." The Iconoclast was striding out from the treeline, holy weapon centred on Ketta's midriff. "Harrow, are you injured?"

"Just my pride."

"Had you any?"

He got up, and stumbled over to where his carbine lay. "Less now, I think. Is this the place?"

"It would seem," the Iconoclast replied, "that we have reached our objective."

Harrow straightened up, clutching the carbine, feeling his heart dip in his chest. He hadn't been entirely sure what he was expecting to find at the source of the power spikes, but it had never been anything so hopeless as this scorched wasteland.

He stared around him, eyes straining in the darkness. Try as he might, he could see nothing that justified the twelve days trek through thick forest, not to mention being hunted, beaten, shot at and caught on hooks. Just a wide tract of burned, ash-covered ground, broken only by a few pathetic splinters of what must have once been trees; tall shards of blackened bark reaching for the sky.

"I don't believe it," he breathed.

Ketta snorted. "Keep watching, mutant, and you'll see some sights." She made to move away, but a subtle shift in Godolkin's stance halted her. She doubted her ability to dodge a staking pin from so short a range.

"Be still, agent," the Iconoclast told her quietly. "And explain."

"We'd all be safer if I explained past the treeline."

Godolkin shook his head. "Somehow I find the idea of escorting you back into the forest less than appealing. You can explain here."

"By the saints!" She threw her head back in exasperation. "Are all males congenitally stupid, or just those in this galaxy? Look around you, heretic!"

If that was an attempt to make Godolkin lose his aim, it failed. Harrow, however, gave the clearing more of his attention. His eyes were becoming more accustomed to the darkness, and now he could see that what he had taken to be fragments of tree were actually artificial. Each was a tall spire, many metres high; he could see three from where he stood, and the hint of a fourth. When he took that into account, their arrangement became clear. Each stood at the corner of a vast square, surrounding him completely.

"Those towers," he said, mostly to himself.

Ketta nodded angrily. "The mutant has better eyes than you, heretic. Those spires have been charging up for the past half hour, reeking of ozone, and that means only one thing. In the next few minutes, this place will become an inferno all over again!"

"You've seen this before?"

"Just once, but it was enough. Something happens between the towers – it caught one of the Omegas in its wash and flipped him inside out before it incinerated him."

It didn't sound good. "Maybe we should go," said Harrow.

"Very well." Godolkin stepped aside to let Ketta past him, motioning her with the holy weapon. As he did the forward edge of it came close to the barrel of Harrow's carbine, and there was a loud snap of voltage between the two. Harrow saw a fat blue spark connect the two weapons an instant before he felt it stinging his arm. "Ow! Sneck! What was that?"

"Static charge," gasped Ketta. "Come on, for God's sake! It's almost on us!"

There was a rising hum, a shivering. Harrow could feel the hairs on his forearms shift, drawn up by the electricity in the air. When he took a step towards the trees, his boots crackled as they met the ground.

"Run, you bloody idiot!" Ketta yelled, and darted past him. Harrow needed no further encouragement, and began his own flight towards the treeline. He was halfway there when he heard Godolkin snarl behind him, followed by an odd scuffling sound. The sound of a blow, metal on flesh.

Harrow glanced over his shoulder. A second later he had stopped dead, skidding to a halt and dropping to one knee with the carbine jammed back into his shoulder, waiting for the chance to fire.

Hermas was still alive. The Omega was on his feet, and had Godolkin around the throat.

The warrior still had the staking pin through his chest, from his back to his sternum, but it didn't seem to be slowing him down. His hands were locked around Godolkin's neck, despite the pounding he was receiving.

Harrow saw Godolkin drop the holy weapon, free his right arm, and send Hermas sprawling with a punch to the

head. The Omega warrior was just leaping back into the
fray when the towers came alive.

One of the structures was close to where Harrow knelt,
close enough for him see a network of fine lines spring to
life. The lines were made of light; a complex, regular network of sapphire brilliance that covered the tower from
base to point for an instant before they widened, spilling
blue light and shadow across the clearing.

The towers were springing apart, the multiple sections
that formed their outer casing moving smoothly outwards
on hidden pistons, allowing the light that filled them to
escape. Past that painful glare, Harrow caught a glimpse of
the machinery inside the spires, but the devices were too
bright to behold for long. He had to shield his eyes from
them.

The light had appeared rapidly. Hermas and Godolkin
were caught by it like moths in a torch-beam – it was over
them before they had a chance to move. They were still
transfixed when the towers played their final trick.

The tower closest to Harrow snapped out a thread of searing blue light, bright as a laser, that connected its peak to
that of the tower opposite. A moment later the other towers
did the same, and the point at which the two beams crossed
began to spit sparks. Harrow saw, for a split second, those
sparks rain down on Matteus Godolkin's upturned face.

In the next instant the beams intersected at a point of
light at the clearing's centre, a point that seemed to flower
into an autonomous shape. It was a cube, growing as Harrow stared at it, its edges perfectly regular, its faces a
maddening twist of refraction. The cube twisted as it grew,
all six of its faces giving birth to another cube, each reflect-
ing and distorting the image of the first.

Those cubes vomited forth others, in their turn, and those
children did the same. The process accelerated violently,
doubling in speed with each incarnation, until the shape
between the towers was an eruption, a foam of glassy light
and billowing edges.

Before Harrow could shout, it had swallowed the men beneath it. He saw a fleeting image, so quick and so small it could only have been his imagination, of Godolkin's face reflected a million times across the faces of those seething cubes, before it was replaced by fire.

First an image of fire, and then the real thing. Harrow heard running feet behind him, felt something strike him with impossible strength and flatten him into the dirt, just as the cubes and the towers vanished in a firestorm that blotted out the world.

14. CONVERSATIONS UNDERGROUND

There came a point during the journey to Ashkelon when Matteus Godolkin beheld wonders.

It was a very brief point indeed. Much of the trip – for he now knew that he had been transported – consisted of being thrown wildly about in myriad directions all at once. It hadn't felt like movement, exactly, but something altogether more distressing. As though he was shifting through different states of being.

The journey had begun with the Omega's hands around his throat, but as soon as the towers had begun their display he had lost sight of the warrior completely. One moment Hermas was next to him, gazing up in horrified rapture at the rain of sparks, and the next he was gone. Godolkin was in darkness, and falling, as though he had tumbled down a mineshaft.

That had led in turn to the directionless buffeting, the mad shaking from one state of existence to the next, all in complete blackness. Wherever Godolkin spent those first wild moments, it was a place where light did not exist. His eyes were open, but so was his mouth, and he saw about as much through each.

But then came the wonders.

They burst on him quite suddenly, only for a split second. What he saw had nothing to do with vision; his eyes were still dead to him. The wonders came upon him like a flood, over and through him. They made their impressions on his mind because, for that infinitesimal fraction of time, he was a part of them.

Worlds, he saw, countless worlds. Worlds that he knew, countless others he had never heard of. And each place he saw was an infinity, superimposed upon themselves and one another in an insane panoply of possibilities.

Had it lasted any longer than they did, Godolkin's mind would have come apart at the seams, of that he was certain. As it was, the darkness came back to claim him as soon as it had left, followed swiftly by a feeling of deceleration. And with it came another sensation, equally puzzling: that of reduction. Godolkin felt that he was being simplified, translated, reduced, until all that he was had become nothing more than a symbol of itself.

At the moment at which his essence was reduced to its most basic level, the light returned, leaving him to drop several metres through the air onto his head.

He awoke some time later with a pounding headache and images of a billion worlds dancing behind his eyes.

The worlds faded, mercifully, as did the pain. Soon he was able to lift his head enough to see where he was.

The sight did nothing for his mood.

He was in a dungeon. There was no prettifying the description: he was in a windowless space, cylindrical, defiantly subterranean. The walls were lined with glossy white tiles, the floor and the ceiling too, although it strained his neck to look high enough to see it. The dungeon was scrubbed clean, reeking of disinfectant, but Godolkin knew this had less to do with hygiene than with sensory deprivation. A bloodstain or two would give the eye a point of focus in all this gleaming white.

There were a couple of imperfections: the door, a heavy slab of dark metal; a drain in the centre of the floor, and, chained on the opposite side of the dungeon was the Omega warrior Hermas.

Godolkin let his head drop forward again. He, like Hermas, was chained to the wall.

"You're awake, then," the Omega said, without much malice. "You've a thick skull, heretic. When you came down head-first I thought that was the end of you."

Godolkin said nothing. A part of him wished the fall had cracked his skull, had laid his brains on the floor. His desire for self-preservation was, at least in part, diminished.

Hermas, however, wasn't about to content himself with silence. "Won't you speak, heretic?"

"I'd rather not."

"And here I was thinking we'd finally get to know each other."

Godolkin looked up at him. The man was dangling from his chains, unable to properly stand upright in their clasp but looking far more comfortable than he had any right to – given the staking pin sticking out of his chest. "I believe, commander, that I know everything about you that I need to."

Hermas sneered. "You know less than you think, heretic. About many things."

"Heretic?" Godolkin raised an eyebrow. "And what should I call you? Hermas? You're no Iconoclast. You are not even human. There are mutants languishing in the most loathsome dungeons of the Inquisitorium that have more humanity in them than you."

"Like that weasel Harrow? I'm sure you and he had a pleasant little camping trip. What did you bring him for? Entertainment? Some boyish warmth in the night?"

Godolkin let his head drop again. The chains made it hard to keep his gaze level for long, and his neck muscles ached powerfully from the fall. "A pack animal," he replied. "But your comments please me, Hermas. Now I know that Saulus was truly insane, to have chosen the likes of you as the basis for his warrior race."

There was a long silence. Then Hermas said, very calmly, "If I get the chance, heretic, I'll have your tongue for that."

A sore point, then. Godolkin stored it away. "Forgive me, Hermas. I thought that you were built to bring down the

Blasphemy, nothing more. I didn't realise that your condi-
tioning was liable to break down so quickly."

"If you think you can enrage me with such petty sarcasm,
Godolkin, you're a duller blade than I thought." Hermas
had regained his conversational tone. "And for your information, we were never conditioned. Our hatred of the
bitch-saint is as it always was. But we're fewer than we
were destined to be."

"And getting fewer all the time."

"Ketta picks off one of us here, another there. Her private
crusade, in between grubbing for work like a backstreet
assassin." The Omega's voice lowered. "I'll tell you this,
Godolkin. Just as we broke the secret of the shadow web,
so we'll soon crack the code of our own creation. Saulus left
it there for us, locked inside. All we have to do is turn the
key just so, and we'll swarm over Ketta, and your precious
saint, like flies on shit."

Apt, thought Godolkin. "So are you the leader of your
people?"

"I was the first. If that makes me leader, then so be it."

"It probably just makes you older."

"And Ketta thinks me a wordy braggart." Hermas
laughed, the sound deep and resonant within the tiled cell.
"I knew it, Godolkin. You are me, in all but name."

Godolkin's head snapped up. "And now the delusions."

"You can deny it all you like, Godolkin, but the truth
remains: you and I are mirror images. Both elitists. Both
Iconoclasts once, but no longer. Both outcast by the actions
of the bitch-saint Durham Red."

That stung. Godolkin forced his tone level. "Really," he
replied. "I assumed you'd reserve more bile for Major Ketta.
Wasn't it she who brought Saulus to justice?"

"Justice?" The Omega turned his head and spat. The spit-
tle hissed as it struck the floor. "That word has no meaning
to me, heretic! Lord-Tactician Saulus was a genius, a father
to me and my kin! When Ketta brought him low, she took
humanity with her."

"Hermas and his Omega warriors, the last best hope of humankind. Your arrogance is even more astounding than your stupidity."

"And who else will stand against the mutant? You and your line-troops? So crazed with superstition you'll follow your worst enemy on hands and knees after one nip. I've felt the bite of your Scarlet Saint, Godolkin." He turned his head, displaying a pair of ragged scars running from below his ear to just above his shoulder. "Just like you. But unlike you, I'm not so mindless a drone that I believe she has power over me. On the contrary, I'm sure I felt better than she did after the encounter."

"That was your blood on the bridge."

"Some of it was mine."

"Hmph," snorted Godolkin. "Your blood and her vomit. It seems she found you almost as hard to stomach as I do."

The Omega's eyes narrowed. "Your wit will be the death of you, Godolkin. If I have anything to do with it."

"You won't."

It was a third voice, coming from the doorway. The armoured slab had swung aside on silent hinges. Light spilled through, past the figure of a man.

At first glance, his appearance was nothing that would raise comment. Of middling height, quite slender; his hair cut short, his coat long. But Godolkin, who was trained to notice such things, looked past the man's pleasant expression and unimpressive physique. The coat had a waterproof sheen to it, as though it might need frequent cleaning. There were marks on his face from wearing protective goggles, and the way his fingers crooked unconsciously made them seem to be clasping a knife.

A torturer, then. Godolkin, chained in a dungeon, should have expected nothing less.

"I'm afraid," the man said quietly, "that we're on rather a tight schedule today. Normally I'd leave you here for a week, maybe two, just so you could get to know each other.

But my hand is forced. I'll need to work a little more swiftly than I'm used to."

He looked slowly from one prisoner to the other. "You'll forgive me, then, if my methods are more direct than usual. Time is of the essence."

"Good," growled Hermas. "I've spent enough moments in this fool's company."

The torturer smiled at him. "So eager," he whispered. "What a choice! So who will I take first?"

It was another blurred journey. Godolkin was drugged and hooded for his trip to the torturer's lair. His system started to work on the drug immediately it was injected, but the chemical, coupled with the darkness of the hood, still set his head spinning. By the time it stopped, he was in a different place.

He was lying down on some kind of trolley, cold steel at his back, thick canvas straps securing his chest, wrists and ankles. Even inside the hood, he could perceive different smells: more disinfectant, but also blood, metal, thin oil. Human excrement.

He lay still, listening. The torturer's footsteps went past him, unhurried, but there were at least two others close by. Assistants, he decided. Godolkin wondered if the set-up could get any more theatrical or clichéd.

Another needle slipped into his arm and he groaned.

There was a creaking sound. The torturer had sat down beside him. "How do you feel?" the man asked.

Godolkin held his tongue. This new drug was unleashing a flood of emotions in him – fear, mainly, but tinged with undertones of loneliness, bass notes of lust. His heart hammered behind his ribs, then slowed. Nausea washed over him, and sweat prickled his skin.

The drugs were powerful, their effect complex. In anyone but an elite Iconoclast shocktrooper, they would have been hideously effective. But Godolkin's modified system metabolised them within moments, flushing the residue through his pores. No doubt the torturer and his cronies would take the increased sweating as a sign of their work's success.

The smell of his own perspiration stung Godolkin's nostrils, but he ignored it, filtering it out. He was rapidly building up a mental picture of the room around him; how the steel trolley lay in relation to the walls, where its occupants stood or sat. It was a mental technique he had long since learned to perfect. During his elite training, when he had been raised from line-trooper to Iconoclast First-Class, he had often been required to enter combat while blindfolded. Those bloody, gladiatorial exercises had served him well – even lying on his back with a cloth hood on his head, he could tell how far away the walls were by the echoes of the torturer's voice, where the men in the room stood or sat by their breathing, their smell, their heartbeats.

The torturer was still sitting beside him, leaning close, certain of his own safety, his superiority over the captive. One of the assistants was standing on his far side, poised to deliver more drugs. The third man stood at Godolkin's head. And therein lay a problem.

He needed the third man to move, if he was to prevail against the interrogation.

"I'll ask you again, alien. How do you feel?"

"Afraid," he lied.

Faint sounds reached Godolkin through the hood. The man was sitting back slightly. Godolkin factored it into his soundscape of the room.

All three of his interrogators were men. Two had remained silent throughout, but he could gauge their gender by hormonal odour. He was glad that the assistants were male. Godolkin had no compunction against killing women, but, on the whole, men tended to struggle less.

"What are you afraid of?"

"Falling," said Godolkin.

A beat of silence. It was not the answer the torturer had been expecting. Godolkin knew more about the mechanics

of interrogation than most men, and if there was one thing
certain about the art it was that there were no certainties.
The drugs, the needles, the tongs and the blades all affected
different people in different ways. No two subjects were
ever alike.

"Why do you fear falling?"

"My leg strap is loose," Godolkin breathed. "If it comes
away, I'll fall again."

Godolkin was no actor, but his allusion to his recent journey rang true. The man at his head moved at some wordless
signal from the torturer, down to the other end of the trolley.

When he was halfway there, Godolkin sat up.

The strap across his chest sheared, the heavy canvas
snapping apart at the point where it was stitched to the trolley's frame. The effort made his stomach muscles scream,
but his leverage was well-judged. Godolkin had been sur-
reptitiously testing the strength of his restraints since they
had been locked over him, tensing against them to feel how
flexible they were, how brittle.

The lesson he had applied back in Zimri's tower was just
as relevant here. Every system had a weak spot.

The straps around his arms gave him no more trouble
than that around his torso. He tore them both free at once.
A needle brushed his left bicep but he simply reached past
it and grabbed the arm that held it, shattering the thin wrist
bones with one squeeze. One man fell away, allowing
Godolkin to grab at the second assistant, dragging him back
down onto the trolley and slamming his elbow down to
crack the man's skull.

Before the body hit the floor, Godolkin had whipped
around to his other side and snatched at the torturer. He
took hold of the man's throat with one hand and pulled him
close, ripping the hood free as he did so.

The bland face was white with terror.

"Do you have a name, knifeman?" Godolkin asked him.

"Silic…"

"Well, Silic, I must inform you that this interrogation is at an end. But it would be such a pity to waste all this fine equipment, don't you think?"

Godolkin stayed with Silic for twenty minutes, until the torturer's heart stilled from shock.

He'd discovered many things during those scream-filled moments, but one of the most telling facts emerged well before Godolkin began taking Silic apart. It was obvious that the torturer and his masters had never had an Iconoclast First-Class in their midst before. There were methods for restraining someone of his enhanced physical capacities, as Godolkin well knew. But canvas straps on a steel trolley didn't even come close.

He stepped out into the corridor, his hands still damp from washing. He was bare-chested, his battle harness taken from him while he lay unconscious from the fall, but that didn't bother him. He needed no armour to prevail against these effete fools.

As he was locking the door, the lights above him flickered, dimmed, then returned to normal brightness. Godolkin nodded to himself. Silic had told him all about the spate of systems failures that had the Keep in a panic. No wonder the interrogation had been so rushed, so botched. Something was happening to the Keep that no one yet understood, and it had all started when the mutant Durham Red was brought inside.

Godolkin wasn't surprised by that. The Blasphemy drew chaos in her wake like a wedding train.

The lights fluttered again and something in the walls groaned. Godolkin started away. The sooner he discovered where Red was, the more chance he had of leaving the Keep before it collapsed around his ears.

15. RETURN TO NEVERLAND

"What," snarled Vaide Sorrelier, aiming a needle-gun directly at Red's face, "have you done?"

Red kept very still, her boots firmly planted on the shale. Sorrelier was furious, totally enraged. She had never seen him even close to being this angry. All his insolent calm, his languid demeanour, was gone. In the few hours she'd been away, he had been through some serious changes.

His clothes were different, but that was only to be expected. The dark robes he had worn to the Masque – and in which he had gone flying over the balcony, back in the hangar – were replaced by a simpler outfit of blue and gold. He wore a long, brocaded coat, and his dark hair was draped freely over his shoulders.

But he looked untidy. That, even more than his anger, surprised Red.

There was a livid bruise on one side of his face, most likely from where she had hit him, and he hadn't even tried to powder it over. His collar was askew, and there were marks on his sleeves, scuffs on his boots.

Something had gone very wrong for Vaide Sorrelier. Red could see that as clearly as she could see the tensing of his trigger finger, which further encouraged her stillness. She had no doubts about his intentions, nor his aim. Mutant reflexes or not, if she tried anything funny or even said the wrong thing, she'd end her days with a faceful of needles.

And if he had ever truly believed that the surface of Mag-adan was infected, he was past caring.

She held her arms out from her sides, hands open, and wore what she hoped was a calming expression on her face. "I just tried to escape, that's all."

"That's all?" He shook his head. "Sorry, my dear, but that doesn't even begin to cover it."

Red had very little idea of what he meant, but to say so might have tipped him over the edge. She glanced past him, up at the ship he had arrived in, wondering if there was any way she could reach it if she managed to distract Sorrelier and get the drop on him. But as she did so she saw the two sylphs up in the hatchway, aiming needle-rifles with the same lethal precision as their master.

Not good.

The flier had come down close to where Red was standing, angling its landing legs to compensate for the slope of the hills. It was a polished silver torpedo fifty metres long, with a faceted glass nose and slender, curved wings that slid smoothly back into the hull as it landed. As a design it was elegant, classic, more like piece of sculpture than a working aircraft. Red wondered what it was like inside, what luxuries Sorrelier had fitted for his in-flight pleasure.

If she was careful, she might even live to find out. "It's true, Sorrelier. Whatever you doped me up with didn't last. I'm sorry I had to flatten a couple of your sylphs, but they were in my way."

"And you expect me to believe that the skiff you stole was a random choice?"

"Er, yeah."

He sighed, and lowered the gun slightly. "You see," he said, moving towards her. "That's where your story starts to fall apart. There was no way you should have been able to take that boat out of its launch tube. I had my captain call the harbour master as soon as we saw you trying to steal it, but somehow the tube refused to lock down."

That was news to Red. She had thought she'd succeeded in her escape because of her own skills, and maybe a little luck. Equipment failure hadn't entered into it. "Really?"

"Oh yes. Furthermore, all airboat power plants are set to detonate once they go out of traffic-control range. The harbour master tried to take over your instruments, but again the system refused to let him. And then, oh miracle of miracles, your power-core failed to detonate."

Red swallowed. "Bloody hell. Look, if I'd known that I wouldn't have tried to steal the damn thing, would I?"

"Unless you knew that the boat had been modified."

"How the sneck would I know that?"

"You knew because it was part of your arrangement with that little catamite Saleph Losen!"

Red stepped back, hands raised. "That shithead? No way! He's the bastard that had me locked up and drugged in the first place! Anyway, if I'd stolen some extra-safe aircar, it wouldn't have crashed, would it?"

Sorrelier's eyes narrowed. "Crashed?"

"In the swamp." She pointed vaguely over towards the Keep. "Back that way. I had to go wading through a ton of shit to get out, and since then I've been trudging through this bloody wilderness! You think I've got a fetish for blisters?"

"I hardly know what to think."

Red, however, was starting to believe she knew. From what Sorrelier was telling her, someone had let her escape. Let her out of the Keep with a rigged airboat and a broken launch tube, but only to get so far. And while she was out of the picture, Sorrelier had been put through the mill.

She saw nothing wrong with that last part – in fact, as soon as the opportunity arose, she would be having a very final few words with Vaide Sorrelier. But as much as she disliked him, she disliked the idea of being used to bring him down even less.

"We've been played," she told him. "Both of us. Played like a couple of snecking tambourines."

Despite himself, Sorrelier nodded. "Losen."

"Higher up than that."

. . .

Sorrelier had a tale to tell, but it wasn't the kind of story he trusted to the open air. Once he had convinced himself that Durham Red wasn't the initiator of his woes, he was quick enough to invite her aboard.

There was no great risk in what he did. Even if Red had wanted to attack him so early, she'd have the two sylphs to deal with, and their needle-guns were still on her. Instead she did as he bade her, and stepped past into a long central corridor.

It led onto the flier's bridge. Red was shown to a seat, facing the glassy dome of the vessel's prow. It gave a good, if slightly vertiginous view of what lay outside: the glass replaced the entire forward part of the nose, and the bridge was built on frames within it. Red sat, looking down at the grey rocks beneath her dangling feet.

Sorrelier gave a command to the captain, and the rocks dropped away.

Red just about managed not to yelp. The take-off was sudden. She saw the ground shrink beneath her, then the craft began to power forwards.

For a moment Red was convinced that Sorrelier was going to try and fly over the hilltops, and she almost shouted a warning. When she had tried to go past the brow of the hill she had simply turned back on herself, but the flier was a lot bigger than she was. Anything could happen. The vessel might break up, turn itself inside out, or worse.

Luckily, the craft tipped over into a long, powered curve away from the hills, and back towards the Keep. Red let go of the seat's arms. She hadn't been aware of just how tightly she had been gripping them, until she felt the dips in the metal frame caused by her clenched fingers.

"Snecking hell," she whispered.

Once the flier was on a level flight, Sorrelier rose from his seat. "Rimail," he said, addressing the ship's captain. "Back to the Keep, but not too quickly. Take a roundabout route, hmm?"

The man nodded. "As you wish, sire."

"And now, our guest and I have things to discuss. In private."

Sorrelier's idea of "private" was himself, Red, and three sylphs in silent attendance. Two of them were the gun-carriers Red had seen before, and the third was Lise, the woman Red had been scratched by outside the Masque. "Don't concern yourself with them," he told her as he sealed the door behind him. "There's no way to make a sylph speak. They've lost the art."

"Or had it taken from them." Red leaned back in her seat, stretched out her legs, and put her boot heels up on the table. "No more lies, Sorrelier. What do you do to them?"

"Personally? Nothing at all. I buy them from a dealer on one of the common strata. His product is good, but expensive." He glanced appreciatively over at Lise. "Although every now and then one gets a bargain."

Red gritted her teeth. "So what does he do, this dealer? Lobotomise them, or something?"

"Nothing so crude. But we aren't here to talk about the staff, are we? I thought we had more important matters to discuss."

Red folded her arms. Her eyes flicked from Sorrelier's face to the chamber where he had led her – a low-ceilinged place, ornately decorated and dominated by a vast desk of polished wood. A room for conducting business, far away from the Keep. Somewhere secure.

And she was locked in. So far, Sorrelier was being careful. He was a smart one, she had to credit him with that.

"Okay, let's discuss. What are you up to?"

His eyebrows rose. "Me? What makes you think–"

"Oh, for sneck's sake, will you just cut out the bullshit?"

His gaze threw daggers at her for a long moment, then his shoulders slumped. "Very well. You realise I'll be breaking the habit of a lifetime."

"My heart bleeds. Now tell."

He told. Put simply, Sorrelier was plotting against the Magister. It was a plan he had been working on for years.

"I have a small army, raised and trained in secret. Quite enough to mount a serious challenge."

"You're crazy."

"Far from it. This isn't some whim, Durham Red. I've got a thousand elite soldiers dispersed among my domains, weapons caches, spies in every other citadel. I've bribed, blackmailed, bought and sold. I've stolen and killed, and all for this. Never, in all the Keep's history, has anyone been so close to the top."

Red closed her eyes, thinking hard. "Let me guess: someone sold you out."

"Not exactly. To be quite honest, I let my greed get the better of me. I went after you."

"Me?"

"You're a prize, Durham Red. The Magister wants you, wants you badly enough to send Losen out to get you and risk Magadan being exposed to the very universe he fears so much. I don't know why, but I knew that your value to him would be of use to me."

Red opened her eyes and grinned at him. "Flattery doesn't get to me, you know. Much."

"Don't be flattered. As far as I can see, you were a juicy piece of bait, nothing more." He sighed. "They were waiting for me to make a play. And curse my impetuousness, I did. But as soon as you had gone from the Keep, and I tried to return to my domains, I found them under Magisterial Edict."

"They knew what you were up to."

"They do now."

Red shook her head. "Close, but no cigar. Not yet. There must have been other worms the Magister could dangle at you, Sorrelier. Things you wanted more than me."

"Possibly."

"So why go to all the trouble? If the Magister is so scared of the outside universe – and sneck, he's got every right to be – why risk dragging me all the way back here?

No, there's something else. He wants me for his own purposes, not just to draw you out."

"In which case, we both have business with the man." Sorrelier put a finger to his lips, pondering. "I propose a truce. And a deal." He got up, and walked around the table to join her. "If I were to get you to the Magister, what then?"

"Could you do that?"

"If I had your help."

Red looked away, gnawing a fingernail. She would rather have entered into a pact with a shoal of piranha fish, but she couldn't deny that Sorrelier's plan had a twisted kind of merit. The Magister, after all, held the answers she was looking for.

He was also head of a society that used its own lobotomised citizens as slaves and sexual playthings. Sorrelier wanted to take the guy's place, swapping one tyrant for another. Well, when the time came, Red would have something to say about that, too.

"Okay," she said. "Let's do it."

They went back to the bridge, and on Sorrelier's instruction Captain Rimail poured on the power. Red felt the acceleration shove her back into the seat as the flier forged towards the Keep.

As the tower began to grow in front of her, Red turned to Sorrelier. "I just had a thought."

"My mind reels with sarcastic replies," he sighed. "What was it?"

"You said that anything flying out of the Keep blew up if it didn't have the Magister's say-so. How did you get out here?"

"I had the bomb taken out years ago, along with the control locks. You don't plot against someone without learning their little tricks."

"All right, smartarse. If he knows what you're up to, how are we going to get back in?"

He leaned close. "I have agents in one of the flight harbours."

"Really? You've been gone a while. Are you sure you've got anything?"

He sat back, his arms folded. "We'll see."

The craft began to tilt, circling around the Keep. As it did so, something came into view that Red was sure should not have been there. "Is that smoke?"

Rimail started checking his instruments. "Sire, I'm picking up radio traffic from the western harbour. There's been a crash."

"No matter," Sorrelier replied. "Our berth is in the eastern."

"Not any more. Rimail?"

The captain jerked around, startled to be addressed in that manner. "My lady?"

"Head right for that smoke. Get into one of the launch tubes while the place is still going apeshit." She turned back to Sorrelier. "Lesson number one, twinkletoes. When you're busting into a place like this, head straight for the chaos."

"And if there isn't any?"

"Make some."

Close up, the entrance to the flight harbour was a honeycomb of launch tubes, large and small. Several had smoke gouting from them, and Red could see the brilliant yellow sparks of internal fires. As she watched, something inside the harbour detonated with a white flash, followed by a ball of greasy flame that vomited out of one tube. Debris spat past the schooner.

The bridge rocked. "That one," Red told Rimail, her hand on his shoulder. "Six along, two down."

"It's close to the blaze, lady."

"That's the point." She got up from her seat and stood up. "Sorrelier, grab whoever you're taking and get ready. We'll have to jump and run."

"Understood. Rimail?"

"Sire."

"Once we're in, take off again as soon as you can. Find a place to set down and await a signal."

"And make sure you've got sunscreen," Red told him, as she headed for the rear hatch. "The weather's just to die for."

The harbour, as Rimail's radio traffic had intimated, was a ruin. It looked like a schooner-sized vessel had come in at full speed, tearing up a hundred metres of launch tube before shearing through the docking clamps at the inner end and exploding. The debris had ripped through the complex of platforms and walkways, detonating fuel supplies, setting vessels aflame, killing dozens.

Damage control teams had been called, but were quickly overwhelmed. As Red barrelled through the carnage the order was already being given to fall back.

"There have been system failures all over the Keep," Sorrelier gasped, trying to keep up. He'd brought Lise with him, but if the sylph was tiring she made no sign. "They started not long before I left. Small things, mostly, but it has some of the strata panicking."

"Your people? Maybe shaking things up in your absence?"

"Not my style."

"Whatever. It's good for us, anyway. Should take some of the heat off," Red replied. She slowed, unsure of how best to leave the harbour. "Now, which way?"

"The elevator," Sorrelier told her, pointing. As he spoke, something behind him blew up with a shattering roar, shaking the decks and sending shrapnel careening over their heads. "Or the stairs."

The journey took them downwards, strata after strata.

Once they were away from the flight harbour they felt it safe enough to travel by elevator, and for that Red was grateful. She'd been lying about having blisters, but she had walked a very long way. To get down to the Magister's strata completely on foot would have been like doing the whole trip again, from the swamp to the hills, but this time vertically.

Finally, after an hour or so of continual travel, Sorrelier called a halt.

The lower strata became progressively less like self-contained, artificial worlds. They were starting to reach the inner workings of the Grand Keep; the factory levels, the power and support systems. The surroundings were still lush, opulent, but grass had given way to carpet and polished marble, fake sky to gantried ceiling.

The level Sorrelier had brought them to seemed to consist mainly of fountains, great eruptions of water dozens of metres high. They came up from a series of circular pools down on the stratum floor, leaping past and through each other in a ceaseless, gushing dance of brilliant clear water. The stratum was ringed with circular walkways, so long that they faded into threads as they curled away, then vanished behind clouds of vapourised water. The noise was deafening.

Red and Sorrelier stood panting on the upper walkway, leaning against the rail. "What the sneck's this?" Red puffed.

Sorrelier shook his head. "Something to do with purification, I believe. Although whether of water or air I have no idea."

"There must be a million tonnes of the stuff!" Red leaned over the rail, peering down over the sheer drop to the kicking, hissing pools far beneath. "And the Magister's got his home under that?"

"Some distance below this stratum, yes." Sorrelier put his back to the rail. He was sweating, his hair plastered to his scalp with a mix of perspiration and spray from the fountains. "Durham Red, listen to me. This is where things start getting difficult."

"Start?"

"So far this has just been a long walk. The Magister takes his privacy very seriously, believe me. I've only been below this level once, and then only to the outer reaches of his court. The way will be guarded, heavily."

"Great. And I don't even have a gun."

"You don't honestly think I'd be anywhere near you if you did?"

Red gave him a look, then straightened up. "Come on then. Let's see how many heads we can crack."

"It's this way."

She followed him around the walkway to an exit hallway, and in turn to a gleaming, carpeted lobby bigger than Mazatl's entire longhouse. Three sets of sliding double doors occupied one wall. More elevators.

As he saw them, Sorrelier slowed. "That's odd."

"What?"

"No guards."

"How many would there normally be?"

He made a face. "I'm not sure. A lot."

"Wonderful. They must have been called away. Let's get in and go down a few strata before anyone notices they've left the doors open."

She ran forward, hearing Sorrelier and Lise follow. As she reached the nearest set of doors they slid aside and she stepped in. "Come on."

"This isn't right."

"Don't get cold feet on me now, buster!" She reached over the threshold and dragged him in, ducking a blow from Lise as she did so. "Hey!"

"Lise!" Sorrelier regained his balance, and went to stand warily next to Red. "It's all right, Lise. She meant no harm."

"Yet," Red grinned, showing him her fangs. Hers were still a lot longer and sharper than his. By the look that crossed his face, he knew it.

Sorrelier pressed a control, the lowest one on the board. The elevator doors slid closed, and Red felt the floor drop below her. On the control panel was a series of indicators, glossy jewels set into the brass. The top one lit, then went out as the next one down came on. As it did so, there was a faint chime.

Red smiled wryly to herself. Twelve hundred years from home, and some things stayed exactly the same. "Sorrelier?"

"What now?"

"Just so I know what to call His Majesty once we get in there, what's his name?"

The man shrugged. "I have no idea. We're only told the name of a Magister once he dies. Only the Board of Arch-Domini know the identity of the living Magister."

"Because they elect him."

"I'm impressed."

"Don't be. It's pretty snecking obvious when you think about it."

The chimes continued, faintly, as the elevator continued to drop. "Almost there," said Sorrelier, after a few seconds. "Be ready."

"I'm always ready."

"Are you? I had no idea." He arched an eyebrow. "You must be a very popular girl."

Red was weighing up whether she should break Sorrelier's spine and spare herself any more of his wit when the lowest indicator lit up, and chimed. "Here we go," she growled, tensing.

There was another chime, then, seconds later, another. "Sorrelier, we're still going down."

"That can't be."

Red watched him turn to the panel and begin pressing randomly at the controls. Despite his denial, the lift was not only still descending, but doing so at an increasing rate. She could feel the floor vibrating under her, hear the faint whine of its systems rising in pitch, in volume.

Something was definitely, horribly wrong. "Sneck. I knew we should have taken the stairs."

Without warning, the lift slammed to a halt. The floor bounced hard enough to knock Sorrelier off his feet. Lise caught him, blurringly fast, just as the doors snapped open.

Red dived out. If the elevator had suffered one of the

Keep's mysterious systems failures, she had no intention of setting foot inside the thing again. Next time she'd walk, blisters or no blisters.

A moment later, Sorrelier followed, with Lise hanging onto his arm. The man looked thoroughly shaken. "Mutant," he muttered.

"What? Don't blame me for that. You're the one who pressed the damn button."

He waved her to silence. "Mutant, we are here! The inner court!"

Red glanced about. The elevator doors had opened onto a space so big that, for an instant, she hadn't even registered that they were indoors.

It soared away from her in every direction, the floors polished so close to a mirror finish that it was like standing in mid-air. The distant walls reared up in sheets of pastel amber, meeting columns of blinding white at every intersection. Red couldn't even gauge the exact shape of the place, let alone its size. There were chambers leading off chambers, stairways and balconies and halls, linking and interlinking in awesome, airy profusion.

It was a city made from cathedrals, each one knocked through into the next. "Sneck me," Red whispered.

Sorrelier seemed just as enrapt by the sight as she was. He stood with his neck craned backward, his eyes wide. "Incredible. I've never imagined anything like this." His voice, hushed as it was, echoed around the pale walls.

"Never mind that, Sorrelier. How did we end up here?"

"The elevator?"

"Yeah, the snecking elevator. Except it wasn't even supposed to come down this far, was it? What do you think that was, one of your crazy systems breakdowns? No chance." She stalked away from him for a few paces, out across that gleaming floor. "No guards upstairs, no one down here, and the elevator just happens to go mad and drop us on the exact floor that we want?"

"What are you saying?"

"That the Magister wants us down here. In fact, he's wanted us down here from the start."

He paced over to join her, Lise just behind him. "For what reason?" he whispered.

"Search me. But he's the one whose been screwing us both around since Christ-knows-when, so it's no surprise he's still at it now." She began striding off, aiming herself directly away from the elevator door. "Come on. The Magister's made it really easy for us to get down here so far. He's not about to start making it difficult now."

"As flawed logic goes, that's so skewed as to be practically circular."

Red nodded ahead at the door she had spotted. "Oh yeah?"

It wasn't quite that easy. The door lead to an empty hallway, rather than to the Magister himself, which led in turn to a similar chamber. In all, five more chamber awaited them – a full twenty minutes of brisk walking – before they reached what Red decided had to be the last door. It was easily the biggest and most ornate of them all, for one thing. For another, she wasn't sure how much further they would be able to walk in a straight line before hitting the opposite wall of the Keep.

"This is it."

"You're sure about that." Sorrelier drew something small and slender from his coat pocket. The needle gun.

"Sure enough." And she drew her foot back to kick the door aside.

They opened, silently, before she could connect, and the aborted kick took her a few stumbling paces beyond the doorway. Almost to the feet of the man who sat within.

He was seated on a vast golden throne, set atop a circular dais of jewelled steps. He wore a suit of black silk, a frilled white shirt, and a collar fixed with an ruby the size of an eyeball. Straight hair, jet black, framed a cold, imperious face, and a heavy moustache drooped over a sensual, slightly smiling mouth. He was looking right at Durham Red.

"My," said Simon D'Isis, the Gothking. "You really have taken your own sweet time."

16. RISE AND FALL

By sunrise the perimeter of the clearing had stopped burning. Judas Harrow was able to venture out past the treeline again, into the wide space between the towers.

The air in the clearing was foul, thick with acrid smoke. It was still rising from the ground, trails of it mixing with the morning mist, forming a nauseating miasma that caught Harrow's throat and made his lungs ache. Still, at least the ground had cooled down a little. The last time he had tried to walk here, his boots had caught fire.

That had been hours ago, not long after the inferno. He had still been groggy from Ketta's blow, not thinking straight, and had wandered out into the flame-shot darkness without even a weapon. After his soles had started to smoulder Ketta had darted out and dragged him back, and moments after that he had collapsed again. When he came round the sun was already casting shafts through the forest, and the pounding in his head had diminished enough for him to speak. He had asked Ketta why she had dragged him back into the relative safety of the trees.

Her answer was no surprise. "You'd have attracted attention, blundering around out there. I didn't want another encounter with the Omegas so soon."

And that was that. Ketta had busied herself with preparations: sharpening her knives, testing her poisons, making sure the guns were loaded and oiled. She didn't speak to Harrow, and he didn't speak to her, but he found watching her oddly fascinating. She tended the tools of her bloody craft the way some women might tend children, or their own beauty.

Perhaps it was better that she lavished her care on bullets and blades. Harrow found the thought of Ketta even being near a baby quite disturbing. She seemed such an unashamedly lethal thing, devoid of any trait or talent not directed towards destruction. It might have just been her demeanour in front of a mutant – her enemy, after all – but Harrow wondered if she had ever felt anything but blood-lust in her life.

Still, for whatever reason, she kept watch on him while he ventured into the clearing.

The ground was warm beneath him, but no longer smouldering. He trudged through the ash to where Godolkin and the Omega commander had been when the lightshow began, and crouched there, sifting through the carbonised muck with his fingertips. There was little to find – powdered ash, mainly, wood or soil so blasted with heat it had been reduced to smuts. Scraps of stone, patches of sand turned to brittle glass. Nothing much.

He was about to give up when he discovered what he was looking for, and pulled it free with a small smile of triumph. He got up, cradling his find in his palm, all the way back to where Ketta crouched.

"Here," he said, handing it to her. It was a scrap of blackened wood, finger-length and slender.

She didn't take it. "And what 's that supposed to be?"

"A twig."

Ketta blinked at him, her huge eyes dark and impenetrable in the smooth sand-brown of her face. "I'm sure I'll regret even asking this, but–"

"It's a twig. Just a twig, don't you see?"

"Yes, mutant, I see what you're getting at. How could you find a burned twig, but no bone?"

He nodded. "Bones are tough, even normal human ones. If Godolkin and that Omega had been burned–"

"Harrow," she interrupted. "He's dead. Face it."

"I think you're wrong."

She pointed over to their left, deeper into the woods. "The Omega I saw killed by the towers is over there. I buried him myself. If you like, I can dig him up for you."

"No, thank you."

"Do you want to know what a human skull looks like turned completely inside-out? Because I can show you."

"I said no!" He stalked away, back to the treeline, and stood looking across the clearing. "There's no sign of them because they weren't here when the fire came. I'm certain of it."

"Yes, but you're an idiot."

Harrow stood quiet for a time, then turned back to her, unclipping the dataslate from his belt. "We'll see."

Being so close to the towers when they activated had given Harrow all the information he needed. The dataslate had been picking up their power signatures the whole time, and sending it back to *Crimson Hunter* for processing by the ship's on-board computer. Where before Harrow had been relying on long-range scans, blocked by a hundred kilometres of solid forest, now he had accurate, close-up data direct from the source. And it told him a great deal that he hadn't known before.

"There," he told Ketta. "That's the point of maximum output. *Hunter*'s sense-engines lost all resolution at this point, on every long-range scan."

They had retreated back to Ketta's campsite. Harrow was showing her the dataslate output, the modified recordings he had recently downloaded from *Hunter*.

The day was already starting to warm up. Ketta had discarded her jacket, and now wore nothing above the waist but a black vest. She seemed quite unaware of any effect her figure might have on Harrow, but he was finding it difficult not to be distracted.

Instead, he concentrated on the dataslate, and the thought that there were more important things to do than consider the body of a woman who would kill him as soon as her use for him was finished. Whatever that use might be.

The slate was showing Ketta a field of static. She raised one eyebrow at him, very slightly. In response, he advanced the data a few seconds, until the static was gone. "There."

"Which tells me what, mutant?"

"Nothing at all. But if we go back to that point, and factor in the new information we have about the towers…" He advanced the scan again.

This time there was no obscuring static. Just an explosion of flame, billowing out from the centre of the towers in a cluster of superheated gasses before spurting upwards. In a few fractions of a second, a spine of fire had risen up from the clearing and whipped out of sight.

"The sense-engines never picked it up before. They were scrambled by the initial spike."

"A take-off," Ketta muttered. "Mutant, I take it all back. You're not a complete idiot after all."

The evidence, now they could see it with the raw voltage from the towers filtered away, was clear. Something had appeared in the centre of the clearing at the same time as Godolkin had disappeared and launched itself on a column of fire towards the stars.

Crimson Hunter had told them it had seen no orbital traffic since they had arrived, and that was true. That wasn't to say there hadn't been any, just that the ship hadn't detected them. Judging by this, at least four starships had left Ashkelon in the past twelve days and no one had been any wiser as to where they were going, of where they had come from.

"It must be some kind of transportation device," Harrow ventured. Ketta opened her hand for the dataslate, and he passed it to her. "The ships start off somewhere else, maybe on the other side of the planet, or even another world close by, then transport via the towers and lift off."

"Why? That's an insane waste of power." Ketta was tapping at the dataslate with her forefinger.

"I don't know. Maybe they come from a world with much higher gravity, and use the towers to accelerate. What are you doing?"

"Factoring this filtering equation into some scans of my own."

Harrow leaned close. The renegade was operating the slate quicker than he had ever seen it done, taking his equations and working them through a new series of returns, linking back to another source which could only have been her daggership. Within a few moments the screen changed, flipping over from a 3D representation of the clearing to a flat sheet of interlocking lines and panels. "There," she breathed.

"What?"

"The Omega's landing site. I've been looking for it ever since I got here, but their damned shadow web defeated me. Now I have those towers out of the way, I can see where they've hidden themselves."

Harrow frowned. "And what are you going to do with that knowledge?"

Her look was open, almost innocent. "What do you think?"

"Something involving flayer missiles."

"Oh, at the very least." Ketta got up, rising to her feet with an easy grace. "Mutant, I've had these bastards on my back for months, ever since I delivered their creator to the Ordo Hereticus. They hate me almost as much as they hate your Durham Red. If I've got a chance to bring them down, I'll take it, without hesitation."

Harrow got up as well. He could feel his usefulness to Ketta wearing rapidly thin. "You seem to have done all right so far."

"Really?" She turned her head slightly, raising her chin to show him the scar. "I heal fast, Harrow. Do you know how much it takes to put a mark on me? Hermas did that, with a vibrablade. He had my jawbone in half."

"Ouch."

"I escaped by blind luck, and that's how I've survived this far." She was looking past him, consumed by a private horror. "But luck runs out."

He had to ask. The question had burned on his lips ever since he had seen her there in the clearing, with guns flaring in her hands. He knew it would invite retribution, but if she had her map and was done with him, he may as well have been damned.

"Ketta? Why did you turn renegade?"

She blinked, as if waking from a reverie, then turned her gaze on him. It seemed surprisingly calm. "I'd spent too long with your Saint. The Ordo took me when I went back after Lavannos, but even after they'd declared me purified I knew there was no future for me. And after what they'd done…" Momentarily lost in a reverie, she then stated, very quietly, "Saulus killed himself before the Ordo could take him. If I'd had the sense, or the courage, I would have too."

Abruptly her mouth curled up at one corner. "Anyway, that's enough. I've got work to do." She reached down for her bolter. "I know you want my ship, Harrow. Yours is a wreck. But I've become rather attached to it, I'm afraid."

"Which leave me in something of a pickle."

She smiled. "That's a quaint turn of phrase. Hers?"

"Yes."

"Thought so." She paused. "You could come with me, you know."

Harrow stared. Of all the things he might have expected her to say, it was probably the least likely. For a second he wasn't even certain whether his own panicking mind had decided to betray him, to calm him with hallucinations before the blow fell. "Excuse me?"

"You seem useful enough in a fight, and you're not half as arrogant as most males I've met. Maybe another pair of eyes would come in handy."

"Ah, you're not proposing–"

"Don't get any funny ideas. I'm not into men. But there's profit to be had, if you live long enough."

He spread his hands, helplessly. "I'm sorry. I have to find her."

Her belongings were bundled into a small pack. Apparently she didn't need much to survive, even on Ashkelon. "Don't think that just because Godolkin's not here, he's still alive. He's more than likely just a wet smear on someone's launch pad, half a world away. Your Saint too, if she escaped via the same route." She lifted the pack and swung it over her shoulder. "No, you're right. It wouldn't work."

"I'm sorry," he said again.

"So am I. You know I can't let you follow me."

Here it comes, Harrow thought. He wondered if he had a chance of reaching his carbine before Ketta got him first, but quickly realised that he didn't. "Make it swift, agent."

"Oh, don't be so melodramatic," she said, and shot him down.

The blow was hard, but not lethal. Harrow came to his senses a few minutes later, with water hitting his face.

In the moment between oblivion and wakefulness he was treated to a quite delicious delusion – that Durham Red, the Scarlet Saint herself, had returned to him. She was sitting close by, glass of cold water in hands, dipping her fingers into it and sprinkling droplets over him. "Wake up, sleepyhead," she breathed.

His eyes flickered open and she was gone.

The water was coming down hard, in fat, fast gobbets. He had to shield his face with his hand as he sat up; if any of those watery missiles had struck him in an open eye it would been painful at best, possibly damaging. If this was rain, he decided, his head spinning, he regretted not bringing a hat.

But it was neither rain nor Durham Red with a glass of water. It was coming down off the trees, from high up in the canopy. And not only water, but leaves, twigs, small creatures, all pouring down on him from on high.

The forest was being shaken.

Harrow staggered to his feet. If it hadn't been for the clump of detritus on his head he would have been convinced Ketta's blow had set him rocking, but he was more stable than the trees and vines around him. The ground beneath his feet was convulsing steadily, a rhythmic quaking, like a giant's heartbeat hammering under the forest's skin. It was making the wildlife shriek, the canopy sway.

Not far away, a tree must have lost its roots to the shaking. Harrow heard the groan and howl of overstressed wood, the succession of rustling crashes as the trunk battered its way groundwards, crushing everything beneath it. He looked about wildly, suddenly aware that any one of the trees around him might suffer the same fate, flattening him if he was too close. Not for the first time, the forest was a dangerous place to be.

But as soon as the thought presented itself, the shaking began to subside. Within a few seconds it had abated entirely, marked only by a slowing fall of canopy water and the fading screams of the animals.

He stood, in the ruins of Ketta's campsite, breathing hard and wondering what to do next. If he stayed where he was, he reasoned, there was a very good chance of being pulverised by falling trees if the forest erupted again. He had seen no evidence of such activity; the forest had seemed remarkably stable before the event. But if Harrow knew anything about seismic quakes, it was that one tends to beget another.

Besides, the campsite wasn't far from the clearing. The other Omegas must have known that Hermas had been there, although where he was, was a subject for conjecture. Harrow had thought about waiting between the towers in the hope of following the same path as Godolkin, or maybe even Durham Red, but there was little logic in it. It might have been days before the towers activated again. If exposure didn't finish him, the Omegas certainly would.

No, his only real option was to keep moving. But where to?

Crimson Hunter was too far away, and Godolkin had taken most of the survival equipment with him into the fire. Even if he was mad enough to attempt the journey, he'd never make it. Ketta had taken the dataslate, and with it his only compass. He'd be lucky if he could even make it back as far as the ruined town, but what would be there for him if he did? An empty courtyard, some bones, and a slow death from starvation. Ketta would be long gone.

As far as he could see, he had only one option. He could make contact with Ketta again, try to appeal to her better nature, and hitch a lift back to *Crimson Hunter*. Once there he could try to rig a long-range distress transmission, and hope that some Harvesters or sympathetic Tenebrae picked him up before an Iconoclast patrol found him.

If he had the ship up and running, he could use it to search for Durham Red. After all, that was what he had originally bought it for.

His choice, then, was made for him. He retrieved his carbine from where Ketta had left it, found where she had hidden the magazine – a further delaying tactic on her part – and set off towards the spot she had marked on her map. He knew enough about the workings of the dataslate to read her diagram as a location as soon as he saw it.

The day was still young and the sun burned low in the sky. The shafts of misty sunlight it threw between the trees were further marked by the dust shaken into the air. Harrow aligned himself with the trees, readied the carbine, and walked into the forest.

His destination wasn't far away. Maybe, if he hurried, he would find the Omega ship before Ketta did.

The sun was higher and the day hotter than any Harrow had so far experienced. The heat made the perspiration run down his face and his chest in streams, gluing his shirt and jacket to his back.

Not all his sweating was done at the sun's behest, though. Fear played its part. He was walking straight

towards the greatest concentration of Omega warriors on
Ashkelon, hoping to beg help from an Iconoclast special
agent – put so badly, the thought almost stopped him in his
tracks.

A distant rumble, far off among the trees, lent him speed
once more. Another quake, perhaps, or the launch of Ketta's
daggership – he wasn't sure which, but either could result
in his death. He increased his pace, battering down any
undergrowth in his path, skirting any patches that would
defeat his hands or the butt of the carbine. Ketta had taken
his vibrablade.

The track he was on had climbed steadily for the past
thirty minutes, exhausting him still further. Even in the
clearing it had been difficult to gauge the topography of the
forest. From inside it, where the furthest he could see
through the greenery was only a few metres at a time, it was
quite impossible to determine what ground features lay in
his path. He might have skirted mountains and never
known it.

It was no surprise when the end of the track almost
became the finish of Judas Harrow, too.

There was a bed of vines in his path, pulpy things as thick
as his thigh that curled and corkscrewed their way out of
the ground to wrap around nearby trees, protecting their
soft innards with an arsenal of needles and thorns. Harrow
couldn't see a way past them and so had resigned himself
to fighting his way through, turning the carbine around and
using its folding stock as a blunt axe. The vines had put up
a fight, but his ferocity had been a match for them and
within a minute or two Harrow found his way clear. He
stepped through, feeling pleased with himself and promptly
fell off a cliff.

He yelled, twisting as he tumbled, losing the carbine but
gaining a grip on a smashed length of vine. For a few seconds he hung there, staring at the rough rock face of the
cliff, trying to get a purchase with the toes of his boots, until
his weight proved too much for the vine and, as if in

revenge for the beating it had taken, it sheared through and let him drop. Palms full of needles, he fell.

The drop was frightening, but not all that far. Still, Harrow would have broken a limb if he hadn't landed in water.

The impact knocked the breath from him, and the shock of cold water almost stilled his heart. Struggling, choking, he fought his way back up to the surface, lungs aflame, until his head broke through and he dragged in a gasping, shuddering breath. His clothing was not made of a fabric that absorbed moisture in great quantities, and he was able to tread water for a moment or two while he got his bearings.

The section of sodden vine drifted past him. He eyed it sourly as it bobbed away.

There was a narrow, steeply shelving beach at the base of the cliff. Harrow swam towards it, his feet finding purchase when he was a few metres from shore. He waded up the slope, until he left the water entirely, then turned to try and make sense of his surroundings.

Something must have been wrong with Ketta's map, or his interpretation of it. He hadn't found the Omega base camp. He'd found a lake.

It had been a crater once, back in the distant past, and a huge one. Harrow looked across two or three kilometres of open water to the far shore, where a cliff of similar proportions to the one he had fallen from rose up. To his right loomed a dizzying wall of rock, jagged and sheer – if he tumbled down that, he thought with a start of horror, he would dash his brains out on the water's surface.

Over to the left, though, things seemed friendlier. The side of the crater must have collapsed in that quadrant, spilling itself into a series of low hills, now covered with forest. The shoreline widened out there, too.

Harrow didn't waste time looking for his carbine. It was in the lake somewhere, and while it was quite waterproof it was also heavy. He'd never find it. Instead he began walking along the shoreline, heading towards the wider part.

He had been walking for no more than a few minutes before he heard the rumbling again. It was ahead of him, this time; there was no mistaking its source, because a great cloud of flying creatures billowed up from the forest on the low edge of the crater, their distant cries mingling with the seismic growl to form a sound that set Harrow's teeth vibrating.

The rumbling had become a rougher sound, a sharper one. Harrow stopped where he was, eyes wide, as the forested hills began to shake, a juddering vibration so fast that it blurred his view. It was nothing like the heartbeat shaking of the quake he had felt back at the campsite. This was the surface of Ashkelon quivering until it fell apart.

Chunks of tree began to fly upwards, joined moments later by a fog of debris. And then, when Harrow thought that the hills themselves would start to fly apart, something erupted from the forest with a cacophony that had every flier leaping from every tree, their screams filling the crater.

A shard of black stone, as big as a cathedral spire, crashed upwards through the canopy, tottered for an awful moment, and then fell towards Harrow.

It goaned as it fell, trailing arcs of dust and pulverised soil. Harrow didn't move – if the shard missed him, he would live, and if it came close he would die. There was no running from it. All he could do was stand and witness its fall.

It hit the lake a hundred yards from him, blasting a wall of water into the sky.

The water moved him more than the rock. Harrow ducked away from it as the wall came back down, hitting him and battering him sideways across the shoreline. It didn't knock him off his feet, but it soaked him to the skin a second time.

He cursed. His clothes had only just started to dry.

Behind him, the lake was still rocking, waves crashing backwards and forwards as though chasing each other to destruction. The hills had stopped their convulsions when the shard appeared, but the surface of the water seemed to have taken on their violence. Harrow backed away, still too close to the cliff wall to go far, his head ringing from the sound of the quake, heart leaping in his chest as he contemplated what a further impact below the lake's surface would do to him.

The water was beginning to surge upwards. Gas, he thought. Some titanic reservoir of toxic fumes must have been released from the lakebed, breaking as he watched.

The water continued to seethe and its swell kept getting bigger, far beyond the point at which it could have supported itself. Smaller streams ran off it in sparkling rivulets, as if from glass or something even more transparent.

Like a ship with a shadow web.

"Sacred rubies," he whispered. The Omegas had hidden their ship under the lake, and now they were trying to lift off before any more rock spires came down on them.

He started to run along the shoreline, still watching the ship rise. He saw more domes break the surface, shimmering, water pooling in the air between them, then slabs and planes, the cylinders of great drive nacelles. The ship was a big one, corvette-sized or greater.

It wasn't alone, either. Three smaller vessels accompanied it – they were heavy interceptors, oddly shaped things twice the size of *Crimson Hunter*.

By the time he had made it to the shard's flank the Omega corvette was out of the water, shedding tonnes of spray. It couldn't engage its main drives yet, or its thrusters. Gravlifters would work when they were submerged, but if the Omega captain tried to power up a thruster while it was full of water he might cause a steam explosion. If he was lucky he might blow the tube clear, but if not, then the superheated steam could take the whole assembly off.

Antimat fire carved up from the vessel's lucent, glittering flanks.

Harrow ducked, but the fire wasn't aimed it him. It snarled overhead, its heat ripping the air, streams of it converging from invisible turrets. Water scattered as the interceptors started to turn.

There was only one thing the Omegas could be shooting at. Harrow covered his head and forced himself against the wet side of the shard.

Ketta's daggership howled across the lake, its drives torching out great streams of flame, weapons spitting ragged bolts of blinding energy. The agent must have started her drives while she was still on the courtyard, letting the air in the tubes heat up before she turned the power up. She'd had time to prepare. The Omegas, jolted into action by the falling shard, had not.

The daggership thundered past Harrow and under the corvette's belly, strafing it from wing to wing.

Deafening explosions tore downwards, vomiting fire and debris into the lake. As the rain of hot metal hit the water steam blasted up, meeting the fires that were falling down, the whole mess surrounded by coruscating patterns of colour as the shadow web began to fail. Harrow saw the ship flashing, flickering into view, sections of it still invisible but others losing their camouflage, turrets still chasing the darting daggership.

There was no way this could end well. Harrow abandoned his hiding place and ran, heading up the shoreline as fast as his legs would carry him.

More explosions sounded behind him, but he didn't look back. The Omega vessel, for all its might, was being ripped apart by Ketta's modified gunship. With their drives full of water, neither it nor the interceptors stood a chance.

Harrow had been running for a minute, maybe two, when there was a blast from the lake so powerful it knocked him flat.

He rolled over, in time to see the corvette roar overhead, its shadow covering him, blocking out the sun as it careered away. It was sliding in the air, burning as it went, its drives ablaze, its turrets still spitting fire like a severed vein spits blood. Fully visible for the first time, it thundered past him and out into the forest, losing height all the time.

An interceptor exceeded its velocity, flickering with damaged camouflage, and blew up in mid-air. Seconds later, the corvette touched the forest and shattered.

Pieces bigger than Ketta's entire ship flew through the sky, comet tails of fire and smoke following their arcing paths down to the trees. Secondary explosions began to hammer out from behind the hills, battering Harrow in waves as Ketta's ship screamed across the canopy.

One of the surviving interceptors tried to follow her, its drives stuttering with steam detonations, but a whirling section of the corvette came too close, and batted it out of the air. Harrow saw it strike the canopy and crash through, rolling to a messy halt among the trunks.

And then silence – save the dull rush of forest fires, and the crack of debris surrendering itself to heat.

Shaking, ears bleeding, Harrow forced himself to sit up, then to stand.

Everywhere he could see, the forest had gained new pathways, burning, pulverised tunnels through the undergrowth, where pieces of the Omega's hidden warship had tumbled to earth.

Maybe, when the fires were out, he would use those paths. There didn't seem to be anywhere else to go.

Some time later, Harrow wasn't sure how long, Ketta came back.

Her daggership drifted down in front of him, as he climbed the first of the hills where the shard had emerged. She didn't land it, just kept hovering a few metres above the ground. It must have been set to automatic, because within a minute or two a side hatch opened, and Ketta put her head out.

"Hello, mutant," she called down.

Despite himself, Harrow put up a hand and waved. He was too tired, too assaulted by events, to do much more.

She crouched in the hatchway, looking down at him with a slight smile on her lips. "I wasn't expecting to see you here. I thought you'd have stayed with the towers."

"I thought about that," he called back. "But it wouldn't have worked. Too much company."

"Don't think it's all gone. There was a skeleton crew on those ships, nothing more. The forest is still swarming with them, and there'll be more waiting for me elsewhere. Hermas wasn't an idiot."

"Unlike me?"

She appeared to shrug, although it might have been the downdraft from the daggership's grav-lifters, catching her clothes. "You're no idiot, Harrow. I'm beginning to think quite highly of you."

"Really?"

"Freedom does strange things to a girl. Anyway, have this." She threw something down to him.

Harrow caught it before it hit the ground. It was a small plastic case, no larger than a volume of scripture. "What is it?"

"A gift for your saint, if you happen to see her again. I picked it up on Biblos. Oh, and you can tell her she won't hear from me, either. I'm done hunting mutants."

"She won't believe you."

"I know. Harrow, I've got to be away. You should too – there are fissures opening up in this world's crust, not far from here. I don't know what's happening on this planet, but it's nothing good. Get away while you can."

"That might be difficult."

"Not really. Head northeast, and keep your wits about you."

Harrow glanced in the direction he thought she meant. He could see nothing there but debris. "Ketta?"

"Goodbye, mutant." She stood. "Try not to fall in love with her."

He grinned. "Too late."

"I know that."

With that, she was gone. The hatch closed up, and a moment later the ship turned in the air and darted away.

Harrow felt the backdraft tug his clothes. He watched the daggership slice the air over the canopy, heading north-east.

Its wings waggled a few kilometres away – a signal? – and then the ship pointed its nose to the stars and powered upwards. A heartbeat or two, and it was out of sight.

The case was heavy in his hands. He stared at it, turned it over, triggered the catch and lifted the lid a fraction.

And slammed it closed. "My God," he breathed.

It would take him a couple of hours to get to where Ketta had indicated with the tilt of her wings. After seeing what lay in the case, he knew that was where he needed to be.

Could an Iconoclast special agent and a mutant of the Tenebrae cult be allies? Even for an hour or two? It was insane. Then again, Judas Harrow lived in an insane universe. Anything could happen.

With that thought fixed in his head, he headed off, up the hill and into the burning trees.

17. THE LAST SUPPER

Durham Red was utterly without words.

She had thought that she was beyond shock or surprise. This deranged universe had delivered shock after shock to her, battering her with wonders from the moment she had climbed out of the cryo-tube on Wodan. She had seen spiders as big as cities and monsters the size of worlds, had watched planets burn and whole populations put to the sword in her name. She had walked on the surface of the Moon with only a coat to protect her, had stood before a spinning pulsar and felt its warmth on her cheek. Yet none of these things, or a hundred like them, had rendered her as speechless as seeing this one man sitting in front of her.

It seemed to amuse him. But then, by now, most things did.

"You're gaping," said the Gothking. "You have pretty teeth, my dear, but please close your mouth. You have no idea what might fly in."

"You're not real," Red breathed. She shook her head, slowly. "You can't be."

"Oh, I can assure you that I am. As real as I was, oh, when did we last meet? Lethe, I believe." He sat back and steepled his fingers, still with that faintly amused half smile on his lips. "I told you then that you weren't much to look at. Your dress sense hasn't improved much in the last twelve hundred years."

"Nearly thirteen," Red murmured absently. "And these aren't mine."

"I'm so glad to hear it." He turned his attention to Sorrelier, who took a step backwards in what seemed a reflexive jolt of guilt. "And Sire Vaide."

Sorrelier looked both confused and acutely uncomfortable. There was no way he could have known who the man sitting up on the dais was, merely the anonymous ruler he was intending to assassinate, but the Magister's reaction unsettled him. "My Lord," he muttered.

"I'm almost sorry your little plot fell at the first hurdle, Vaide," D'Isis purred. "It would have been fun to see it unfold, and I always try to encourage forward-thinking among my subjects. But you might have spoiled the last dance, and that would have been a pity."

"Dance?" asked Red. Her brain was starting to get back into gear, slowly. "What dance?"

"A little soiree I've arranged in your honour, my dear." He stood up, leaning slightly on the cane he carried in his right hand, a metre of polished ebony topped with a silver skull. "Nothing much. A few friends, a little wine. Just a diversion from the coming troubles, but it should still have its charms." He looked from Red to Sorrelier, and back again. "Well now, you might try to look a bit pleased. It's not often I grant an audience these days, and rarer still that I offer hospitality."

"Hospitality!" Red shook herself, and stepped forwards. "Look, this is insane. You should be dead a thousand years, and instead you're standing here inviting us to a party!"

"I'm sure you have questions," said D'Isis, starting down the steps.

"Snecking right I do!"

The interruption brought a warning glance. "Manners. There are clearly things you'd like to know. And you will, believe me. When the time comes, you will."

"But–"

"Ah!" He raised a hand to silence her, then turned the gesture to one of invitation, motioning her to one of the chamber's doors. "I'm sure you wouldn't like to keep any-one waiting."

She followed him, along with Sorrelier and Lise, out of the chamber and along a narrow, ornate corridor. The décor of the Magister's rooms was nothing short of breathtaking, a dizzying fusion of marble and jet, diamond and gold. Light came from illuminated ceiling panels, hand-wrought with startling scenes of erotica, and the floor was a polished chequerboard of inlaid gems.

Red walked some distance behind the Gothking, watching his every move. There had to be some flaw in his perfor-mance, something about the impostor striding ahead of her that would reveal the truth of him. There was some trick here, some falsehood, of that she was certain. The only other explanation was that D'Isis had walked into a cryo-tube not long after she had, and she couldn't believe that. It didn't fit the history – he wouldn't have had time to found the Magadan colony if he'd been frozen.

Besides, it simply wasn't his style.

She felt Sorrelier draw close to her as she walked. "What's going on?" he said. "What in the name of the Prime were you two talking about back there?"

Red opened her mouth to explain, then closed it again. There wasn't time, and she didn't have the energy. "Trust me, you don't want to know."

"I'll be the judge of that."

"No, you'll be the bloke with the gun, okay?" He started to protest but she waved him away. "Listen, just keep that needler handy. And when I give you the word, don't hesi-tate. I've got a really bad feeling about this."

"You're not the only..." Sorrelier trailed off. "What are they doing here?"

"Who?" Red's attention had been on Sorrelier, she hadn't seen the Gothking stop at the end of the corridor. He was waiting next to a door, both hands clasped over the top of his walking cane.

Four men had appeared to stand alongside him; two at his left hand, two on his right.

"Guards," Red muttered. "It figures."

"Those aren't guards. Those are servilants." Sorrelier slowed, hanging back. "I don't like the look of this."

As Red got closer to the new arrivals she began to see what Sorrelier meant. There was nothing martial in the servilants' dress or bearing, just a slack-jawed emptiness, a lifelessness that made sylphs look vital and alert. They stood as though their shaven heads had been nailed to the air, and their bodies left to dangle below.

All of them were dressed in long, glossy coats of pale green, studded with pockets and fastenings. Bright, gleaming things stuck out of those pockets in neat rows.

There were stains on the servilants' coats, dots and smears that made Red's nose itch as she stepped alongside.

The Gothking turned to flash Red a smile. "It's time," he said. "As you are my guests, I'll announce you."

Seeing that smile, Red's stomach knotted. There was something horribly wrong besides the Gothking's anachronisms. She could hear noises coming from beyond the panelled door, muted shufflings and murmurs, the scrape of furniture on polished floors. That, and a kind of rapid, repetitive tapping, as though someone with a wooden spoon were beating a faint tattoo upon a china plate. "Gothking–"

"Please," he said gently. "Call me Simon. You're among friends here."

He pushed the door open.

Red cried out, covering her mouth with one hand. Dimly, she heard Sorrelier curse behind her, and then D'Isis, with surprising strength, grabbed them both by the shoulder and propelled them into the room. "Ladies and gentlemen, Sire Vaide Sorrlier, and the Lady Durham Red!"

It was a dining hall, long and high-ceilinged, lit by chandeliers and dozens of flickering candles. The walls were white marble, trimmed with gold and set with panels of rose quartz. The furniture – a long dining table and chairs, side-tables and consoles hugging the walls – was smooth oak and soft, wine-dark leather.

The stench was indescribable.

As D'Isis had intimated, there were guests here. In fact, of the twenty or so chairs available, only three stood unoccupied. In the others men and women sat, facing the table as though in anticipation of a feast. From what Red could see of them, though, eating was the last thing on their minds.

The Gothking's guests had been bound to their chairs, stout leather straps tugged tight into protesting flesh, and each bore a catalogue of wounds. Some ghastly fusion of surgery and torture, mutilation and cuisine, had taken place, like a gourmet's most surreal and bloody nightmare. Several of the guests were plainly dead, lolling in their straps, but the majority were still, distressingly, alive.

None, though, had been left capable of speech.

Red saw a man whose whole skull had been flayed, the skin of his face cut into strips and served to him on salad. There was a woman with her mouth opened into a gaping, circular wound, head down over a bowl of blood and teeth. Across the table was a quivering wreck, rendered sexless by its injuries, with skin more cut and sliced than intact. Horrible visions, every one, the living mewling and mumbling in their agonies, the dead swollen and stinking where they sat.

"I'd like to introduce the Board of Arch-Domini," said D'Isis. "You'll forgive them for not getting up. Impolite of them, I know, but we can't have everything. Oh, here's a friend of yours."

He touched the shoulder of one of the ruined men. Red saw the eyes roll towards her, agonised and beseeching. His eyelids had been sliced carefully away, and he stared out from twin puddles of congealed blood. Below that, his lips had been stitched shut, but worse still were the man's hands. The skin and muscle had been carved away from them, leaving skeletal claws, held together only by strings of tendon and random shreds of muscle.

On the plate in front of him were the parts he was missing: eyelids, tongue, the meat of his hands, arranged on the china-like nouvelle cuisine, and as he shivered and quaked in shock his finger bones rattled the plate – the tattoo she had heard from outside.

"I'm sure you recognise Sire Saleph Losen," the Gothking said, smiling down at the man. "I had high hopes for this one, but he proved something of a disappointment. He encouraged Sorrelier to kidnap you at the Masque, led him on quite atrociously, just so they could expose his plots to me." He patted Losen's quivering head, as though comforting a favourite dog. "And there's Sire Brakkeri, with whom he conspired." He began moving along the line of bleeding Domini. "Normally I'd ignore their little indiscretions, even applaud that sort of behaviour, but to be honest I no longer have any use for the game."

"You're snecking insane," Red managed to say. She was barely staying upright, shock and nausea threatening to unbalance her at any second. Just as she thought she had seen some of the most shocking sights in the universe, she had thought herself immune to horror before she had stumbled into this awful feast. She had been wrong on both counts.

Sorrelier stepped unsteadily past her, his eyes fixed on Losen's wreck of a face. "Insane," he agreed, gasping. "A madman. By the Prime, I wished this whelp dead enough times, but…" Words failed him, and he trailed to silence, shaking his head as if to dislodge what he had seen.

Red started backing away. D'Isis looked up at her. "Leaving so soon? I'm not sure I can allow that. After all, I went to a lot of trouble to arrange this."

As he spoke, the four servilants stepped in through the doorway, moving with clockwork precision. As one, they reached into pockets in their discoloured garments, drawing forth glittering metal objects that caught the candle-light; shears and hooks, needles and saws. All the instruments that had flayed Losen and the Board, eager for more harm.

Red stopped where she was, caught between the servilants and their master. There was nothing remotely sentient
about these drooling surgeons, she could see that at a
glance. They were puppets, and the Gothking had their
strings. "Call them off, D'Isis."

"Sit down like a good girl, and they'll be gone."

"No chance."

"A pity. We have much to talk about, you and I."

"There's been enough talk," Sorrelier snarled. He had the
needle-gun in his fist, and Red saw it come up, smooth and
fast to centre on the Gothking's face. "No!" she cried, in
spite of herself. "Don't–"

Sorrelier's finger whitened on the trigger.

D'Isis didn't move. It was Lise that sprang into motion,
darting up behind Sorrelier and ripping the gun from his
grasp. A single needle sprang up, striking crystal from a
chandelier.

Sorrelier span, gaping. "Lise!"

"I'm sorry," said the Gothking. Bizarrely, he sounded as
if he meant it. "She's programmed. I'm the one person she
can't possibly let you harm."

That final betrayal was too much for Sorrelier. Maybe he
could have taken the horror all around him, braved the
atrocities, but for his beloved sylph to turn against him
must have been the final crack in his mental armour. He
howled, wordlessly, into his Magister's face, then turned
and bolted towards the servilants.

They stepped aside, and he ran between them.

Red heard his footsteps vanish down the hall. Beside her,
D'Isis was leading Lise to one of the empty chairs. She sat,
blank-faced as ever, between two men gutted wide open.
"At least one of my guests has the grace to sit."

"This has gone far enough, D'Isis. Or whoever the sneck
you are." From the corner of her eye Red saw the servilants
banding together again. She wasn't going to be allowed out
as easily as Sorrelier. "I don't know what the hell you're
playing at here, but it ends now."

"You're absolutely right," he replied. "All this has gone quite far enough." He made an airy, all-encompassing gesture. "And this is where it ends."

She lashed out in fury, sweeping dishes from the table. "Will you stop talking in bloody riddles!"

"Sit, then. And I'll explain."

"You're mad!"

"I don't enjoy being defied, little girl," he growled. The smile was gone from his face, and behind her Red heard the servilants take a reflexive step forwards. "And I'm disappointed that you, the great predator, would shy away from a little meat. So sit down while it's still a voluntary action!"

As the words left his lips, the chandeliers dimmed.

It was only for a moment, a second or two while the room's power levels dipped, but it was enough. Red actually heard the drop in electricity, a barely audible lowering of a background hum so pervasive she'd not even noticed it was there. She also heard the servilants shift position very subtly, as though their master's control of them was affected too. One of Sorrelier's system failures, maybe.

Whatever the cause, to Durham Red it was an opportunity to put an end to this insanity once and for all. She leapt at the Gothking.

She was fast, she knew, blindingly so, and her fury leant her even more speed. No matter how the Gothking had survived all this time, no matter what power he had in this world, she was going to put an end to him. She came at him like a missile.

He stepped aside, and batted her across the room.

It was like being struck by a sledgehammer. Red went spinning past the table, catching a corpse with her foot, a living man with her hand, and the three of them struck the wall together. A console shattered as they struck it, pieces of oak hitting the ceiling. Red bounced from the wreckage and rolled onto the floor. The guests she had plucked from the table, both corpses now, fell with her, chairs and all.

The Gothking was stronger than she could have imagined.

She struggled out of the wreckage, expecting him to come after her, but he left it to the servilants. Two of them were hurtling across the dining room towards her, blades at the ready, hooks dripping. She felt a flensing knife part the air above her head.

She brought her foot up, planting the sole of her boot against the servilant's chest, and shoved him back. He crashed away, spitting blood. She'd kicked him hard enough to cave his sternum in.

The second one came at her, but she was on her feet, and he never stood a chance. She grabbed his face and leapt, powering up and away from the wall, riding the servilant all the way over in an arc until his skull shattered against the hard floor. Grey pulp and circuitry spattered across the tiles.

Red jumped away from him, and dived at the Gothking again.

He struck at her a second time, but she was ready for that. She ducked under the blow, twisting her body sideways as she went past him, reaching out to grab the walking cane and tear it from his grasp. As she came up behind him she whirled with it, swinging the metal skull at the end around in a humming arc that terminated, with shattering force, on the side of his head.

There was a crunch that Red felt all the way up her arm, and the cane shattered. D'Isis twisted clear around, and then sagged onto the floor, the right of his skull caved inwards. There was a dent in his head she could have put her fist into. Red dropped to her knees next to him, ignoring the pain he had ignited within her, and sank her teeth into his throat.

As soon as she did so she realised that it was a mistake. The texture of his skin was wrong, the smell of him was wrong. Even his sweat was a warning, a sterile mix of water and artificial grease. But her fangs were already biting through to the core of him, the vampiric reflex so strong in her that she couldn't unlock her jaws again before it was too late. Beneath the Gothking's throat, its workings tasted sour, warm and metallic, as Red's teeth parted its inner covering.

There was a brilliant flash, and a feeling like being hit full in the face with a baseball bat. The floor came up and hit her in the back of her head. She was flung away from her potential meal so fast and hard that she hadn't even felt herself move. She was simply there one moment, and on her back the next, with a mouthful of skin.

Not even his flesh was real. She spat it out and rolled over, trying to get to her feet before the Gothking could recover and finish her. But he was going nowhere. Half his neck was hanging off, with fluids gushing across the marble – not blood but greyish, watery stuff, shot through with sparks and wisps of smoke. The Gothking's body jerked and twisted rhythmically, the same motion over and over again. He was broken, a clockwork toy with his gears knocked askew.

"Oh, snecking hell," Red groaned. She spat, purging the taste of voltage from her mouth. "A robot."

"You make it sound so mundane," sighed D'Isis. His head was calm, despite the convulsions of his body, the eyes swivelling to look at her.

Red got to her feet. "I didn't think they made these any more."

"They don't. It's an antique. A duplicate, from when I still had an empire. I used to have hundreds, but this was the only one that survived."

"So all this time I've been talking to a bloody droid?" She walked over to the table and picked up the needle gun.

"Don't be hasty. You've been speaking to me through the robot." The eyelids dropped closed over roving eyes. One of them came up, but the other was frozen. "Things have changed around here, Durham Red. I have a little power now, more than I've ever had. The systems failures have let me take control of a few machines, but I'm still a prisoner. I need you."

"You're doing that riddle thing again."

"It's a hard habit to break." The voice was fading, attenuating. She drew closer to hear it. "I'd tell you everything right now, if I could. You deserve it. But we're out of time. You have to come and find me."

"So where are you?" She hefted the gun. It was small and heavy, fully loaded. Not a weapon she was familiar with, but she could soon learn. "And why the sneck shouldn't I just walk out of here right now?"

"Because you'll never leave Magadan unless I tell you how." The eyes weren't moving at all. "Come down and find me, Durham Red. I'll guide you. Find the real me, and I'll tell you everything. Every…"

The head stilled. Red nudged it with the toe of her boot, but it gave no reply.

"Shit."

There was one more thing to do before she left, a promise to keep. When she first resolved to kill Saleph Losen if she ever saw him again it had been in the form of a threat. But in the space of a few hours, it had passed from a threat to a duty.

She took the needle gun, went over to the mewling thing that had been Sire Losen, and fired a single toxin dart into the back of his neck. Then, as he fell silent, she did the same, carefully and systematically, to every other guest at the table.

All but one. Lise was still sitting in place. Her face was blank, her body motionless, but her eyes followed Red everywhere, flickeriing plaintively between her face and the gun.

Red perched on the edge of her table. "I don't know how to help you," she said simply. "I wish I could."

The sylph gazed up at her for a long moment, and in that haunted look was all the answer Red needed. Even if it wasn't the one she wanted to hear.

"I understand," she said.

Slowly, Lise closed her eyes.

18. NO PLACE LIKE HOME

There was no sign of Sorrelier on the way out. He was obviously long gone from the court. The only signs of his passing were a couple of bloodied footprints near the door, where he'd trodden in seepings from one of the dinner guests, and a puddle of greasy bile in the next hallway along. Red saw that and felt nothing. Her own guts were in turmoil from what the Gothking's servilants had wrought in the dining hall.

She was glad that Sorrelier had gone, in more ways than one. The man was a menace, a conspirator and a fool. He'd kidnapped her, and set Ketta upon her, and Red had the uneasy suspicion that he'd done worse to her in another life. She still couldn't shake the conviction that she knew him.

Not only that, but if she saw him again she might have to tell him about Lise.

D'Isis had only given her one clue as to his location, before the damage Red had done to his robot duplicate had taken its toll. She knew that she had to go further down into the Keep, though she didn't know how far or how she might arrive there.

Red ran until she reached the elevator, through the five halls, across the mirrored floor. The elevator doors were closed. Sorrelier must have rode the elevator back up to the stratum of fountains. Red pressed the call control, expecting a wait, but the doors opened for her immediately.

She stepped through them, impatient to be away, and found her foot dangling in empty space.

Red cried out, just about managing to scramble back before she lost her balance completely. The elevator was gone, as she had suspected, but the doors had opened anyway.

"Snecking system failures," she said out loud, feeling a little breathless. She was going to have to watch her step; whatever dissolution was affecting the Grand Keep, it was becoming lethal.

If the elevator was above her, she couldn't see it. The shaft was dark, only the light spilling in from the open doors partially illuminating its interior, which seemed to go on forever, upwards and downwards. Red stared into it for a few moments, then stepped away. "D'Isis?"

There was no answer, save the echo of her own voice. She tried again, more loudly this time. "Hey, Simon. You said you'd guide me. Now would be a good time to start!"

Nothing. Either the Gothking had been lying, or he couldn't reach her yet. In either case, she would need to find her own way.

She leaned back into the shaft. After a few moments her night vision came into play, enhancing the meagre light coming in through the open doors.

There were dozens of pipes and ducts hugging the walls, some of which might provide enough of a grip to enable a short climb. A narrow ledge ringed the shaft at floor height. Red scanned these features quickly, and dismissed them with similar speed. She didn't want to be spidering around the inside of the shaft if the elevator decided to reappear. No, there had to be another way.

And there it was, over to her right. Above the ledge, a small hatchway.

Red stepped into the shaft, gripping the walls wherever she could find purchase, inching her way above the dizzying drop. By the time she reached the hatch her fingers were aching, and the oily smell was starting to get to her. She was glad she'd not been stupid enough to try climbing the pipework.

The hatch, thankfully, was not locked, and slid easily aside on hidden runners. Behind it was a cage just about big enough for an engineer – or one very tired and hungry mutant in uncomfortable boots – to stand up in. A service elevator.

Red stepped gratefully inside. "Shirts and haberdashery," she muttered. "Going down."

The elevator, according to its indicator panel, could take Red six strata below the inner court. She still had no idea how far down the Gothking might be, but she pressed the lowest button anyway. She could work her way up from there if she needed to.

The journey wasn't as swift as in the larger elevators, but it was far more interesting. The service elevator had no solid walls; it was basically a cylinder of steel mesh on grav-lifters, and many parts of its surrounding shaft were laid wide open. Red saw more of the workings of the Keep in this one short trip than she had done on her entire journey with Sorrelier.

First was the space below the inner court, a cavernous level that seemed to stretch away into infinity. There were no walls, and it was no higher than a couple of storeys, but it was a maze of systemry; forests and cabling and pipework, endless ducts and thousands upon thousands of support braces. This, she realised, was merely the court's underfloor area, the structure between strata. There was probably one of these under every inhabited level.

Huge machines hummed, glowing with power. Gravity nullifiers, giant companions to the service elevator's own system of motion, had been set into the space. Red felt the heat of their radiators and marvelled. This was how the Keep extended so high, she realised. Each floor negated the mass of the one above it.

Suddenly, the idea of power failures within the Keep became even more terrifying.

Further levels brought further wonders. She passed down through a stratum that was clearly one enormous flight harbour, many times the size of those she had seen before. A ring of starships, ranging in size from yachts to caravels, was arranged around the perimeter. From the ceiling extended a series of oddly shaped towers. Decks and gantries surrounded the ships, which were attended by cranes and mobile grabs. Cargo and fuel were being loaded, and the hangar seethed with people running in every direction. They seemed to be in a state of high agitation. One man, close to the shaft, looked in as Red went past. His face was a mask of terror.

It looked as though the whole statum was preparing for an exodus, although no exit was visible. If a ship lifted off from one of those inward-facing berths, Red wondered, how would it leave the Keep?

She headed further down, through more braces and support levels, more ducts and tunnels, to the bottom of the shaft.

The elevator sighed to a halt and opened. Red slid the hatch aside and stepped out of it, glad to be free of its confines. Her boots came down on steel mesh.

It was hot. Steam came up through the floor, and disappeared through a ceiling made of the same material. The mesh deck had four, maybe five, similar levels both above and below it. Light came from tubular lumes bolted to the ceiling at intermittent points, issuing simultaneously from up and down, but a greater source of illumination could be glimpsed glowing at some distance ahead.

There were machines everywhere, pumping and hissing, complex assemblies of black metal and chrome. Pipes hung from them, dangling like jungle vines, and cables snaked across the floor. The service elevator had taken her right into the guts of this place, whatever it was, into the heat of its bowels. There was nothing appealing or pretty here.

No workers, either. The place must have been largely automatised, or else the engineers and their sylphs must have been scattered by the same panic gripping the hangar decks above.

"What the sneck," she breathed, "is all this?"

"You're in my domain, Durham Red."

She whirled. His voice was everywhere, coming down from concealed sounders. "Where are you?"

"I'm close. You'll have to come and find me, Red. I'm not as fit as I was. You've weathered the years far better than I."

"Thirteen hundred years of hibernation is great beauty treatment." She started forwards, deeper into the maze of machines. "So it really is you."

There was a long, soft, synthetic-sounding sigh. "In a manner of speaking."

"Quite a coincidence. Of all the planets, in all the systems—"

"Please don't continue with that awful paraphrase, my dear. You're far smarter than that. And trust me, there is no coincidence at all. I looked long and hard for you, and it took some considerable effort to bring you to Magadan."

Red was still pacing forwards, heading for the light. After a time the rows of devices gave way to a railed walkway between them, curving slightly away to left and right. Like most places in the Keep, the Magister's domain must have been laid out in a vast circle. "So you could do to me what you did to those poor bastards upstairs?"

There was an exasperated noise from the sounders. "Don't waste your sympathies on those monsters, girl. If you want to grieve for someone, take a look at the inside surface of one of the sarcophagi you've been passing by."

Red paused. The rows of blank devices had given no clue as to their purpose. It wasn't until she turned around and studied one up close that she saw the machine was faced with a window, a curving glass panel taller than she was. Red wiped steam from it so she could see what was inside.

It was a man. He was very young. His skin was pale and slicked with sweat, criss-crossed with the straps that held him in place. His arms were outstretched, his legs held straight and his feet together, crucified on a gantry of gleaming surgical steel. He was naked, apart from the straps and a device that covered his groin; pipes led from that device into the floor. More pipes came in from the sides of the machine, terminating in bright steel plugs bolted directly into his skin between each pair of ribs, into his armpits, the insides of his elbows, the backs of his knees. His body was a forest of shaking, pumping cables.

His head sprouted slender tubes connected to what appeared to Red to be a skullcap. Then she wiped away a little more steam, and saw that the man wore nothing on his head – not even bone. The entire top of his skull had been sliced away, exposing the grey mass of his brain.

The thin tubes ended in needles, and these were pushed into the man's brain tissue. Fluids inched up out of them, slowly, constantly. He was being fed by the pipes below, and drained by the tubes above.

Red backed away, horrified. From where she stood she could see hundreds of similar machines; row after row, rank after rank, thousands ringing the stratum, hot and rattling, a man or woman trapped in every one of them.

"You see?" said the Gothking, his voice thick. "They built this, those creatures you felt such sympathy for. Generation after generation of Arch-Domini have added to it, sacrificing their own people." He gave a derisive snort. "And you thought *I* was evil."

"Why?" Red stepped back from the encased man, and saw his eyes follow her. "What's this all for?"

"For me," the Gothking said. Then suddenly his tone switched, adding a sense of urgency. "Durham Red, there's someone down here."

Red tensed. "Who? Guards?"

"No, they're gone." There was a heartbeat of silence. "He's on this stratum, close at hand. I have some eyes and ears down here, Red, but I'm not omnipotent. Far from it. You'd better keep moving."

"Where to?"

"Follow the light."

For once, Red did as she was told. She aimed herself at the greatest source of light and ran.

She passed ten rows of machines, ten great rings of human captives, crucified and drained by the Board's sarcophagi. The same number, maybe even greater, occupied the levels above and below. The total count was something Red couldn't let herself think about.

She ran through an open area, only stopping when she reached the huge windows that lay beyond.

There was a kind of observation gallery here, the windows tilted inward at the top, so tall that they stretched past her level and into those above and below. The gallery was circular, surrounding a space as big as the Masque stadium. Red put her hands to the nearest pane and looked down onto a sea of glowing machinery.

These weren't the coffin factories that had surrounded her, but something else entirely. Tubes of glass and steel, spire-topped, gave off a fitful blue light. There was a forest of them, a sea of them, so closely packed that she couldn't have walked between them, each one bigger than a starship set on end.

Above them was a cruciform walkway, four bridges of narrow mesh meeting at the centre of the space, where they joined a stepped disc. And there, on the circular top step, was a house-sized cylinder of black metal. Pipes, thick as tree trunks, hung down from above the gallery to join the top of the cylinder.

"I can see you," Red whispered. The Gothking was hiding in that drum of black steel. She knew it as certainly as she knew her own heartbeat. Here, at the very centre of the Keep, was the real Simon D'Isis.

Now all she had to do was find a way down.

"And I can see you," D'Isis replied. "Be careful, Red. I can't imagine that this fellow means you well."

"I don't see him."

"No, I think that's the way he wants it. But I can't help you from here. If you need an ally, you'll have to bring him closer."

She glanced about wildly, peering through the heat-haze. As she did so, a pale form stepped out from behind one of the machines, three or four rows away and part-hidden by steam.

Red almost laughed with relief. "It's okay, D'Isis. That's a friend. It's Godolkin."

Even half-hidden by vapour, and lit only by the fitful shafts of light from above, there was no mistaking that colourless skin, even from a distance, or the powerful muscles that rippled beneath the charm-tattoos covering his naked torso. He wore his black uniform trousers and heavy boots, but his battle harness was gone. Maybe he had stripped it off in the heat.

She raised a hand to wave, and saw the figure move towards her. He started to run.

"I've seen Godolkin before," the Gothkin said forebodingly. "And I don't think that's him."

"What do you mean, you've seen him? When did you – oh, *sneck!*"

It wasn't Godolkin. His hair was too short, his charm-tattoos too sparse. His eyes were covered with round-lensed goggles.

It was Hermas, the man whose blood had almost eviscerated her on Biblos.

He was pounding towards her now, his boots hammering the mesh. Red hauled the needle gun up, squeezing the trigger to send a burst of toxin barbs lancing out at the Iconoclast, but if they struck him he didn't seem to notice. A moment later he was upon her.

There was no subtlety to his attack. He just ran into her, shoulder first, crushing her against the window.

He was fast, and brutally strong. The blow slammed her with incredible force back into the glass. She felt it crack behind her as her skull smashed back into it, felt one of her ribs give way with an a creaking snap. Pain flooded her, and she cried out.

Hermas yanked her away from the window, and shoved her back into it again. "That's the spirit, bitch-saint! Scream for me!"

"Yeah," snarled Red. "I bet you love it when they do that."

His face twisted in rage, and he reached for her, but she had the measure of him now. She ducked away, letting his momentum carry him past, and powered her elbow into the back of his head. This time it was his skull that collided with the glass, face-first. Cracks spiderwebbed across the window.

There was something sticking out of his back, a metal cylinder as thick as two fingers. A staking pin, crusted with dried blood. A memory of pain sparked in Red's mind. She knew what that felt like.

Hermas span around to face her. She darted back, sweeping her foot around at head-level, the steel toe of her boot cracking his jaw. He roared and caught the boot, twisting Red over, but she wrenched herself away and leapt at him.

They went through the window together.

It was a long way down. Red could see the sea of blue-lit machines spiralling up at her, the slender spires atop each one, sharp as a blade. She twisted, trying to get Hermas beneath her, but he was too strong. When they hit, she was mostly underneath the Iconoclast.

They didn't hit the towers, though. It was the walkway that exploded into Red's back.

The impact was awful. Red's vision sparked to black, pain erupting through every part of her. The broken rib was a blowtorch in her side, joining up with fires in her back, her limbs. She screamed, weakly, blood and bile choking her.

Hermas had rolled away, and was getting to his knees. He staggered up, standing over her, then slowly reached around his own back.

"I saved this for you, Blasphemy," he gasped, and then tensed the muscles of his arm. There was a slick, grinding sound, a sucking, and the point of the staking pin disappeared back into his chest.

Blood came, filling the space it had vacated. Drops fell onto Red, striking her in the belly, and they began to burn. Unable to move, barely conscious, she moaned as the pain of the corrosion added itself to the symphony of hurt already playing upon her nerves. It was all she could do to keep her eyes open, to watch Hermas drop to his knees and raise the staking pin, two-handed, above his head.

The point of it was aimed at her heart, and there wasn't a damn thing she could do about it. Unlike Hermas, a stake through the heart would finish her once and for all.

At least it was traditional.

"In the name of the Patriarch," Hermas breathed. He swept the stake back, readied himself for the blow.

A thread of light touched him between the eyes, and his head exploded.

The detonation was instantaneous, utterly without warning. Everything above his lower jaw was gone, a cloudy shower of crimson steam and debris. Red found enough strength to jerk back from it, as the scarlet cloud started to rain blood and pulverised tissue down over the walkway. Hermas sank forward, his emptied neck spilling ruin onto the mesh. He toppled.

The staking pin, still clutched in his two hands, struck the metal between Red's knees.

She staggered up. "D'Isis?"

"Right here." His voice, so close to the source, reverberated with power. "A communications laser. I had it installed a very long time ago, and then made sure it was forgotten about. I'm so glad it still works."

"Me too." Red paused, wincing, then straightened herself up in one sharp heave. Agony flared at more points in her than she could count, but then began to fade. "I wish you'd just say what you mean once in a while. 'Get him close to the big black thing. I've got a laser' would have been a start."

"And imagine our mutual disappointment if it hadn't worked."

"True." She moved closer. "So, do we do this face to face, or what?"

"It's always been my favourite method. But be warned: I'm not the man I once was."

There was a sound, a heavy metallic thump. Red felt it through the mesh. It was followed by another, and another, accelerating, and as the sounds came, so the metal cylinder at the heart of the Keep began to open up. Each thump was a bolt unlatching, and each allowed a section of the casing to hinge upwards, until they hung above Red like the petals of some outlandish flower.

She walked forwards, towards the massive tank of fluid that the petals had revealed. And there, finally, she saw the Gothking.

He filled the tank, parts of him pressing against its sides, bobbing in a vile soup of nutrient fluid. Pulpy folds of grey tissue, shot through with pumping veins, slid greasily past the glass as the currents within moved him.

There were still a few scraps of humanity in the muck. A withered twist of limb, an eye milky with multiple cataracts, a tooth or two. But in essence, Red was looking up at a brain tumour the size of a house. Its constituent mess must have weighed tonnes.

"Oh sneck," she breathed.

"Nice to meet you too," the Gothking replied. "Now, I think it's time we had a chat. There's still a little time before the end."

19. DECODED

"I warned you," the Gothking told her.

Red shook her head. "I've seen worse. Believe me, I really have. That thing in Lavannos…" She stepped right up to the glass, and put her hand on it. It was warm. "I still don't understand, though."

"There's no way you could." The thing in the tank moved, fitfully. "And now that you are finally here, I'm not even sure how to explain it all. So much happened after we met on Lethe, Durham Red. And I don't know how much time we have."

"I've worked one thing out for myself. The Board were keeping you alive."

"That, and the myth of the Magister. Every now and then they would find some poor devil, have him killed, and sorrowfully announce to the citadels that another glorious ruler was dead. They'd give him a new name, paint a portrait, and the job was done for another decade or two. No one wanted to reveal that the Prime Magister was still alive." He sighed. "If you can call this living."

Red most definitely did not. "So what happened? Who did this to you?"

"You did," he said simply, as if it was the most obvious thing in the world.

"I think I'd remember."

"Not really. You were asleep."

She nodded. "I get it. Whatever happened, happened after I got frozen."

"Some years after, from what I can gather. Although it all started on Lethe. Once you'd won your contest with me, and I took the price from your head. I didn't realise how much face I would lose on account of that, until it was too late."

"And I thought it was just the money."

"Oh no, my dear, it was never just the money. After Lethe, my whole empire fell. It took a decade or two for the rot to really set in, but the decline was inexorable. When the profits stopped coming, the protection stopped, and the forces of law began to close in. By the time the authorities had me where they wanted me, everything I'd had was gone. Because of you."

Red had started to pace around the tank. D'Isis didn't look any prettier from a different angle, but she needed to keep moving. To stop her injured joints from seizing up, if nothing else.

"So I won after all. I finally brought you down."

"You did. All it needed was patience, a quality that you rather lacked until the lid of your cryo-tube closed. But yes, you won in the end."

Red had reached Hermas again. He didn't look any prettier either. "What happened?"

"They parcelled up the remnants of my empire, all my Gothlords and their families, the few chattels I could legally hold on to, and they banished us here, to Magadan. In a way, we were lucky. Execution had gone out of style."

Red frowned. "They didn't put you in prison?"

"There were a hundred thousand of us. Few prisons have such capacity. Anyway, they didn't want us to get out. We were to be wiped from the face of the universe, and that's exactly what they did. Look on any star chart, Red, and you'll find no trace of Magadan."

Red felt a hard spike of panic at her very core, ice-cold and shuddering. "What do you mean?"

"There were two worlds in this system's biozone, Ashkelon and Magadan. Now there's only one. They put us here, and then…"

The voice trailed off. Red stepped forward and slapped the glass, hard. The talk of vanishing worlds was bringing back memories she didn't want in her head any more. "What, D'isis? Tell me what they did!"

"They encoded us."

It wasn't the answer she was expecting. "Come again?"

The transcendant remains of the Gothking gave that breathy, metallic sigh. "We were encoded. They confined us to one part of the planet at first, an island. We thought it was going to be some kind of prison camp, but there was more to it than that. We saw them setting machines up around us. It took a year for them to finish doing that, and another to calibrate the system. And then they switched them on... Dear God, the panic!"

"What happened?"

"We were turned inside out." There was a chill to his voice, now. The memory of what he was relating must have been torturous. "Every one of us, unmade, in front of each other. We were reduced, folded, crushed so small, but conscious of it the entire time. They reduced us to symbols of ourselves, and then wrote us down where no one would ever find us." He must have seen the blank incomprehension on Red's face. "Don't you see, girl? If you want to store a mass of data, what do you do?"

"Compress it," she replied, her voice weak. "Encode it."

"Everything. The very stuff of us, our flesh and bones, our thoughts and feelings, the ground beneath our feet. The air we breathed. The entire centre of the island was encoded."

"They zipfiled you?" Red scraped her hands back through her hair, her mind spinning. How could a world, a people, be reduced to code? It was deranged, impossible. And yet...

All she could think about was the hilltops, and the mist that covered them. She hadn't been able to cross to the other side of the hill because they didn't *have* another side.

Dear God, he was telling the truth. For a thousand years or more, the Gothking and his people had been reduced to data.

She stumbled away, turning her back on the tank and its ancient occupant. Her mind was reeling. It was bad enough that entire worlds could be moved, sent off to hell, and then retrieved with living cancers at their core. It was bad enough that her home planet had been torn from its orbit and sent away into the depths of space. But now, to discover that the world she now stood on was no more than an encoded representation of itself, a series of symbols that walked and talked and thought themselves real...

Durham Red herself no longer existed, except as code.

The Gothking must have suppressed the knowledge from those that came after. He invented myths about the outside world being diseased, so that no one would travel to the end of the world and find out how close it was. He told his engineers to build upwards, rather than outwards, because there was no territory to colonise beyond their immediate field of vision. "This code. They must have hidden it somewhere."

"From what I've been able to work out, about a cubic kilometre of active silicon is buried somewhere on Ashkelon, transported by some new technology of theirs."

"But you found a way out. The Logic Gate."

"It took a long, long time. Longer than I would have lived."

"So you changed yourself." She stared into the tank, through the greasy nutrient soup to the pulsing matter beyond. "It started small, didn't it? A drug to make you smarter, another to get an extra few years. But you couldn't stop. You got addicted."

"You've got it half right. Once the Logic Gate opened, that first time, I was ready to stop. But the Gate relies on me. Without my control, it's nothing."

Suddenly, the machines around them grew dim, and then brightened again. The very structure of the Keep seemed to groan. Red backed away, looking wildly around her. "That's you, isn't it? The systems failures, the power outages, this is because of you..."

"They wouldn't let me die," he whispered. "I've been like this a thousand years, and they wouldn't let me go. I had power over nothing but the gate, so I couldn't stop them, couldn't kill myself or allow myself to die. I've not slept in ten centuries…"

And then Durham Red finally realised what was happening. Why she'd been brought to the Keep, why the power was failing, everything.

The Gothking wanted to die.

The Board had kept him in suspension for a thousand years, just so they could continue to use his Logic Gate. They had preyed on their own people, feeding them to him, and there wasn't a damned thing he could do about it. All he could do was control the Gate.

Maybe they gave him a little light interrogation every now and then. He'd always been subtle, and he'd manipulated Losen and Sorrelier somehow. All it must have taken was a few scraps of advice in the right places.

D'Isis had learned that she was still alive somehow. "You keyed the Logic Gate to me, didn't you? So things would start to go wrong once I came through it."

"You always were brighter than you gave yourself credit for, Red. And yes, it was the only choice I had. The Gate is as much a part of me as I am of it – there was nothing else I had power over. But I did have a piece of your genetic code."

Red closed her eyes. There were a thousand places he could have stolen it from. "The Gate's allergic to me."

"Crudely put, but more or less true." The mass in the tank seemed to settle, and as it did the lights dimmed again, and fluttered. "I'm sorry, Durham Red. You were the only weapon in the universe I could use."

In the silence, footsteps sounded on the walkway. Red turned, and saw Matteus Godolkin striding toward her.

For a moment she was so stunned to see him that she couldn't even speak, so pleased that she could have rushed forward and hugged him. And then she realised it wasn't the real Godolkin she was looking at, any more than she was the real Durham Red. He was an encoded version of himself, a symbol, a few scraps of code enscribed into a block of active silicon somewhere under the crust of Ashkelon.

He was looking down at the corpse. "Impressive. I can only assume, Blasphemy, that your weaponry is more effective than your tailor."

"Nice to see you too," she said thickly. "I mean it. Really."

"Hmph."

She turned back to D'Isis. "How long?"

"I can't say." His voice was faltering. Red saw Godolkin frowning at the ceiling, trying to place the source of it.

"Blasphemy?"

Red patted Godolkin's shoulder. "I'll tell you later. Just watch my back, okay?"

"Thy will be done."

"D'Isis, listen to me. The people in the Keep, they don't deserve this. The Board did, but you've had your revenge on them. You can stop this now."

"It can't be stopped. It never could. Soon the first gravity nullifier will suffer a failure, and then it's all over. The Grand Keep will implode."

"You'll kill thousands!" She flung her arms wide. "There are children out there, scared stiff, wondering why the lights are going out! Are you going to slaughter them, just so you can die?"

There was silence. Below her, the walkway shifted and groaned.

"Please," she breathed, moving close to the tank again. "You've got what you wanted. If it's going to come down, then so be it. But please, don't take them all with you."

For a long time, all she could hear was her own heartbeat, and the groan of the failing machines around her. Then the Gothking spoke.

"What have we become, Durham Red?" D'Isis whispered at last. "A frozen bounty hunter and a drug dealer in a tank. How did it come to this?"

"I wish I knew."

Something was moving on top of the tank. It was the communications laser, the one that had taken Hermas's head off. Red saw it swing up, swivelling on its gimbals until it was pointing directly upwards.

A dish was dropping from the ceiling, far above. A second later, a thread of crimson light connected the two, flaring off the dish like a minor sun.

"People of the Grand Keep," the sounders roared.

The voice was deafening. Red had to clap her hands over her ears to shut it out. She could feel the hammer of it coming up from the walkway, vibrating the glass in the windows, shaking her in her boots. Even Godolkin was wincing.

"People of the Grand Keep, this is your Magister. Hear me!"

The voice must have been echoing around the entire Keep, thought Red. Only with the systems failing could the Gothking make this connection – the Board would have stopped him in an instant, had they been in control.

"By order of the Magister, Lord High Knight of the five Citadels, all citizens of the Grand Keep are ordered to evacuate by any possible means! The outside world will not harm you, its diseases have been conquered. But power failures are causing the Keep's structure to collapse, and the end is at hand. Get to your ships, my people! Flee while you can!"

The laser dimmed, and when the Gothking next spoke it was to Red alone. "I'll warn them for as long as I can," he said.

"Thank you."

"Don't be so quick with your thanks, girl. Most won't go, they'll be too afraid. But we'll save some. Oh, and by the way…"

"What?"

"I'd start running, if I were you."

Running wasn't easy, but it was all she could do. Red didn't know how long it would be before the gravity nullifiers gave out – it might be hours, or just minutes. But the Keep was moaning and shivering like a beast in pain, and

Red certainly didn't want to be around when the ceilings started to come down.

By the time she reached the service elevator she was almost totally out of breath. Godolkin, in contrast, looked as though he had been out for a stroll. "We need to go up several strata," he told her. "The hangar deck. During my pursuit of Hermas I noticed towers there that are twin to those on Ashkelon."

Red nodded. It made sense. Assuming the Logic Gate acted as its name implied, the ships on that stratum would only have to launch forward to be swallowed, decoded and spat back into the real, solid universe.

Godolkin eyed the lift carefully as she slid the hatch aside. "This was how you arrived, Mistress?"

"Yeah. What about you?"

"Other methods. However, this would seem more sensible, considering your injuries."

"I'm fine. Just get in and scooch over, okay? This is going to be a bit cramped."

All things considered, Matteus Godolkin's body was not the worst thing Red had ever found herself crushed up against. The pressure of her body against his gave a welcoming warmth, even though it made her broken rib ache. Once they were ascending she took the opportunity to smile up at him. "It's good to see you, Godolkin."

He snorted, but kept his silence. Red realised that he was embarrassed.

She grinned, and increased the pressure, just for the hell of it.

The elevator reached its destination a little soon for her liking, but not soon enough for the Iconoclast. Red opened the hatch and stepped out. He followed, keeping his face impassive but obviously relieved. "What?" she grinned. "My deodorant not making the grade any more?"

"Harrow is waiting for us on the other side of this Logic Gate, Blasphemy. Considering that Major Ketta and a large number of Omega warriors are there with him, haste would seem more appropriate than humour."

"Okay, okay. Don't rush me." She glanced around, looking for the best ship to steal, and then noticed Godolkin's attention wasn't on her any more. He was walking slowly away, his gaze fixed on something she couldn't see. "What?"

"Blasphemy…"

She trotted over to join him, pushing her way through the throng of scuttling workers, then finally she saw.

There was a window, a towering wall of glass like the one she had seen up in Losen's domain. Through it she could see the mottled landscape of Magadan, its swamps and forests, the low hills rising in the far distance, wreathed in their impenetrable mists.

Above this, up in the clouds, dark motes were swarming away. Every flight harbour must have been emptying itself of airboats, every schooner and skiff filled with escapees wondering if their power cores would go critical before the diseases killed them.

Neither would actually happen – although what lay in store for the Magadani out in the wilds was unknown. Things were going to be different for them, that was for sure.

She shook herself. "Godolkin, stop gawping. We've got to go, okay?"

"I concur. I suggest we take one of these vessels aloft, and wait for the Magadani to activate the Logic Gate."

"What? It's not working now?"

"When it is, Blasphemy, you will know it."

She took a deep breath. It was going to be close. "Okay. Pick a ship."

The hangar was in turmoil. Techs and sylphs were running everywhere, trying to avoid the vast crowds of Domini invading the strata. Fights were breaking out, sylph against sylph, citizen against citizen. A panic was ripping through the Grand Keep, and eating it away from the inside.

It was horrifying. For every Magadani taking off from the flight harbours, another ten were unable to get there in time or too frightened of the diseases outside. It was little wonder. They had grown up in fear of the tainted surface of their world, had its lethality drummed into them from childhood. Even with the Gothking's voice hammering out through the internal sounders, few could bring themselves to trust him.

Of those who did, a considerable number seemed to be in the hangar deck, trying to fight their way aboard the starships berthed there. The situation was so disorganised that Red and Godolkin were able to break into a ship before anyone knew what they were doing. It was only when Red had engaged the thrusters and torn the ship free of its moorings that a few shots tapped at the hull.

The ship was small, a bullet of burnished bronze, its cockpit fronted by a glass canopy. Red watched the deck in awe as she took the ship around in a wide curve. "Christ, look at this. They're going crazy."

"Fear turns men into beasts, mistress."

She nodded, turning her attention back to the controls. "So," she growled, taking the ship around on a second circuit. "Are they going to turn this thing on, or what?"

"Have you considered, mistress, the ramifications of doing so?" Godolkin was still glaring down at the rampaging Domini below. "The universe will fill with homeless Magadani."

"Well, I hope they've got enough sense to head outside the Accord. Can you imagine that lot between the Iconoclasts and the Tenebrae?"

Godolkin grimaced. "I fear for my people."

The Gate still hadn't come on. Red was taking the ship around in a third circle when the hangar shook.

Even from the air, she felt it. It was though the entire ceiling had dropped a metre, compressing the inner walls of the Keep, sending vast sheets of metal splitting away from the

hangar's sides and toppling down into the crowds below.
One scythed down into a fuel store, and seconds later was
blown clear across the stratum by a billowing fireball.

Fuel canisters began to detonate, careening upwards on
columns of flame.

"Godolkin! We're too damn late!" Red hauled on the controls, swinging the ship around as a piece of ceiling the size
of a house broke free in front of her and went spiralling
down onto the deck. It flattened the wing of a starship that
was just taking off, slewing it into its neighbours. A drum
of blazing fuel shot past her in the other direction. "The
Keep's coming apart!"

"The Gate," he snapped in reply. "It's activated!"

Harsh light had flooded the hangar.

For a second Red thought the light was from more fires,
but this wasn't the yellow-orange of burning fuel. The
downwardly inclined towers had opened into complex jig-
saws of blue light and silver machinery, and were spilling
out beams of sapphire brilliance. At their point of intersection a cube of golden, glassy light was expanding, sprouting
smaller cubes from its faces, which sprouted more in turn.
In seconds, it billowed into a great cloud of shining, revolv-
ing facets.

"Blasphemy, the Gate is open."

Red sat, dry-mouthed. "You came through that?"

"I did, although my journey was unshielded."

"Okay. Let's get out of here. I don't want to be encoded
any more." She gunned the engines.

In front of her, the hangar ceiling detached itself with a
shriek of tearing metal. A gravity nullifier dropped through
it to explode against the deck, and then the air was a storm
of debris.

The Keep was coming down.

There was no way to get to the Gate now. Red swung the
bronze ship around, opening up the drives in a searing column of plasma, and dove straight at the windows she had
looked through earlier.

There was no glass in the frames. It lay in heaps inside the hangar, or was already spiralling down to the surface of Magadan. Red saw the gaping openings rush towards her, reach out to brush her with the last few shards they possessed, and then they were gone.

The bronze ship raced away from the Grand Keep, as the entire edifice began to tear itself apart.

20. THREE TALES OF THE FALL

The Gothking had many eyes. The ones he had been born with were quite useless to him now, just pallid blebs of milky flesh drifting with him in his tank of nutrient, but there were thousands of others. Visula pickups all over the Keep were showing him the destruction he had wrought.

If his own eyes had been working, he would have wept from them.

He had seen the Grand Keep in the days when it was a few scattered towers, gradually roofed over to provide more shelter from Magadan's driving rains. He had overseen construction as the first gravity nullifiers came online, and the second stage began to be built above the first. He had watched the society of the Magadani form itself from the embittered remnants of his criminal empire, slowly growing into the advanced and ultimately debauched culture it had become. And although he hated what he had created with a passion, he loved it too. They had modelled themselves on his example. They were his children.

And now their house was coming down around their ears.

He had stopped shouting now. Everyone who could have left had done so; the flight harbours were empty, the hangar deck in turmoil. The Logic Gate had been activated, too late for many. That part of the Keep was beginning to collapse.

Minutes were left to him, if that.

He wondered if Durham Red and her Iconoclast companion had made it through the Gate. He hoped not. The surviving Magadani would be leaderless, lost in the swampy wilds of their encoded world. They could use someone like Durham Red to band them together, to start again.

Maybe she would help them build another Logic Gate. After all, it needed an immortal to make it work.

D'Isis could feel the vibrations of the Keep's structure now, riding up through the support braces beneath his tank. It heralded his own impending death, but he gloried in it. So much so that he failed to see Vaide Sorrelier running up the walkway towards him until the Domini was standing at the foot of his dais.

"It's true, then," the man was gasping. His face was a riot of emotion: terror, triumph, nausea. "This is the almighty Magister, ruler of Magadan. A brain in a bubble."

"Hello again, Vaide." D'Isis turned an eye or two towards the Domini. He could spare their vision. "I'm glad you're here. It will be nice to have some company at the end."

"Oh, don't get used to it. I'm not staying. I just wanted to see you with my own eyes, before I left you to rot in this teetering junkpile."

More fool you, thought D'Isis, but he said nothing. "That's a shame. And we were getting on so well."

"I saw the mutant run out of here, with her slave. Did you tell her about me?"

"About what you did to her? No, I spared her that." Up in the citadel of Trawden, a dozen of the Gothking's eyes died as a thousand tonnes of stone and metal sheared free of the main tower, ripping a great track down the side of the Keep. "It wouldn't have been fair. If she'd discovered that you were the one who sold her to the Osculem Cruentus, she'd have wanted to hunt you down and eviscerate you personally. The fact that she could never see you again would have infuriated her."

"Don't be too sure. We might–" Sorrelier's face darkened for a moment. "What was that?"

"What? I'm a little cut off in here."

"I'm sure I heard something."

What Sorrelier had heard was the Logic Gate, exploding into frenzied life above him. The decryption algorithms that formed it were unstable, thanks to the influence of Durham Red's DNA, and the Gate was beginning to fail. But not in the way that D'Isis had predicted. He had expected it to collapse in on itself almost immediately. Instead it was feeding off of its own energies, becoming a storm, a whirlwind that was eating the launch hangar from within.

Spikes of decryption were starting to rip through the walls.

Sorrelier must have felt that too. A look of panic crossed his features for a moment, replaced quickly by oily determination. "Time to be gone."

"Oh, say it's not so," D'Isis chuckled. "We've so much to discuss. Please, sit a spell. Take the weight off."

The Domini was already starting away. The Gothking watched him go, counting his footsteps.

He got to fourteen before the end came.

It was very quick, at the finish, although not as quick as Sorrelier might have liked. Through the Gothking's multiple eyes it seemed that a number of things happened almost simultaneously.

The structures supporting the five citadels failed as Sorrelier took his fourteenth step, their titanic weight immediately crushing the stratum below before the immense towers, each massing millions of tonnes, began to fall away from each other. The support braces below the Magister's tank shattered, the mighty weight they supported splintering immediately, exploding out through the host of voltage regulators surrounding them. And at the same moment as the power finally failed, the launch hangar collapsed, the strata above it imploding as they crashed downwards through the ceiling, taking the Gate towers with them.

Uncontained, the Logic Gate erupted. Tendrils of raw decryption lashed out in every direction. One of them came down through the ceiling of the Magister's chamber, and swept through Vaide Sorrelier.

D'Isis saw it happen, through multiple eyes, in the final fractions of a second before the Keep came down on top of him. He saw the Domini unfold, shrieking, his body expanding into a profusion of surfaces: skin, bone, brain. Just for that last, endless second he was less a man and more an origami figure in glistening red paper, opening up and out until he was as thinly spread as the air.

The Gothking's final thought, before the untold billions of tonnes of masonry above him hammered down, was how substantial, how loud, Sorrelier's screams still remained.

Judas Harrow had just reached the Omega ship as the inferno began. He had been tracking it along the path its impact had carved through the forest, trekking towards the point where Ketta's daggership had executed that jaunty flip of its wings before vanishing into the sky.

He had been able to see the vessel for some time, and had slowed his pace as he realised how intact it still was. It had been batted out of the sky by a piece of debris from the Omega corvette, and had slammed down hard in the forest, rolling for some time before it came to rest. But the armoured shell seemed intact, the bulbous pressure cylinder undamaged, the angular mass of pipework that fed the main drives barely scored. It was a worrying testament to the resilience of Omega technology.

Harrow could see, as he got closer, how the name of the ship's owners had been stencilled along one flank. "Moon of blood," he cursed softly. "How arrogant can you get?"

Behind him, the jungle turned to fire.

He ducked on reflex, and whirled around, bringing the carbine up, but there were no Omegas behind him. The wash of orange across the forest wasn't the burst of cleansing fire that he feared, but a cube-shaped blaze.

As he watched, stunned, the edges of it billowed out above the canopy.

Arcs of raw voltage were spilling upwards and outwards like captive lightning. Whatever they touched flashed into fragments, and they were touching an awful lot. In moments the air around the clearing was a tornado of scorched wood and tumbling tree-boles.

This wasn't the same as before. Harrow began to retreat backwards towards the Omega ship.

The outlines of the cubes were ragged, swelling like thunderclouds. Harrow felt the warm metal of the ship at the same moment the inferno seemed to intensify, swell, and then vomit something vast into the sky.

It wasn't a starship, not this time. No space vessel surging upwards on a column of flame.

This was part of a building.

Harrow could do nothing except stand and stare as the immense structure came arcing through the air towards him. It was half a tower, a curve of glossy blue stone, unfeasibly vast. As it got close, its droning roar tearing the air, he could see the smooth side of it studded with thousands upon thousands of windows.

The other side was a mess of masonry, but Harrow saw gigantic floors and decks poking out of the shell, stacked above each other and pouring debris down into the forest.

The tower tumbled end over end, whirling through the sky. For a moment it blocked out the sun, and then it was gone. Seconds later it touched the ground, and the force of its destruction made the ground shake as badly as the seismic quakes earlier.

Harrow scrambled to his feet, shaking pieces of forest out of his hair. The tower's fall had knocked him prone, and the sound of it was still beating his ears. Past the Omega ship huge chunks of stone were still bouncing and spinning away; towards the clearing, more masonry was spitting out of the inferno.

It was raining skyscrapers. Harrow's stomach suddenly swooped with the realisation of what would happen should the next flying castle come any closer to where he stood.

He still had the data pick. His fingers were shaking so much, so slick with sweat, that he dropped it the first couple of times he tried to use it. By the time he finally got the interceptor's hatch open, the sky was dark with stone.

Durham Red's stolen ship was in the air when the Keep finally collapsed. She saw it happen through the side of the canopy – she had turned to circle the tower after leaving through the hangar windows.

The destruction of the Keep happened with an agonising slowness, yet with impossible speed. When a great piece of Trawden tower detached itself from the rest of the citadel, it seemed to do so lazily, scraping downwards in an unhurried fashion. Then Red remembered that even that small part of the tower was probably a thousand metres tall, containing dozens of strata, and suddenly its destruction didn't seem so slow any more. The Grand Keep was shattering itself with incredible force.

Chunks of outer wall, some the size of starships, were flung away from the main structure by the weight of the sections above. Red had to dive under one as it ripped through the air towards her. She looked across to see it carve a two-kilometre furrow in the swamp beyond.

Godolkin had to grab the control board to steady himself as the bronze ship rocked. "Blasphemy, this is insane. We should get out of range before the entire Keep falls!"

"Not yet."

"What are you waiting for?"

Red glared at him. "Just trust me, okay?"

"Mistress, lead will become gold before that occurs."

She couldn't help but grin at that. "Put it this way. I spent a long time wading through that rain-sodden sneckhole down there. If there's any chance of not spending the rest of my life dodging angry Magadani through the mud, I'll take it."

"Should any more debris come that close, you will not have to... Blasphemy! The towers!"

Red could already see it. The five citadels had sheared free from the main body of the Keep, and were toppling.

Most of them were spilling outwards. One was tumbling in on itself, the gravity nullifiers that had held it together now powerless to prevent it coming apart. It fell, in a dense cloud of pulverised stone and smoke, into the centre of the Keep. Any remaining scaffolds and construction machinery were wiped away in moments.

As Red watched the other four citadels flower outwards, golden light burst from the centre of the Keep.

The Logic Gate had billowed out as the hangar collapsed. Somehow it had become self-sustaining, feeding on itself and the titanic shards of stonework falling into it. The Keep was not only collapsing in on itself under the pull of gravity, but was being dragged into the Gate at the same time.

Red gave a whoop of triumph. "That's it!"

"Blasphemy, if you intend to enter that maelstrom, you are truly insane!"

"You know I'm mad. You say it all the time."

"Yes, but this time I mean it."

Red swung the bronze ship around, and slammed the main drives to full thrust. "Too late. In we go."

"I embrace death," Godolkin muttered. Red laughed out loud, and hammered the ship into the heart of the Logic Gate.

The air between her and the Gate was filled with tumbling stones. Red began to twitch the controls, ducking under a giant slab, then swooping up and over half a stratum that spun past like a boomerang. Dust and pebbles were ringing off the hull, but she couldn't waste her attention on them. It was the pieces of stone slab the size of battleships that she needed to avoid.

A stone column, bigger than those in the inner court, slammed into the port wing, and Red shouted, dragging on the controls so hard that she bent their levers. The ground welled up towards her, covered with tumbling, bouncing debris, and then dropped away. The Gate, twisting and pocked with fireballs, reared up ahead of her.

The sky went dark. Red was flying directly under a citadel.

She couldn't have guessed which one it was, and at that moment it didn't matter. All that Red could see was the storm of light in front of her, the sea of stone above. The tower was sagging as it fell, unable to hold itself together. The thousands of windows studding its curved flanks were dripping corpses.

The bronze ship whirled through a hail of bodies, of stonework and furniture, trees and gantries and statues as it raced for the Gate.

Red glanced down at her controls, then up at the falling tower. It was impossibly close. She could see the cracks in the stonework, the faces on the corpses falling from the portals.

She wasn't going to make it.

A gilded statue came down directly over the ship's back. Red cried out, feeling the vessel slide away from her, then slam back in the opposite direction as another chunk of stone came down on the wing. Then the ship was tumbling, spinning out of control, and all she could see out of the cockpit glass was darkness.

And then, light.

A tendril of the Logic Gate had swept them up, enveloped them in a storm of glassy polyhedra.

The light vanished, leaving Red in absolute darkness. For an infinite moment she hung suspended, motionless, utterly without feeling. In the next instant she was pounded by a million jackhammers.

The ship was shaking with incredible force, although she could neither see nor feel the vessel itself. All Red could experience was pain, an awful battering that seemed to fling her in every possible direction at once. It was so horribly violent that she thought she would come apart at the seams. Red tried to hold onto the chair arms, but couldn't feel her hands.

She was dimly aware of someone screaming, and realised that it was probably her.

A flash, at the back of her mind, sent cartwheels of light into the space between her eyes. The buffeting took on a new direction, over and over and through herself, then slamming into her again. It was a storm of motion, shot through with bolts of searing light and pain, one phase after another crashing into her like waves in a tempest.

Just when she thought that her head would shatter, and her brain come flying through the wreckage to join all the other debris in the Gate, the light came back.

Not just light, but the universe.

Stars in their millions crowded in on her, worlds without end, without number. It wasn't one universe she was seeing, but many – suns overlaid upon suns, galaxies eclipsing themselves a million times over. An infinity of worlds, each one the same and yet each one subtly different. But in every one of these realities, bursting into her senses like hammer blows, there was one constant.

It was terrifying. She saw what was out there, looking back on her with infinite eyes, and she howled.

She was still howling when the jungle came up and hit her in the face.

Somehow, they had survived the Logic Gate. Red wasn't awake to see what happened immediately after – the onslaught she had suffered, coupled with her hunger, exhaustion and injuries, had put paid to her senses for a while. She would find out later that Godolkin had dragged her out of the wreckage just seconds after the bronze ship had flipped out from between the towers and ploughed into the burning forest beyond. Just moments before the Logic Gate had expanded to a size and ferocity even greater than that she had seen swallow the Keep.

It was still blazing an hour later, when the ship came to find them, adding its violence to multiple fires already burning in the forest. Red was conscious again by that time, mainly due to Godolkin. He had opened one of his veins for her, allowing the hot blood from his wrist to drip into her mouth while she lay insensible. It wasn't much. It wasn't even enough. But it sent her back to the land of the living, for a while.

The ship that came for them wasn't one she recognised. It seemed to appear from nowhere, flickering into view as it hovered, wobbling, above the trees. Red initially put that down to her own addled state of mind, but Godolkin knew better. "That's an Omega vessel, a heavy interceptor. The shadow web has just disengaged."

"We should get going, then." Red wondered how fast she could run, if at all. Godolkin shook his head.

"I don't think so. Omegas are skilled warriors. Whoever is in control of that ship–" He broke off as the vessel wallowed, belly first, into the ground a few metres away, throwing up fountains of ash and soil. "–is not."

A hatch opened in the ship's battered, bulbous flank, and Judas Harrow jumped out of it. "Holy one!" he yelled, breaking into a run.

"Jude!" Red gathered enough strength to grin at him. "You got us a new ship!"

"A gift from Major Ketta," he said, skating to a halt. He saw the look on her face and shook his head. "Don't ask. Oh, and I must warn you. It has a very annoying voice."

Godolkin eyed the inelegant vessel with some disdain. "My torments continue."

"Nice to see you again too," Harrow smiled. "Major Ketta gave me something else to pass on to you, Holy One. A parting gift."

"It's a bomb," Red growled. "Dump it."

Harrow put a hand to her shoulder. "Come aboard," he said softly. "I think you'll be surprised."

EPILOGUE – FINAL ITERATION

The Logic Gate would take a long time to die.

It was like a star down there. Looking at it from orbit, Red could see it still spitting fire at the forest, or sending another vast chunk of stone into the air. Most of the Grand Keep had ended up burying itself in the jungles of Ashkelon, although some took longer than others to arrive. Maybe, Red thought, their journeys had been as strange as hers.

As soon as that notion came to mind, she pushed it away. Her trip through the Gate wasn't something she wanted to think about now, or indeed ever again.

There couldn't be many others who had come through it alive that day. Maybe a ship or two got free before the hangar was crushed, but no one left in the Keep could have survived. The Gothking had finally gained the peace he craved, ending his millennium of loneliness and despair, but he had taken many thousands of his progeny with him. An entire race had almost died.

But some had got away. Even through her haze of exhaustion, hunger and pain, Red could take a little satisfaction from that. If there was one memory of this adventure she would have liked to keep in her head, it was the sight of hundreds of airboats howling away from the citadels, carrying off those Magadani brave enough to venture out into the world before the roof caved in.

There would be a lot of changes on Magadan in the coming years. Wigs and face-powder would go out of fashion very quickly indeed.

She stayed on the Omega ship's bridge for a time, watching the Logic Gate flare and spark below her while Godolkin tried to get used to the controls. The ship was essentially an Iconoclast design, so it wouldn't be difficult for him to master. But Harrow had been right about its voice. Its alert system wasn't based around the usual cacophony of chimes and gongs, but on a nasal, whining word-system that achieved results simply because no one could bear to listen to it for long. Godolkin contended this was the reason the Omegas abandoned the vessel after it crashed. They simply couldn't stand to hear it talking any more.

Harrow said nothing; he smiled and kept his own council. Red, who had seen the corrosive bloodstains around the airlock and on the ceiling of the vessel's bridge, knew better.

After a time, Red grew tired of listening to Godolkin argue with the ship, and went to find herself a cabin. There was no more reason to stay on the bridge anyway. The Logic Gate was still blazing, the seismic destruction of Ashkelon quieting now that the decryption was over. Red had never been more exhausted in her life. She left the bridge to Godolkin and Harrow, exiting with dire warnings about what would happen should either of the two men be foolish enough to disturb her for the next week or so.

Sleep, however, wasn't the first thing on her mind.

Red chose a cabin, one of five in the pressure cylinder, and moved in. It was very small, like all the cabins on the ship, and moving in didn't take long. Everything she had owned in this universe was gone. Clothes; weapons; perfumes, soaps and souvenirs – all were still aboard *Crimson Hunter*, buried in the depths of the forest. With all the attention Ashkelon would be attracting soon, it would never be safe enough to go back and retrieve them.

All she had left now was her soiled costume from the Masque, the dismantled auto-chetter, which Harrow had been carrying in his backpack for the past two weeks, and the case of data crystals that Ketta had left for her.

She sat on a hard, narrow pallet and picked the case up, turning it over in her hands. It was a small thing to have cost so much, to have taken her so far. She wondered if its contents could ever be worth the price.

Her fingers sought the locks, not through impatience, but in the hope that the case might occupy her mind for a while, maybe even make her memories of the Logic Gate go away.

Later, she lay back in the dark, listening to the throb of the light-drive as the Omega ship powered away from Ashkelon. Red had made Godolkin stay there longer than he needed to, but finally the ship's nasal voice announced the arrival of dreadnought-sized warp-echoes, and the Iconoclast had opened the main engines up to full thrust and headed away.

The data crystals, and their translated contents, lay strewn on the pallet around her. The case hadn't been locked, and its contents were unencrypted. It was startlingly easy to read the data she had crossed half a universe to find.

Opened and unfolded, the case had configured itself as a compact library unit, the lid housing a holoscreen and controls while the base held the crystals, set into polyfoam inserts by clever Aranite hands. Alongside the crystals themselves was a series of crypt-discs, brimming with whatever scraps of information the Aranites had rescued from the ancient matrices. All Red had needed to do was to choose a disc and slot it into the lid, for the secrets of the translation drive project to open themselves up to her.

In one way there had been a very great deal of information, terabytes of facts, figures and diagrams. In real terms, however, there was so little useful data on the discs that she came close to throwing them out of the nearest airlock in frustration.

Nearly every byte that the Aranites had recovered was test data of the most esoteric kind. Red found herself poring

over volumes of temperature comparisons, endless lists of
seismic readings in exacting detail, page upon page
detailing power fluctuations totalling hundredths of a volt.
It was stultifying, mindless stuff, fit only for transfer from
machine to machine, never intended to be read by living
eyes.

Disc after disc gave her more of the same, until her retinas felt burned through by tracks of glowing figures. Only
when she reached the summary pages, on one of the last
remaining discs, did she find what she was looking for.

There was a proposed parts manifest which listed, in the
most general terms, the kind of systems required to build a
network of orbital translation drives, just in case something
eighty times the mass of Earth's moon ever needed to be
moved. A series of authorisation requests hinted at a
timescale of four years for the end of testing, while reports
of a memo from some unnamed yet powerful official body
spoke of the need to cut that timescale by half. Lastly, there
was a communiqué from an observatory in Mars' orbit,
summarising a matrix of jumpspace triangulation tests,
along with a list of recommended target points.

Rumours and whispers, proposals and recommenda-
tions. Red should have expected nothing more, given that
the Lavannos incident had taken these crystals on their
fateful journey while the translation drive was still being
tested. But the target points were impossible to dismiss –
although there were a fair number of them, they clustered
around one area of space.

And Red knew where it was. If the data was correct,
Earth lay somewhere in the Vermin Stars.

One day she would study the data again, hunting for
more nuggets of hard information. And then she would
begin to trace her homeworld. But for the moment, with
her head throbbing, her ribs aching and her stomach
empty, she'd had all the revelations she could take.

She still couldn't close her eyes without reliving what
she had seen in the Logic Gate.

Godolkin said he had witnessed a similar phenomenon on that awful trip, but dismissed it as nothing more than an intriguing illusion. Red sometimes wished she shared the Iconoclast's lack of imagination. Maybe then she would be able to ignore the infinity of Reds that had stared back at her from that sea of realities, each one different and each one the same. Not illusions, not optical or psychological tricks, but flesh-and-blood versions of herself with as much life and as much of a past as she. Some bizarre side effect of the encoding process had given her a window looking into uncountable alternative universes, but, in the same instant, the Reds in those other universes had been given a similar view of her own.

How many other versions of her were out there right now, thinking those same thoughts? How many had perished on Magadan, or never made it out of the Gate? They might have been leaving Ashkelon in every direction; some heading into certain death, others into glory. Some living; some dying; some crying in pain; some shouting with pleasure. An infinity of Durham Reds.

All those histories, all those futures. Hers only one among billions.

It was too much. She had already been folded up into a data packet, and spent days as no more than threads of data slipping around a buried block of active silicon. Even if she could believe that she had been reconstructed exactly as she had been before the encoding, the presence of an infinite number of variations upon herself, each now aware of her existence, made her grip on reality even more fragile.

Was she the real Durham Red? Was there even a real one?

It was too much, too mind-blowing. Suddenly the cabin offered her no solace. Often, after her adventures had come to a close, Red would seek out a place of solitude, somewhere to sit and mull things over without any distractions. Right now, she could think of nothing worse. She went for the door, stepped back into the corridor, and headed back to the bridge.

She would sleep later, when it didn't remind her so much of death.

ABOUT THE AUTHOR

Peter J Evans has over four hundred pieces of published work to his name, ranging from the back covers of videos to big articles about Serious Stuff. He has produced regular columns for gaming magazines, short fiction, long fiction, reviews, interviews and a sticker book. His first novel, *Mnemosyne's Kiss*, was published in 1999 by Virgin Publishing, under their worryingly short-lived Virgin Worlds imprint. Evans previously contributed towards Black Flame with *Judge Dredd: Black Atlantic* (co-written with Simon Jowett) and *Durham Red: The Unquiet Grave* and *Durham Red: The Omega Solution*.

Vampire, mutant, total babe
– careful boys, she bites!

THE UNQUIET GRAVE
1-84416-159-5

THE OMEGA SOLUTION
1-84416-175-7